Views on Black American Music

SUCH
SWEET
THUNDER

Edited by MARK BASZAK   Photography by EDWARD COHEN

Views on Black American Music

SUCH SWEET THUNDER

Edited by **MARK BASZAK**   Photography by **EDWARD COHEN**

THE FINE ARTS CENTER UMASS UNIVERSITY OF MASSACHUSETTS AMHERST

Such Sweet Thunder: Views on Black American Music

Copyright © 2003 by Mark Baszak, Photography © 2003 by Edward Cohen
Published by the University of Massachusetts Fine Arts Center

ISBN 0-9726785-0-6

Library of Congress Control Number: 2002117233

Printed in Canada
First Edition

for Fred Tillis and Horace Boyer,
who believed in me and in this project,
for Antoni and Florence Baszak,
who encouraged me to get an education,
and for Jeff Stone…

Editor and Project Director Mark Baszak

Photography Edward Cohen

Book Design and Layout Craig Malone

Cover Design Mark Baszak and Craig Malone

Project Consultants/Editorial Review Board Horace Clarence Boyer, Terry Jenoure, Glenn Siegel, and Frederick C. Tillis

Copy Editing Dianne Bilyak and Ella Kusnetz

Transcriptions of Panel Discussion Audiotapes Charlie Apicella, Mark Baszak, and Janice Webster

Artist Biographies Charlie Apicella and Mark Baszak

Chapter Introductions Mark Baszak, Horace Clarence Boyer, and Glenn Siegel

Contributors/Essay and Panel Discussion Transcript Texts B. Dexter Allgood, Teōdrōss Avery, Jean Bach, Playthell Benjamin, Milton Biggham, Patti Bown, Horace Clarence Boyer, Clarence "Gatemouth" Brown, Phyl Garland, Leonard Goines, Leslie Gourse, Daphne Duval Harrison, Jon Hendricks, Luther "Guitar Junior" Johnson, Paul Kahn, Bill Lowe, Peter Manuel, Portia Maultsby, Amina Claudine Myers, Vernon Reid, Hildred Roach, Billy Taylor, Frederick C. Tillis, Jeff Todd Titon, Steven Tracy, Peter Watrous, and Marvin Winans

The title *Such Sweet Thunder* was inspired by Duke Ellington and Billy Strayhorn's *Such Sweet Thunder* – a twelve-part orchestral masterpiece based on the plays and sonnets of William Shakespeare ("I never heard so musical a discord, such sweet thunder" — Hippolyta from Act IV Scene I, *A Midsummer Night's Dream*).

Our twelve-part book documents eleven harmonious years of Black Musicians Conference and Festival events at the Fine Arts Center on the Amherst campus of the University of Massachusetts, plus one chapter of artist biographies.

THE FINE ARTS CENTER UMASS UNIVERSITY OF MASSACHUSETTS AMHERST

CONTENTS

Acknowledgments

MANY THANKS TO THE ONE HUNDRED-PLUS PERFORMERS, ARTISTS, writers, educators, and Distinguished Achievement Award recipients who participated in Black Musicians Conference and Festival events from 1989 to 1999. Your insights and artistry made annual conferences and festivals a richly entertaining as well as an educational experience, and they will continue to inspire once again with this book.

Such Sweet Thunder: Views on Black American Music is dedicated to an exceptional trio of artistic leaders. This book would not have been possible without the visionary leadership of Frederick C. Tillis, who was director of the Fine Arts Center from 1976 until 1999, and of the conference's artistic directors — Roberta Uno (1989–90) and Horace Clarence Boyer (1991–99) — who each provided the thematic vision that shaped annual proceedings.

In preparing *Such Sweet Thunder* for publication, I would like to thank the former staff members of the Department of Multicultural Programs at the Fine Arts Center. Special thanks to Riki Hing, who provided administrative support to Horace Boyer in his first years as artistic director, and to Janice Webster, who assisted both Horace Boyer and me, and spent many hours transcribing panel discussion audiocassettes and scanning hundreds of pages of essays and support materials. Thank you to Charlie Apicella, my intern, who researched and prepared many artist biographies, helped edit panel discussion transcripts, and kept my spirits up with his infectious enthusiasm for the material we had in our possession.

Extra special thanks to Ed Cohen. His black-and-white photographs are the essential ingredients that brought printed words to life. A huge thank you to designer Craig Malone, who shared the vision of presenting *Such Sweet Thunder: Views on Black American Music* as a work of art. I was extremely fortunate to have worked with a fabulous team of research assistants and project consultants, including Dianne Bilyak, Jack Harrison, Terry Jenoure, Jihyon Kim, Ella Kusnetz, Ryan O'Donnell, Glenn Siegel, Brian Sparrow, Helen Wise, and Pablo Yglesias. Ed Cohen would especially like to thank Rick Grant (Brother Rick), who taught him so much about Black music, and the late Yvonne John, whose advice and support kept him going during tough times.

This book would not have been possible without the financial support of the Fine Arts Center, the UMass Arts Council, and the Massachusetts Cultural Council. Finally, I would like to thank all the staff of the Fine Arts Center who helped to facilitate the annual Black Musicians Conferences and Festivals and who were patiently involved in bringing *Such Sweet Thunder* to publication after all these years.

Mark Baszak, editor

General Introduction

A UNIVERSITY ARTS CENTER SHOULD BE A PLACE OF VISION — A LENS that crystallizes our inner dreams, a mirror that reflects our community, and a window that opens to the larger world. By taking a look back at our past through views into the annual Black Musicians Conference and Festival, the Fine Arts Center at the University of Massachusetts, Amherst, is celebrating its legacy and making a contribution to the study of American music.

The story leading up to the publication of *Such Sweet Thunder: Views on Black American Music* began thirty-two years ago. The W.E.B. Du Bois Department of Afro-American Studies first established the Black Musicians Conference in 1971 to recognize the important contributions that Black Americans have made to American and world music, and the impact that these contributions have had on contemporary thought.

In 1983, under the leadership of Frederick C. Tillis, director of the Fine Arts Center, and Roberta Uno, artistic director of the Office of Third World Programming, the staff of the Fine Arts Center began to program a successful series of weeklong activities. Horace Clarence Boyer, associate director of the Fine Arts Center, assumed artistic leadership of the conference in 1991.

The 1999 festival was the unheralded finale to the nearly three decades during which the University of Massachusetts had honored stellar accomplishments in Black American music. The conference was phased out shortly after Horace Clarence Boyer and Frederick C. Tillis retired from the University.

Views on Black American Music is a companion publication that provides written and visual documentation of Black Musicians Festival and Conference events. Covering 1989 through 1999, this fourth and final issue of *Views*, which we titled *Such Sweet Thunder*, is the culmination of a three-year research and editing project coordinated by staff members of the Fine Arts Center Department of Multicultural Programs.

We are delighted to be able to contribute our collection of essays, panel discussion transcripts, and photography to what is already in print on the subject of Black American music. Although much of the factual information is widely known and available through other sources, *Such Sweet Thunder* presents information directly from "the source" — musicians who created the music, and others who were there to witness the creative moment. Our unique anthology of firsthand accounts of music with such a rich oral history made a lasting impression on us, and we are confident that it will make an equally lasting impression on you.

The book discusses a variety of musical genres (jazz, gospel, and blues) and touches upon a variety of topics within the overall context of music pioneered by Black Americans. *Such Sweet Thunder* also highlights the sublime beauty of Edward Cohen's black-and-white photography.

In gathering the wealth of documentation left behind, compelling themes and common threads emerging from the material seemed to prove the old adage, "the more things change, the more they stay the same." For example, race-related issues are frequently mentioned. Please keep in mind the time period in which a selection was written, the social and political contexts underlying any discussion of Black music, and the work's current relevance to the revolutionary achievements of the music's creators.

In particular, panel discussion transcriptions were purposefully edited to maintain conversational flow and retain the unique characteristics of a live presentation. The passion, humor, and expertise of each author were very evident at panel discussions and in audio transcripts, and I am hopeful that these qualities extend in translation to the printed page.

By tracing the music back to its source and taking a look into the Fine Arts Center's own rich history through annual Black Musicians events, *Such Sweet Thunder: Views on Black American Music* provides fresh insights into the considerable contributions to music by Black Americans.

In conclusion, I challenge my colleagues at arts organizations around the country to continue the important work the Fine Arts Center started, by exploring the latest issues, trends, and developments in contemporary Black music. The entrée of Black American musical forms into the academic arena teaches us that what we are hearing today on radio and television, and in clubs, concert halls, and college campuses around the country, may very well be what we will be studying tomorrow.

Mark Baszak, editor

Upon completion of this book project, the complete archives of the Black Musicians Conference and Festival will be donated to the archives department of the W.E.B. Du Bois Library at the University of Massachusetts. Proceeds from the sale of *Such Sweet Thunder: Views on Black American Music* will support future Black music educational programs at the Fine Arts Center.

Foreword

"…culture is cumulative and centered in the life, love, and work of individuals, and … they are the building blocks of what we call humanity."

Howard Klein, former *New York Times* music critic and
past director for arts at the Rockefeller Foundation

THE ESSAYS, PHOTOGRAPHS, AND TRANSCRIPTS OF PANEL DISCUSSIONS IN THIS BOOK offer a broad range of views and insights regarding music, art, and culture in America. For me, the book marks a definitive moment in time that is a landmark among the many contributions in arts and culture that have distinguished the character of the University of Massachusetts' Fine Arts Center and its legacy.

Thunder carries a profound mythology. It can be light, dark, and frightening. Or, it can reflect sweet or bitter memories. In the eyes and ears of some African drummers and griots, thunder is poetry and inspiration for creating rapture and tantalizing melodies in rhythm. Ultimately, it is like many things in life – unpredictable and a mystery.

In this wonderfully provocative and intellectually engaging book, *Such Sweet Thunder: Views on Black American Music* AND culture tell us compelling and passionate stories about important sequences in the history of America. Echoes of the prophetic and definitive book, *An American Dilemma* by Gunnar Myrdal, the brilliant Swedish social economist reveals just how much "progress" we have or have not made on matters of race here and now in the 21st century. I remain optimistic about the future because the spirit and flesh are willing. This book can enlighten us regarding past and future trends in American culture.

Frederick C. Tillis

Black Music and Social Change

18th Annual Black Musicians Conference

May 1 to May 6, 1989

"It was either live with music," Ralph Ellison explained, "or die with noise, and we chose rather desperately to live."

BLACK AMERICAN MUSIC IS INSEPARABLE FROM BLACK AMERICA'S struggle for freedom and equality. From the subversive messages embedded in spirituals and the tribulations chronicled by itinerate blues singers, to the overt political dimensions of the "fire music" of the 1960s and the confrontational attitude of rap, Black music reflects Black life — a life fundamentally affected by the racist practices of a White majority.

Through music, Black Americans have been able to create an elegant language. Under the peculiar circumstances imposed by White America, it is a triumph of the human spirit. At once an antidote to ugliness and an act of cultural preservation, Black American music is understood and appreciated universally because it speaks to common experiences of beauty, anger, reverence, and fear. More than literature, drama, or the visual arts (avenues of

Odetta
FINE ARTS CENTER CONCERT HALL

May 1–6, 1989, Schedule of Events
BLACK MUSIC AND SOCIAL CHANGE

Monday, May 1, 5:00 PM
Reception, Augusta Savage Gallery
Art Exhibit: graphic works by Mahler Ryder,
May 1–19

Wednesday, May 3, 7:30 PM,
Cape Cod Lounge/Student Union

**Panel Discussion: Black Music and Social
Change**
Amiri Baraka, "Black Music and Social
  Change"
Playthell Benjamin, "African American Music
  as an Agent for Social Change"
Patti Bown, "Black Music as a Force for Social
  Change"
Vernon Reid, "Sound Track of Survival"
Dr. Frederick C. Tillis, moderator

Distinguished Achievement Award Recipients
Benny Carter
Odetta

Concert: featuring Jackie McLean Quartet

Thursday, May 4

Slide Presentation/Reading: Valerie Wilmer,
slides and selected readings from her book,
Mama Told Me There'd Be Days like These
Buckley Recital Hall, Amherst College, 1:00 PM

Art Exhibit (April 27–May 4)
paintings by Ellen Banks
5:00 PM , reception, Hampden Gallery

Saturday, May 6, 8:00 PM
Fine Arts Center Concert Hall
Concert featuring Odetta and Thokoza

The 1989 Black Musicians Conference was a project of the
Fine Arts Center Office of Third World Programming and was
funded in part by the Fine Arts Center Concert Series, UMass
Arts Council, the Chancellor's Office, the Dean of Humanities
and Fine Arts, the Office of Third World Affairs, Afrik-Am, the
Distinguished Visitor's Program, the Student Government
Association, the Special Activities Support Fund, the Gradu-
ate Student Senate, and the Union Programming Council.

expression once largely denied Black Americans), music has always been integral to Black culture.

"It was the one vector out of African culture impossible to eradicate," Amiri Baraka (LeRoi Jones) wrote in *Blues People.* "And in the evolution of form in Negro music it is possible to see not only evolution of the Negro as a cultural and social element of American culture, but also the evolution of that culture itself."

Record companies, club owners, and critics have historically treated Black music as either a purely commercial or musicological phenomenon. The social and political history of Black America — and its effects on the music — has been, for the most part, an ignored subtext.

In New Orleans during the latter part of the 19th century, for example, Legislative Code III and various separate-but-equal statutes forced more well-to-do, European-influenced Creoles of color into the poor uptown neighborhoods of Blacks, creating a new social stratification based on race, not economics. The forced integration of Blacks brought the blues together with music literacy, forming a fertile basis for the development of jazz.

Black music not only reflected changing circumstances; Black musicians helped to create change as well. During the 1950s and 1960s, for example, record labels such as Saturn (Sun Ra), Debut (Charles Mingus and Max Roach), Strata East (Stanley Cowell and Charles Tolliver), and Watt

Jackie McLean
CAPE COD LOUNGE/
STUDENT UNION

(Carla Bley and Michael Mantler) were established to circumvent a record industry that has always exploited musicians. "I was once told by a very social record producer that a musician shouldn't expect to make a living from records," Ornette Coleman recalled. "Yet as he told me this, *he* was making a good living from records that musicians had made for *him*."

Similarly, musician collectives such as the Black Artists Group (St. Louis), Underground Musicians' Association (Los Angeles), Jazz Composers' Orchestra Association (New York), and especially the Association for the Advancement of Creative Musicians (Chicago) have provided teaching and performing alternatives for Black musicians.

Repeatedly, new developments in American music have resulted from the desire of Black musicians to revitalize their music, to reclaim their art. By the time the stunning big band arrangements of Fletcher Henderson, Don Redman, and Duke Ellington became cliché in the hands of commercially successful dance bands, young Black innovators had turned elsewhere. "We are going to get a big band started," Thelonious Monk told Mary Lou Williams. "We're going to create something they can't steal because they can't play it."

The impulse among Black musicians to continue to grow artistically represents the need to express life's new realities. The restless inventions of bebop during the 1940s cannot be separated from the insurrections in

Amiri Baraka
CAPE COD LOUNGE/
STUDENT UNION

ABOVE
LEFT TO RIGHT
Playthell Benjamin, Patti Bown, Vernon
Reid, Amiri Baraka, Frederick Tillis,
Yvonne Mendez
CAPE COD LOUNGE/STUDENT UNION

ABOVE, RIGHT
Thokoza
FINE ARTS CENTER CONCERT HALL

Harlem and Detroit, the Double V campaign for Victory Over Racism, or the protests of Black servicemen against Jim Crow treatment in the army, any more than today's rap music can be separated from the growing frustration of the Black underclass.

During four hundred years of violence and oppression against Blacks in this country, what could not always be expressed openly was given a voice through music. This tenacious impulse to express feelings through sound will undoubtedly endure.

"You can steal my tongue," Bernice Johnson Regan warns, "go on and try to hush my song. My scream of freedom will flood the air of your children centuries unborn."

Introduction by Glenn Siegel

Essay

African American Music as an Agent for Social Change

By Playthell Benjamin

AFRICAN AMERICAN MUSIC IS THE MOST consistently original and representative artistic expression evocative of the American milieu, and it is subversive by nature. As a product of African American culture, Black music is imbued with a sensibility and vision that reflects the socialized ambivalence most Black people feel toward the ideas, values, and standards of White society. As an indigenous American art form, Black music launched an assault on European musical conventions from the giddy-up, resulting in an expansion of the language and an extension of the canon of Western music. In the various genres of African American music, one finds both a reflection of, and inspiration for, some of the most dynamic changes in American civilization.

During the long night of slavery, when the Southern "slavocrats" did their best through word and deed to convince African Americans that they were outside the pale of common humanity, it was the message in Black music that sustained them. One need only listen to the poetry and pathos of "Nobody Knows the Trouble I've Seen," the triumphant spirituality of "Oh Freedom Over Me," or the deep religious faith of "I Couldn't Hear Nobody Pray" in order to recognize what this music must have meant to our enslaved ancestors.

The late poet, philosopher, and activist prophet W.E.B. Du Bois tells us in his essay "The Sorrow Songs":

> I know little of music and can say nothing in technical phrase. But I know something of men, and knowing them, I know that these songs are the articulate message of the slaves to the world. They are the music of an unhappy people, of the children of disappointment; they tell of death and suffering and unvoiced longing toward a truer world, of misty wanderings and hidden ways.

Sometimes the music offered up apocalyptic images that spoke of retribution and punishment for their oppressors. Songs like "Go Down Moses," "Joshua Fit the Battle of Jericho," and "Everybody Talkin' 'bout Heben Ain't Goin' There" all speak to the tradition of resistance and subversion in African American music. It is not surprising that Nat Turner was a religious mystic enamored with the Old Testament prophets of the apocalypse. It was said of him, by

African American music was the catalyst for profound psycho/spiritual changes in millions of White Americans.

everyone who saw him preach, that he appeared to be surrounded by an aura of mystery and power. I am certain that it was the singing of these songs by powerful Black voices in unison that created much of the mystical omnipotence Nat Turner possessed. It was through the agency of the African American religious tradition, of which music is the bedrock, that the most effective slave revolt was organized.

The power of this vocal tradition, which was performed a cappella, has been preserved in the repertoires of Black college choirs. The brilliance of the music's original singers has been captured in the memoirs of contemporary White ministers and musicians who heard them. Consider the comment of the Reverend Samuel Davies after preaching to a Black congregation in Virginia during 1747: "The Negroes broke out in a torrent of sacred harmony, enough to bear the whole congregation away to heaven."

It was this same powerful tradition of Black church singing that created much of the appeal of Martin Luther King's Southern Christian Leadership Conference which sustained the entire Civil Rights movement. We must remember that just like Nat Turner's revolt of a century earlier, the Civil Rights movement was born and nurtured in the crucible of Black religion. It is now clear to all thoughtful observers that without the participation of the Black church with its liberation theology, there would have been no Civil Rights revolution. And for those of us who were there, it is equally clear that it was in the singing that a sense of community in struggle, and a feeling of inevitability of the triumph of our cause, was created and sustained. While much of the movement's music was either modern gospel or secular folk styles, spirituals and the sacred music of slave society continued

to exert their influence.

African American music often conveyed messages that were not so clearly stated but nevertheless called the listener to an ideal of socio/psycho/spiritual liberation. It was not necessary to say it outright because the message was in the medium. Consider the role of women in the world of blues and jazz performance. In spite of some recent argument to the contrary, musicians like Mary Lou Williams, Hazel Scott, Dorothy Donegan, Nina Simone, and Shirley Scott, as well as singers such as Ma Rainey, Bessie Smith, Lady Day, Dinah Washington, Betty Carter, and Nancy Wilson, exercised absolute power over their male sidemen in musical and business terms. They were living paragons of liberated women, and they no doubt inspired the self-confidence of many other women. This is why Black women writers often employ women blues singers as a metaphor for female self-determination. Consider Alice Walker's Shug Avery or Alexis Devoe's panegyric to Lady Day.

Black women instrumentalists have not been given equal attention by creative writers, but D. Antoinette Handy has taken giant steps to fill in the cane breaks of our knowledge with her scholarly studies of Black women in American instrumental music. Women often played important roles as managers and entrepreneurs in the music business. Witness the heroine of Alice Childress's novel, *A Short Walk,* or real life figures like Loretta Carson of *Loretta's High Hat in Pennsauken, New Jersey*, Motown's Suzanne DePasse, or attorney/manager Glenda Gracia, who handles Phyllis Hyman's career.

From the turn of the century, African American instrumental music reflected the complex changes taking place in American society. In the lively cadences and syncopated polyrhythms of ragtime, one hears a sound portrait of an urban society in the advanced stages of industrial revolution. Ragtime was the background sound for the cakewalk, sing-alongs, and house parties that created the ambience of an era now referred to as the "gay nineties." In its basic attitude toward life, this music represented an antidote to the grim puritan vision that still held sway over American society.

African American music was the catalyst for profound psycho/spiritual changes in millions of White Americans. When James Reese Europe became the musical director for the White dance team of Vernon and Irene Castle (the most famous dance duo of their time), Black music and dance began to influence the style and attitudes of Whites in a myriad of ways. Music and dance of African Americans was so influential to the character of turn-of-the-century American culture that E. L. Doctorow named his epic novel on that era *Ragtime*. The most compelling character is "Coal House Walker," a ragtime pianist who quotes Scott Joplin.

As the 20th century progressed and American society became more complex, so did African American music. Black music is so closely identified with the cultural reflections of dynamic change in American society that whole decades are characterized by African American musical styles. F. Scott Fitzgerald dubbed the 1920s "The Jazz Age"; the 1930s and 1940s are popularly referred to as the "Swing Era." Urban White intellectuals such as Jack Keruoac and Norman Mailer called the 1950s the "Beat Generation" and the age of the "White Negro," a phenomenon inspired by the bop revolution of Charlie "Bird" Parker, Dizzy Gillespie, and Thelonious Monk.

In the 1960s, Black music was both the inspiration for, and accompaniment to, a movement that brought the greatest political and cultural changes that American society has experienced in this century. From rhythm and blues antecedents Chuck Berry, Bo Diddley, Ray Charles, and Little Richard, and the guitar innovations of Jimi Hendrix, White musicians appropriated the music and came up with hard rock music. For young Whites of the 1960s who were bewildered by the racism and vulgar materialism of their parents, this music became the basis for a countercultural movement. Whether it was the Beatles or Mick Jagger and the Rolling Stones thumbing their noses at the conventions of respectable society, or Elvis Presley and Jerry Lee Lewis teaching White folks to rock and roll, all acknowledged Black music as the source of their art.

For Black Americans, the creators and major players of the great drama of the 1960s, music was essential to the struggle. We listened as Sam Cooke assured us, "A Change Is Gonna Come"; Curtis Mayfield told us, "We're Movin' On Up"; James Brown bragged, "I'm Black and I'm Proud"; and Nina Simone cursed, "Mississippi Goddamn!" and then told us what it was like to be "young, gifted and Black, with your soul intact." Art Blakey brought us a message from Kenya, Dizzy took us on swingin' nights in Tunisia and resurrected the kingdom of Kash, Sonny Rollins offered us a freedom suite, while Max Roach and Abbey Lincoln insisted on freedom now! Sun Ra taught us that space was the place; John the Prophet gave us a love supreme and then took us out of this world.

For those of us who thought of ourselves as radicals, the art form of jazz was the ultimate model of what human society could aspire to. Having reached

In the 1960s, Black music was both the inspiration for, and accompaniment to, a movement that brought the greatest political and cultural changes that American society has experienced in this century.

As a product of African American culture, Black music is imbued with a sensibility and vision that reflects the socialized ambivalence most Black people feel toward the ideas, values, and standards of White society.

its apotheosis in the late 1940s and 1950s with the bop revolution (a revolt against the restrictions of dance-oriented big bands), African American instrumental music became a living example of the great American ideal of freedom and equality. The jazz band might well be the only society in the world where these ideals are fully realized.

In an essay titled "Jarvis Tyner and the Struggle on the Left: A Portrait of a Real Black Radical," I looked at the connection between the jazz aesthetic and the rise of Black radicalism in the sixties. Jarvis is the brother of the great pianist McCoy Tyner and was chairman of the New York State Communist Party. Like myself, Jarvis came of age politically in Philadelphia. I wrote:

Coming of age in Philadelphia during the chilled-out fifties proved to be an excellent prelude to the turbulent sixties. In the fifties, most of us who would become politically active in radical politics in the sixties were jazz lovers. This was a very important development because jazz is an art form that is philosophically committed to participatory democracy, free expression, individual liberty with social responsibility and the promotion of radical ideas. And what is more remarkable is that it achieves these uniquely American ideals in practice.

There was jazz everywhere and we began to conjure up new visions of human freedom as we swung with Art Blakey and the Jazz Messengers or the Miles Davis Sextet with John the Prophet and Cannonball. Of course, Jarvis was down with this whole scene

because he was a practicing musician for a minute. And McCoy was playing with great masters like Professor Maxwell C. Roach while still a teenager. For young Black men there were many positive lessons to be learned from jazzmen. To begin with, they were performing a complex art form that they created and speaking a language they invented. And whenever you went to see them play, there were always groups of well-dressed white folks hanging on to their every gesture and wildly applauding every flight of virtuosity. Jazz musicians were elegantly dressed, serious Black men who seemed in charge of things and gave the impression of being really free. As image, they were the diametrical opposite of the ineffectual comic buffoon that was so pervasive in American racial iconography.

When a well-known White jazz critic read this passage, he told me with a bemused stare, "I never thought of jazz in that way." I'm sure most White folks had never thought of Bessie's blues the way the male protagonist in Baraka's *Dutchman* describes it — that she was telling White society to kiss her Black ass!

African American music is subversive by nature. As the premier art form of oppressed people, it seems destined to be an agent for change as well as a medium of catharsis, as blues and gospel music surely are. As the great Chicago bard Amus Moore told us, "We are the hip people . . . the two motors of justice." Historical records will verify that it was Black music that fueled the engines of our struggle, and like rapper Doug E. Fresh of Get Fresh Crew's New Jack Swing says, "We Just Keep Rising to the Top!"

Essay

Black Music as a Force for Social Change

By Patti Bown

THOSE WHO CLAIM TO LOVE BLACK MUSIC so much must take personal responsibility for what does not happen to publicize this music in the United States, and we must begin to speak out about this matter. Due to political pressure during the 1960s, Black studies programs began to emerge in universities all over America. These programs encouraged the study of standardized Black educational curricula and encouraged the presence of many Black artists of all kinds in university settings. Black art, music, and drama were promoted to Black students and to all who desired more information about the "Black Diaspora."

In the 1980s, we witnessed the muscle being taken out of most of these programs. A few years ago, I performed in public junior high schools all over the five boroughs of New York, and although there was heavy minority enrollment in every school I visited, I was astounded that most students did not know the name Duke Ellington. Blame cannot be placed on students for their lack of knowledge of the most famous Black American composer; blame must be placed on the educational system, and also on us for not demanding that our children be taught Black music history, including hearing the stories of Black heroes of this music. Our children must be inspired to suc-

ceed in a country that, unfortunately, is still plagued with the evils of racism.

A finger must be pointed at a special offense — the lack of support from print and television journalism. Television, newspapers, and magazines only mimic the views of their owners, and most Black periodicals are more prone to promote the latest "pop" record or recording artist than a jazz artist.

We have an obligation to promote the scholarly study of the complete spectrum of Black music, which covers an unusual heritage of music dating back to slavery times. If we truly believe in the importance of Black music, then we must demand that proper promotion and respect, like the respect that is bestowed upon European classical music, be given to all Black music, especially jazz. Symphony orchestras in this great country of ours must begin performing the music of established and current Black composers. Music schools in America must also teach the art of improvisation, which will help to develop a wealth of new music for our ears.

Our children have not been told how important it is to make contact with music that's in their ears, or how to express it. It is absolutely necessary to tap their own creativity, rather than teaching the way I was taught. My teachers stressed playing "good

Essay

Our children must be inspired to succeed in a country that, unfortunately, is still plagued with the evils of racism.

music," the so-called serious music. Composers such as Bach and Beethoven were considered far superior in form, content, and ideals than Black musicians and composers.

I was 2 years old when my mother bought a piano for ten dollars from a neighbor. I discovered I could play by ear and that I also possessed perfect pitch. Being older, my sisters were given music lessons right away, but I was told that I was too young, and I remember that at that time I felt slighted. But it was a blessing in disguise, because when my sisters went to school, I could play the piano all day. I imitated everything I heard on the radio; and when we finally got a record player, I started copying all the sections in big band arrangements. I could play anything I heard, and I am positive that the advantage of having a very musically talented family constantly playing around me helped me to develop as a musician. Paradoxically, I am firmly convinced that if I had taken piano lessons at 2 years of age, I would not be performing Black music today.

There were no schools to study Black music when I was growing up in Seattle, Washington, like there are today. To study music then meant learning from someone who was not aware of the Black musical experience. Every time I went back to Seattle to give interviews on radio or television, I kept mentioning the fact that there was not a department of Black music at either university I attended. Finally, in 1988 one university established a jazz studies department, which has only Caucasian teachers on its faculty. There is a great need that an organization form to address the practice of racism locally and nationally, especially in our schools.

We must accept the fact that Black music is a uni-versal art form performed around the world. We must also acknowledge that the originators and creators of this music have not been accorded their just acclaim. Pursuing the highest standards of excellence, personal conduct, and artistic growth should be taught to students of Black music. They should be instilled with a great sense of respect for those musicians who came before them, and who helped to pave the road for them today.

We need to find ways to motivate our children despite the increasing dropout rate in our schools, the plague of the "crack" epidemic, the high unemployment rate among young Black youth, poverty, and crime. My firm belief is that it is necessary to reinforce the role that Black churches have played since slavery times. Bring Black music, especially jazz, back into the churches, and make it affordably priced so that those less fortunate will have an opportunity to enjoy the music and be inspired by it. Those who are affluent in our community should be approached to contribute money and time to insure the success of these programs.

Musicians and other writers need to write books that tell the history of Black music and its musicians. Black music libraries should be built to house these books, videotapes, films, photographs, and records, which will help to preserve this rich heritage before materials are lost. Black churches and private donors should promote programs and also give scholarships for the study of Black music, and be a strong community force to educate the old as well as the young.

Expert exponents of Black music, musicologists, and other interested educators must address themselves to the education of the whole family and the cultural importance of this music. Parents must work hand-in-hand with the Black church to rebuild the lives of our youth with fresh ideas and images. Our children should see the difficulties Black artists continue to face, and be exposed to those who triumphed over adversity.

Films and videos should be made about Black music telling the true story of the music past and present: visual documentation that stresses the importance and creativity of the musicians rather than exploiting the personal problems of their lives. Once a national Black music organization is formed, we should become very vocal about offensive images in films, movies, and television. We must set the groundwork for such an organization to flourish if we want to implement any of these ideas.

Black churches must also embrace the complete spectrum of Black music and hold it close to their hearts: not just Negro spirituals, gospel, and European-influenced hymns, but also blues and jazz, which are too often associated with night clubs, and sometimes, houses of ill repute. Black churches would then have the opportunity to increase their memberships and revenue for such programs, and thereby resume playing a role they have always played in Black life.

Most Black parents are not able to teach their children a lot about the complete spectrum and significance of Black music because they were never taught about the music at home or at school. Because of budget cuts, the first programs to be eliminated in our schools are always art and music. I wonder how long it will be before the budget-cutters and legislators become fully aware of how Black music has attracted people in other parts of the world to the ideals of democracy and the American dream.

Our prisons are overcrowded with people who have to find fresh new concepts and values to rebuild their lives. I have performed in many prisons where I saw first-hand how Black music contributes to more positive behavior. Those in the medical profession will also gladly attest to the power of music to heal the sick. In the past, women were not given the same opportunities as men to develop their musicianship, and they must become equal partners in the performance and preservation of this music.

We live in a society that is influenced by youth-oriented, Madison Avenue marketing campaigns. Hollywood movie and record companies are also guilty of giving more credence and opportunities to younger musicians, rather than opting to record middle-aged and older musicians who undoubtedly have more skill and more experience. Care must be exercised in searching out these very talented older musicians who have been ignored by record companies, and who deserve to be heard. To ensure that we do not lose this music, we need to see the formation of recording companies devoted to the preservation of these overlooked Black musicians.

I realize the implementation of most of these ideas — the promotion of Black music as a viable force for social change — will be tedious and expensive, but I learned very early from my parents to only think big. To me, the key word is *devotion* — devotion to the music, and also devotion to Black music's receiving its proper place in American music and in the history of world music.

> I wonder how long it will be before the budget-cutters and legislators become fully aware of how Black music has attracted people in other parts of the world to the ideals of democracy and the American dream.

Essay

Sound Track of Survival

By Vernon A. Reid

Sorrow is not the only emotion expressed in Black music. One of the keys to its greatness is its ability to express joy in the midst of suffering, to laugh in the face of terror.

THE SOUND TRACK OF SURVIVAL IS THE sound of people torn from their land and loved ones, and forced to endure unimaginable hardship. It is the sound of people robbed of language and custom, and that most precious gift — freedom. It is the sound of people who were bought and sold like animals, and treated far worse.

Those who sought to maintain old ways of singing, playing, and maintaining the drum were taught in the cruelest ways that this was not acceptable. Still, the rhythm of that ancestral sound survived in the field shouts and early hymns, in the joy and sorrow of the Mississippi Delta, in Congo Square, on Beale Street, in St. Louis, Chicago, and New York. The rhythm survived, thrived, and grew in the sanctity of the Pentecostal church, in the sweaty sensuousness of after-hours juke joints, at tea dances, socials, and on the vaudeville stage.

Through his pain and shame, the traveling minstrel kept the ancestral spirit of the griot alive. It is a spirit that is strong within rappers of today's hip-hop. If you listen closely, you can hear the sound of that first wail and cry of the African bondsman in the majesty of Mahalia Jackson's gospel praises and in the misery of Billie Holiday's "Strange Fruit."

Gospel music sings of the possibility and necessity for redemption and salvation from the trouble in this world. The blues talks about that trouble and how to deal with it in this life, not the afterlife. That wailing sound is also in the scream of John Coltrane's horn and in the feedback of Jimi Hendrix's guitar.

Sorrow is not the only emotion expressed in Black music. One of the keys to its greatness is its ability to express joy in the midst of suffering, to laugh in the face of terror. Joy and laughter are essential components of Black music's ability to speak directly, passionately, and unsentimentally to the heart of the human condition. The kernel of this truth is in the magnificent orchestrations of Ellington and Basie, and it's there in the uncut funk of James Brown and George Clinton. Its truth is also there in the dense futurism of Ornette Coleman and Cecil Taylor.

If Black music is to be understood as a medium and force for social change, one has to learn to listen to it with new ears. Not the way we listen to it when we're going out to a club on Saturday night, not the way it's listened to in church on Sunday morning when the minister berates us for the previous night's excesses, and not the way it's listened to at the bar of a smoky jazz club, or at a concert, supermarket, mall, or park, or any of the myriad places it's listened to as entertaining background music. Black music has to be

How can it be that Paul Whiteman is crowned the King of Jazz, Benny Goodman the King of Swing, and Elvis the King of Rock and Roll? Talents of the aforementioned gentlemen notwithstanding, the perceived necessity of crowning White musicians over Black musicians in their own kingdom is a racist attempt to keep African Americans second-class citizens of their own art, and it exploits the prejudices and fears of the mass audience.

heard for what it really is — the sound track of African American survival, theme music of a story so powerful it transcends race, religion, class, and geographic boundaries.

Black American music's influence is felt worldwide, and even extends back to its roots in Africa. In order to appreciate the depth of Black music as a social force, we must begin to hear it as a continuum that is not bound by prejudices of popular taste and opinion. Nor can it be limited by categories forced upon it by the commercial needs of the music industry, which benefited incalculably from the music's power, and far too often at the expense of Black musicians.

Practically all categories of American music owe a great debt to Black music, a debt that is often unacknowledged. How can it be that Paul Whiteman is crowned the King of Jazz, Benny Goodman the King of Swing, and Elvis the King of Rock and Roll? Talents of the aforementioned gentlemen notwithstanding, the perceived necessity of crowning White musicians over Black musicians in their own kingdom is a racist attempt to keep African Americans second-class citi-zens of their own art, and it exploits the prejudices and fears of the mass audience.

Black music has always fought against the nega-tion of the African American and won. Seen in this light, musicians such as Jimi Hendrix, Charlie Parker, Thelonious Monk, and Ornette Coleman are not only virtuostic visionaries, but are also warriors of Black culture for all who are prepared to really hear it and bear witness to their truth.

To truly hear Black music, one must be inculcated in the ways of its sound, drama, swing, syncopation, melody, subtleties, and rocking stomp. All is lost if one is not trained in how to listen to Black music. The connection between African music of the past and present, and its African American counterparts, can-not be appreciated without study and exposure, par-ticularly near the beginning of one's learning. Unfortu-nately, most young people do not understand the his-tory of Black music, and there has been precious little effort to educate them. If Black music is to be under-stood as the social force that it is, we must begin by teaching the young.

The Time Has Come:
Gospel Music

19th Annual Black Musicians Conference

April 23 to April 28, 1990

THIRTY-ONE YEARS AFTER HER DEATH, MAHALIA JACKSON (1911–1972) is still considered the greatest gospel singer of all time. She sang a kind of music characterized by stories of the Father, Son, and Holy Ghost, the difficulty of living a Christian life on earth, and the anticipated joy of spending eternity in heaven. She performed this music — gospel — in a style marked by full-throated tones, essaying moans, scoops and slides, bent notes, extended melismas (lengthy passages sung to one syllable), accented divisions and subdivisions of the beat, and syncopation. She was most often accompanied by piano, and occasionally by a choir, where the performance style of "call and response" was preeminent.

Miss Jackson excelled in a music that, though less than one hunded years old, has emerged as the most arresting music of the last half of the 20th

Marion Williams, with
Horace Clarence Boyer
at the piano
CAPE COD LOUNGE/
STUDENT UNION

Schedule of Events, April 23–28, 1990
THE TIME HAS COME: GOSPEL MUSIC

Monday, April 23, 4:00 PM, Augusta Savage Gallery
Artist Exhibit & Concert: *Classic Gospel Singers: Photographs by Lloyd Yearwood* (April 23–May 3). Concert by Chris Coogan Gospel Quartet

Wednesday, April 25, 6:00 PM, Campus Center Auditorium

Lecture & Film Screening: *Say Amen, Somebody.* Introduction by Horace Clarence Boyer

Radio Broadcast: "Studs Terkel Interviews Mahalia Jackson," WMUA, 91.1 FM

Thursday, April 26, 7:30 PM, Cape Cod Lounge/Student Union

Panel Discussion:
The Time Has Come: Gospel Music
B. Dexter Allgood, "The Gospel Choir: The Ideal Gospel Sound"
Portia Maultsby, "Has Gospel Music Become Pop Music, or What Shall We Call Take 6?"
Betty Hillman, "Gospel and Negro Spirituals: Differences and Similarities"
Lloyd Yearwood, "Classic Gospel Singers in Photographs"
Frederick C. Tillis, moderator

Distinguished Achievement Award Recipients:
The Reverend Claude Jeter
Marion Williams

Concert: featuring Claude Jeter and Marion Williams, with pianist Horace Clarence Boyer

Saturday, April 28

Vocal Gospel Workshop: led by Richard Smallwood and Horace Clarence Boyer, with David Marshall Jackson and Chris Coogan, pianists
9:00 AM, Grace Episcopal Church

Concert: "Gospel Alive" with Mighty Clouds of Joy and the Richard Smallwood Singers
8:00 PM, Fine Arts Center Concert Hall

Throughout the week, videos of gospel music performers—Mahalia Jackson, Shirley Caesar, James Cleveland, Aretha Franklin, The Hawkins Family, Andrae Crouch, The Clark Sisters, Wentley Phillips, and others—were screened on closed-circuit television in the Student Union.

The 1990 Black Musicians Conference was a project of the Fine Arts Center Office of Third World Programming and was funded and cosponsored in part by the UMass Arts Council, Augusta Savage Gallery, the Chancellor's Office, the Dean of Humanities and Fine Arts, the Five College Performing Arts Fee, Fine Arts Center Performing Arts Series, Five Colleges, Inc., Grace Episcopal Church, the Office of Third World Affairs, Afrik-Am, the Student Government Association, the Cultural Enrichment Fund, the Graduate Student Senate, the Union Programming Council, the W.E.B. Du Bois Department of Afro-American Studies, and the Union Video Center.

century. There is hardly a piece of music written or performed today that does not bear some influence of its style. Gospel was created to complement the services of the first African American Pentecostal-Holiness congregations, and though such congregations began forming in 1886, it was not until the founding of the Church of God in Christ, the largest of these congregations, incorporated in 1907, that ideas of a music especially designed for services began to take shape. These services combined glossolalia (speaking in tongues), shouting (holy dancing), trances and visions, and bodily movements such as hand-clapping and foot-stomping.

The first period of gospel is called the "Conception" and extends from approximately 1907 to 1920. Chief among the singing preachers were Charles Harrison Mason (1866–1962) and Charles Price Jones (1865–1944), both Pentecostal ministers, the Methodist minister Charles Albert Tindley (1851–1933), and the Baptist minister William Henry Sherwood (flourished 1890–1900). Being singers as well as composers, these men inspired a number of soloists and congregations to adopt the gospel style. They were so influential that

Richard Smallwood
conducting a vocal
gospel workshop while
pianist David Marshall
Jackson and Chris
Coogan look on
GRACE EPISCOPAL CHURCH,
AMHERST

Marion Williams and The Rev. Claude Jeter
CAPE COD LOUNGE/STUDENT UNION

the National Baptist Convention, the largest organization of African Christians in the world, joined their ranks and published the first collection of songs to bear the name "gospel" when in 1921 they issued the historic collection *Gospel Pearls*.

The publication of this hymnal signaled the second era of gospel music, the period called "Development," which covers the years 1921 to 1944. It was during this period that singers established a workable solo style and formed both backup singers and independent vocal groups. Uniforms for male and female groups, mixed groups, and choirs were designed. A group of composers dedicated themselves to composing songs for the style, and pianists formed a gospel piano style, borrowing from ragtime, barrelhouse, blues, and Protestant hymns.

Among the earlier singers was a group of blind men and women, including Arizona Dranes and Mamie Forehand, and sighted singers such as Clara Hudmon, known as the "Georgia Peach," Ernestine B. Washington, The Dixie Hummingbirds, The Fairfield Four, The Roberta Martin Singers, Mother Willie Mae Ford Smith, Sallie Martin, and of course, Mahalia Jackson. Thomas A. Dorsey and Lucie Campbell were principal composers of that era.

The years 1945 to 1968 have been called the period of "Refinement,"

Joe Ligon of
Mighty Clouds of Joy
FINE ARTS CENTER CONCERT HALL

Richard Smallwood leading a choir of
Five College and community singers
GRACE EPISCOPAL CHURCH, AMHERST

for gospel's style had been established, an audience had been cultivated, and those singers who had heretofore held down regular jobs gave them up and became "professional" gospel singers, depending on recordings and concerts to earn a living. Among singers of this golden era of gospel were Clara Ward and the Ward Singers, Brother Joe May, Professor Alex Bradford, The Caravans, The Original Gospel Harmonettes, The Pilgrim Travelers, The Blind Boys (of Alabama and Mississippi), and The Nightingales. Composers of the period included W. Herbert Brewster and Kenneth Morris.

With Edwin Hawkins's 1969 recording of "Oh Happy Day," gospel moved into a period called "Fusion," in which the older style of gospel, dating from the 1920s, began adopting the vocal timbre, melodic delivery style, harmonies, and piano style of other Black music such as jazz and soul. This style of gospel, known as "Contemporary" gospel, as opposed to the older style, called "Traditional" gospel, includes such singers as Take 6, The Winans, and the New Jersey Mass Choir. The leaders of this school include the composer-singer Andrae Crouch, along with such composer-singers as Edwin Hawkins, D. J. Rodgers, and Elbernita Clark of the Clark Sisters. From an elementary folk song style to the polished fusion of many African American vocal styles, gospel music has made a compelling impact on world culture and music.

Introduction by Horace Clarence Boyer

PERHAPS ONE OF THE MOST COMPREHENSIVE CONFERENCES OF THE decade, the 1990 Black Musicians Conference reached hundreds of people through multiple venues that included the Augusta Savage Gallery, the Cape Cod Lounge/Student Union, Grace Episcopal Church, and the Fine Arts Center Concert Hall. The conference presented a variety of mediums and disciplines including radio, television, film, a panel discussion, an art exhibit, concerts, receptions, and a vocal workshop.

Five College students and gospel singers from the community
GRACE EPISCOPAL CHURCH, AMHERST

Although each and every program was memorable, one of the most inclusive and participatory events to bring audiences and performers together was a community and Five College student vocal gospel workshop led by Richard Smallwood. Over one hundred members from surrounding communities joined in song to raise the roof of Grace Episcopal Church with inspired versions of Smallwood's "Holy, Holy," "Center of My Joy," and others.

Essays printed in this chapter include Portia Maultsby's "Has Gospel Music Become Pop Music, or What Shall We Call Take 6?" and B. Dexter Allgood's "The Gospel Choir: The Ideal Gospel Sound."

Introduction by Mark Baszak

Essay

Has Gospel Music Become Pop Music, or What Shall We Call Take 6?

By Portia K. Maultsby

LEFT TO RIGHT

Frederick C. Tillis and Horace Clarence Boyer with panel members Portia Maultsby, B Dexter Allgood, and Betty Hillman

CAPE COD LOUNGE/STUDENT UNION

"Take 6 is gospel. Take 6 is also jazz."

JIM NELSON, MUSIC CRITIC

"When we started singing, we sang gospel. It never got recorded, but when we did start to record as r & b artists the feeling of the gospel music was still there. Even today after all that time, the feeling is still with us, we couldn't get rid of it if we tried."

KELLY ISLEY OF THE ISLEY BROTHERS

"When I started singing rock (rhythm & blues) I still felt I was singing gospel..."

BOBBY WOMACK

TAKE 6 IS AMONG THE MANY GOSPEL performers who appeal to audiences outside contexts of religion. The Isley Brothers and Bobby Womack are among the countless number of gospel musicians who crossed the sacred waters to establish successful careers performing blues, rhythm & blues, soul music, and other African American popular styles. In the process, they brought the spirit, feeling, stylings, and even songs from sacred musical streams into the secular waters of American life, and in turn, secular waters flowed back to the banks of the sacred and forged new sounds and messages in gospel music.

The confluence of these two traditions in contemporary Black America continues a practice and revives a controversy of earlier decades and centuries. This essay examines the origins of this practice and the contradictions inherent in the sacred–secular dichotomy.

With its Christian origins and African contradictions, the sacred–secular dichotomy reflects the duality of Black experience in America. At the core of this experience is the struggle to maintain an African cultural identity and simultaneously meet the expectations of society as an American. W.E.B. Du Bois contends that this struggle emerges from the feeling of having a double identity and a double consciousness: "an American, a Negro; two souls, two thoughts, two un-reconciled strivings; [and] two warring ideals ... " [1]

This double consciousness is manifested in religious practices of Black people. While accepting the fundamental tenets of Christianity, they transformed its worship service into an African ritual, one that interweaves oratory, poetry, drama, music, and dance. Through these cultural forms, Black Christians personalize their religious experience and celebrate their Savior in a joyous and spirited manner.

Black religious rituals and practices are expressions of African cultural values and aesthetic ideals, but are they sacred or are they profane? In contrast to the formalized structure of traditional Christian worship, Black-styled rituals are spontaneous communal celebrations in which prayer, praise, preaching, and improvised song are integral to the structure. Missionaries and other observers throughout the 19th century noted the indomitable force of African cultural values shaping the aesthetic for Black religious practices. A visitor from Scotland, who witnessed a service conducted by slaves, observed:

> The sermons occasionally, but the prayers always, are intermingled with the yelling and hooting of the Negroes ... [who] make use of a thousand ... gestures, quite indecorous in a place of worship ... The religious fervor of the Negroes does not always break forth in strains the most reverential or refined.[2]

Religious services of Blacks often ended with the "shout," a religious dance of African origin. The entire congregation participated, shuffling in a ring formation, jerking the body, clapping hands, but without crossing feet (which distinguished it from secular dance), all the while singing a spiritual.[3]

Missionaries disapproved of the manner in which Blacks conducted their religious services. One admonished, "The public worship of God should be conducted *with reverence and stillness on the part of the con-* *gregation* ..."[4] The Reverend Robert Mallard commented, "Considering the mere excitement manifested in these disorderly ways, I could but ask, What religion is there in this? ..."[5] Other members of the clergy simply were unable to relate to the cultural aesthetic of Black worship services. The folklorist Newbell Puckett, in his analysis of Christian practices among various culture groups, argues that "the way in which a people interpret Christian doctrines depends largely upon their secular customs and their traditions of the past. Most of the time the Negro outwardly accepts the doctrines of Christianity and goes on living according to his own conflicting secular mores."[6]

In dialectical terms, the "sacred" and "secular" are intertwined in the cultural fabric of African life. Religion is a way of life rather than a Sunday or prayer meeting activity. African gods are revered and celebrated in a colorful and spirited fashion. The religious expressions of slaves demonstrated their commitment to these principles while exhibiting their resistance to imprisonment by the cultural values and Eurocentric interpretation of Christian doctrines.

Examining the diffusion of the sacred–secular musical dichotomy, missionaries considered the musical practices of slaves to be as unorthodox as their religious services. Accounts of slave singing abound in the diaries and letters of missionaries. They describe their songs, later called folk spirituals, as "strange" and "weird" improvised strains of disjointed affirmations, and wrote about the pledges, which were lengthened out with repetitive choruses interpolated with yells, hoots, and screams and accompanied by hand-clapping and foot-stomping. An observer noted that these features also characterized secular tradition:

Whatever they sing is of a religious character, and in both cases [sacred and secular music] they have a leader… who starts a line, the rest answering antiphonally as a sort of chorus. They always keep exquisite time and tune, and no words seem too hard for them to adapt to their tunes… Their voices have a peculiar quality, and their intonations and delicate variations cannot be reproduced on paper.[7]

Sacred–secular blurring is evident in the texts of both music traditions in which sacred and secular themes are interwoven. In work songs, for example, biblical and secular motifs form the resources for the text:

Michael haul the boat ashore.
Then you'll hear the horn they blow.
Then you'll hear the trumpet sound.
Trumpet sound the world around.
Trumpet sound for rich and poor.
Trumpet sound the jubilee.
Trumpet sound for you and me.[8]

The nature of the slave experience brought the sacred and secular worlds together, since secular experiences often provided the content for religious songs. A former slave explained the process: "My master call me up and order me a short peck of corn and a hundred lash. My friends see it and is sorry for me. When dey come to de praise meeting dat night dey sing about it":

No more peck of corn for me,
No more peck of corn;

No more peck of corn for me,
Many a thousand die!
No more hundred lash for me,
No more hundred lash,
No more hundred lash for me,
Many a thousand die![9]

In their comparative studies of the blues and spirituals, the theologian James Cone and the poet/writer Larry Neal provide a theoretical framework for analyzing the confluence of sacred and secular texts in the Black music tradition.[10] They argue convincingly that both traditions sprang from the same bedrock of experience, that of oppression, and that themes of struggle, endurance, and survival are common to all Black music genres.

Intermingling of sacred and secular traditions continued in the 20th-century Black church. The Black folk church gave birth to contemporary forms of religious music. This church has been described by the music scholar and performer Pearl Williams-Jones as "one whose historical lineage reaches back to the slaves' praise houses which were autonomous provinces not formally associated with independent Black or White denominations."[11] Associated with the Holiness and Pentecostal sects and with some Baptist denominations, these churches did not prohibit the playing of instruments from the "secular world."[12] Therefore, the sacred–secular dichotomy was further blurred when guitars, drums, horns, tambourines, and piano were added to the traditional accompaniment of hand-clapping and foot-stomping. The resulting music style was gospel.

For many years, gospel music was the exclusive property of the Black folk church. According to the scholar and gospel performer Horace Clarence Boyer, "Until the forties, Holiness churches did not allow their members to sing their songs before non-Holiness persons."[13] Gospel music became known to the larger Black religious community and eventually the world through the efforts of Thomas Dorsey. Dorsey was a former jazz-blues pianist and member of the Pilgrim Baptist church in Chicago. He began composing gospel songs in the late 1920s, and by the late 1950s his songs and those of other gospel composers had become standards in the repertoire of many independent Black churches.

The introduction of gospel music in these churches, however, was surrounded by controversy. Some preachers, Dorsey explains, used to call gospel music "sin music." They related it to what they called "worldly things," like jazz and blues and show business. Gospel was different from approved hymns and spirituals; it had a "beat," and it had a "jazzy-bluesy" sound.[14] A rockin' beat, jazz-blues inflections, "worldly" lyrics, and choreographed movements define the "secular" dimension of the gospel tradition.

Performances of jubilee-derived gospel quartets established musical conventions that became standard among quartet groups and others in the secular idiom.[15] Their a cappella vocal arrangements featured a "walking bass." This rhythmic bass line provided the foundation for four- and five-part group harmonies by imitating the "walking" technique of string bass players. Both the walking bass line and vocal arrangements of gospel quartets were adopted from the big band tradition. By the 1950s, with the addition of the electric guitar, stylings from the blues tradition became standard to gospel music performances. In subsequent years, other secular instruments (bass guitar, drums, horns, and synthesizers) were incorporated into the gospel tradition.

Beginning in the 1940s, gospel music was being transformed into popular song by performers who served their musical apprenticeship in gospel quartets and in church gospel choirs. Lou Rawls, a member of The Pilgrim Travelers, left the group for a professional career in the popular idiom. Switching from gospel to pop, Rawls explained, "wasn't hard because it was just a matter of changing words because the beat was there. It was the same thing — only in the gospel music [quartet tradition], instead of having all the instrumentation, it was just voices and your hand on your hip keeping the syncopation."

In 1955 Ray Charles proved this point when he recorded the gospel song "This Little Light of Mine" under the title "This Little Girl of Mine." Versions are distinguished only by the lyrics. Beginning in the 1960s, gospel songs with original lyrics were recorded by performers of soul music; soul music with original lyrics was recorded by gospel performers; gospel songs crossed over into the soul music charts; and various popular music groups added gospel choirs to their recordings.[16] This sacred–secular exchange was possible because the two traditions emerged from the same social and cultural context.

Gospel music is an expression of life. While spreading the "good news," it delivers a message that builds hope, provides encouragement, and lifts spirits. Many of the lyrics in Black popular music are inspired by the gospel message. The soul singer/songwriter Curtis Mayfield explains how his lyrics relate to this message:

> Life itself isn't all a bowl of cherries, and

Gospel music became known to the larger Black religious community and eventually the world through the efforts of Thomas Dorsey.

Take 6 continues a tradition that has its origins in the nineteenth-century Black folk church. Influenced by the a cappella jubilee gospel quartet tradition, they completely obliterate the sacred–secular dichotomy. Their music demonstrates that the sacred and secular worlds of Blacks are cut from and interwoven into the same cloth.

sometimes, when you can hear an entertainer sing in terms of that thought, it can help you face life better.

I've always written in that manner because of the church... Subconsciously, I picked up the notion that music is a great way to communicate with people and relate to them. And I learned from the church how to bring out emotional response in people through words and music, and how to express something that may be rewarding and fulfilling.[17]

"Message songs" of Curtis Mayfield and other songwriters of popular idioms emerged from a spiritual consciousness. The way in which these songs are performed represents an extension of the emotional and tonal qualities inherent in gospel music. The music then becomes available for renditions by gospel performers as illustrated by Shirley Caesar, The Thompson Community Singers, and The 21st Century Singers, who each recorded Mayfield's "People Get Ready." Melba Moore's "Lean on Me" as "Lean on Him" is another example. Recordings of those songs were well received by both camps of the Black community.

In conclusion, let's return to the question, "Has gospel become pop music, or what shall we call Take 6?" Take 6 continues a tradition that has its origins in the 19th century Black folk church. Influenced by the a cappella jubilee gospel quartet tradition, they completely obliterate the sacred–secular dichotomy. Their music demonstrates that the sacred and secular worlds of Blacks are cut from and interwoven into the same cloth. Both music traditions hold spiritual, cultural, and social relevance in both spheres of Black life.

NOTES

1. W.E.B. Du Bois, *The Souls of Black Folk* (Greenwich, Conn.: Fawcett Publications, Inc., 1961), 16–17. First published in 1903.

2. Quoted in Dena Epstein, *Sinful Tunes and Spirituals* (Urbana: University of Illinois Press, 1977), 120.

3. For several descriptions of the shout, see Epstein, *Sinful Tunes*, 278–87.

4. Quoted in Epstein, *Sinful Tunes*, 201.

5. Robert Manson Myers, ed., *The Children of Pride: A True Story of Georgia and the Civil War* (New Haven: Yale University Press, 1972), 483.

6. Newbell N. Puckett, *Folk Beliefs of the Southern Negro* (Chapel Hill: University of North Carolina Press, 1926), 545.

7. James Wentworth Leigh, *Other Days* (New York: Macmillan, 1921), 156.

8. William Francis, et al., eds., *Slave Songs of the United States* (Freeport, N. Y.: Book for Libraries Press: 1971), 24. Originally published in 1867.

9. Quoted in James Miller McKim, *Negro Songs* [1862] in Bruce Jackson, *The Negro and His Folklore in Nineteenth-Century Periodicals*, ed. Bruce Jackson (Austin: University of Texas Press, 1967), 57–60. For other descriptions of the fusion of sacred and secular texts, see Epstein, *Sinful Tunes*, 168, 170–71, 219; and William E. Barton, D.D. "Recent Negro Melodies," in Jackson, *The Negro and His Folklore*, 302–26.

10. James Cone, "The Blues: A Secular Spiritual," in *The Spirituals and the Blues* (New York: Orbis, 1991), 108–142; Larry Neal, "The Ethos of the Blues," *The Black Scholar* (summer 1972): 42–48.

11. Pearl Williams Jones, "The Musical Quality of Black Religious Folk Ritual," *Spirit* 1, 1 (1977): 23.

12. For religious practices associated with this church, see Jones, "The Musical Quality," 23, 25, and Melvin D. Williams, *Community in a Black Pentecostal Church* (Pittsburgh: University of Pittsburgh Press, 1974).

13. Horace Clarence Boyer, "Gospel Music," *Music Education Journal* 64, no.9 (May 1978): 37.

14. Alfred Duckett, "An Interview with Thomas A. Dorsey," *Black World* (July 1974): 5.

15. These quartets include the Golden Gate Jubilee Quartet, The Heavenly Gospel Singers, The Fairfield Four, and The Swan Silvertones.

16. The soul music performers Roberta Flack and Donny Hathaway recorded "Come Ye Disconsolate" and Marvin Gaye recorded "Wholly Holy;" Shirley Caesar and the Thompson Community Singers recorded Curtis Mayfield's "People Get Ready," and Melba Moore recorded "Lean on Me" as "Lean on Him"; Aretha Franklin fused the lyrics from Carole King's "You've Got a Friend" in her rendition of "What a Friend We Have in Jesus"; Edwin Hawkins's, "Oh Happy Day" crossed over to the soul charts; D. J. Rogers and Wee Wee used gospel choirs in their recordings of "On the Road Again"/"One More Day" and "Hold On (to Your Dreams)," respectively.

17. Quoted in Judy Spiegelman, *Soul* (April 5, 1971), 6.

Essay

The Gospel Choir: The Ideal Gospel Sound

By B. Dexter Allgood

THE PURPOSE OF THIS ESSAY IS TO trace the development of Black gospel choirs and their significance to American music, and it is designed to research the techniques used to achieve the ideal gospel sound of choirs by concentrating on mixed choral groups consisting of sopranos, altos, tenors, and basses.

Black gospel choirs can be found today in most Black congregations throughout the United States. These choirs range from children's choirs and young adult groups to male choruses, women's choirs, and senior choirs. It is also significant that gospel choirs have emerged in many colleges and universities throughout the United States.

The earliest known date for the existence of a Black gospel choir is 1931, when Thomas Dorsey, Theodore Frye, and Magnolia Butts Lewis organized a choir at the Pilgrim Baptist Church in Chicago. Later, in 1932, Dorsey organized the National Convention of Gospel Choirs and Choruses (popularly known as the Gospel Singers Convention). Most music for this choir was developed from the pen of Dorsey, who published *Gospel Pearls*, a publication of the Sunday School Publishing Board of the National Baptist Convention held in 1921. These songs were a collection of White and Black gospel hymns and spirituals that were adaptable for choirs and congregational singing. [1]

The convention that was held at the Pilgrim Baptist Church in Chicago attracted over three thousand people. Many of these convention-goers participated in the choir. Dorsey stated, "We had so many voices in the choir, we had to put the director's stand halfway up the aisles and in back of the church."[2] It is also significant to note that the Gospel Singers Convention was the only institution of its kind that was dedicated to promoting gospel music. This remained in existence well into the early 1970s with the emergence of the James Cleveland Gospel Music Workshop.

Although much of the credit has been given to Thomas Dorsey for his contribution to gospel music, it was Roberta Martin who was known during her career for her choral vocal style and piano accompanying. Roberta Martin was born on February 12, 1907, in Helena, Arkansas, but at an early age she migrated to Chicago. She soon secured the position of pianist for the Young Peoples' Choir of Pilgrim Baptist Church. Dorsey and Frye guided Martin through her early career. By 1936, she had organized her own group, the

Roberta Martin Singers, consisting of Eugene Smith, James Lawrence, Robert Anderson, Willie Webb, and Norsalus McKissick. By 1940, two female members were added to the group.[3]

While the Roberta Martin Singers were not a large gospel choir, one can gather much information on how they performed musically. Martin preferred a rich and distinctive sound. Joe Bostic stated, "That's the Roberta Martin Sound, as only they can do it: rich, restful and righteous."[4] Martin developed a distinct way of playing, singing, and arranging gospel music. One can go a step further and say that Roberta Martin was one of the few musician–composers to use male and female voices readily in the 1930s, when many gospel groups were either all-male quartets or all-female groups like the Clara Ward Singers.

Musically, Martin taught her choirs how to perform with specific vocal techniques. Incorporated in her performances were certain colors, vocal textures, dynamics, and harmonic blendings. She also concentrated on achieving a rich sound from the choir in relationship to the soloists. Singers would often use various vocal techniques to achieve the correct sound for Martin's music; they were often asked to use slurs, slides, bends, vibrato, and even to sing from a high to low vocal range. Roberta Martin was the master of vocal control, timing, and phrasing.

One of Roberta Martin's distinctive musical traits was having the soloist "lag behind the beat," a style that influenced many gospel and pop singers of the late 1940s and 1950s, such as Sallie Martin, Sister Rosetta Thorpe, Clara Ward, and Dinah Washington.[5] Martin believed that delivery of the lyrics was essential to singing good gospel music. Always performed in a percussive manner with emphasis placed on most words and syllables, the style most likely emerged from the Holiness church where song and dance make up a great portion of the service. It is the Holiness church that employs the rhythm for the lyrics in the tunes. Tony Heilbut states, "Most of the old Holiness tunes are similarly simple and repetitive. The musical interest lies almost solely in the rhythms, sanctified hand-clapping, and it is a miracle of rhythm complexity and glorious voices."[6]

Perhaps the one individual who was most influenced by Roberta Martin's music was James Cleveland. The Rev. James Cleveland was born December 5, 1932, in Chicago. He patterned his singing and piano style after Roberta Martin, and contends that he was the first to merge the music of the Black Baptist church and the Holiness church. Through his choral arrangements he learned how to achieve a very new and refreshing choral sound in gospel music. He learned how to build tension musically and emotionally by making arrangements more soulful rather than concentrating on a beautiful-sounding voice.

James Cleveland's vocal sound, often harsh and strong, also includes falsetto, groans, screams, and spoken dialogue. He trained many singers, but his prodigy was Aretha Franklin, who began her professional career as a gospel singer. One only has to listen to these two singers to conclude that their singing and piano playing styles are quite similar. His motto as a teacher is that a vocalist must always sing well.[7]

By the mid-fifties, Cleveland was considered the best gospel arranger around. He worked with several gospel groups including the Gospelaires and the Roberta Martin Singers. It was during this time that he composed such tunes as "Stand by Me," "Grace Is Sufficient," "He's Using Me," and "Good Enough for Me."

Roberta Martin was one of the few musician–composers to use male and female voices readily in the 1930s, when many of the gospel groups were either all-male quartets or all-female groups like the Clara Ward Singers.

James Cleveland
trained many singers,
but his prodigy was
Aretha Franklin, who
began her professional
career as a gospel
singer.

Gospel music began to take a new direction in 1960, and James Cleveland was one of the moving forces behind this movement. During this time he began to channel his efforts into gospel choirs, and he was concerned about the sound and tone quality of these ensembles. One of the most popular gospel choirs to emerge during the 1960s was the Voices of Tabernacle from Detroit. When the group recorded "The Love of God," it became an instant hit, and unlike the traditional gospel style of the 1950s, it was a slow ballad but with a soulful beat. Tony Heilbut states, "The Voices were the most musically disciplined gospel choir ever... and The Voices [were] like the Mormon Tabernacle Choir."[8]

Cleveland's third album, *Peace Be Still*, made gospel history. It can be said that Cleveland bridged the traditional style of the 1930s and 1940s with the 1960s. He achieved this by arranging choral works that possessed the piano style and lyrics of the 1930s and 1940s, while introducing the contemporary sound of the 1960s. For the first time, accompanying instruments played a vital role in the music. In a manner that was unique and innovative, Cleveland incorporated piano, organ, and percussion in his arrangements for *Peace Be Still*. Piano and organ arrangements were designed to support the choir and also fill in any empty spaces with arpeggios, scale passages, and jazz riffs. Percussion served as the backbone of the composition, with much emphasis placed on beat 1 of this 3/4 meter work and the snare drum acting as a majestic metronome. The choir tends to have a balanced sound, with dynamics and good phrasing essential to Cleveland's music.

It was also during this time that James Cleveland signed with Savoy Records. His expertise as a com-

poser and choir director allowed him to produce other choirs such as the Charles Fold Singers, the Southern California Community Choir, and the Salem Inspirational Choir of Omaha.[9]

In 1969, another composer–singer by the name of Edwin Hawkins emerged to exert a major impact on Black gospel music. The New York City–based gospel disc jockey Joe Bostic was sent a recording of "Oh Happy Day" by Hawkins's Oakland-based choir, the Northern California State Youth Choir. He was asked to review the recording, an arrangement of a simple hymn transformed into a hand-clapping tune with contemporary jazz harmonies. Bostic was fascinated with the recording and invited Hawkins to New York to discuss future plans for the group. "Oh Happy Day" was first played on WLIB radio and distributed in the Metropolitan New York area. The record became an instant success and requests resulted in its being distributed nationwide. The country was charmed by the sound and style of this group.[10] Horace Clarence Boyer states:

> By 1969, the entire United States and part of Europe were rocking, shouting and dancing to an old Baptist hymn called, "Oh Happy Day." Since the diction on the record was comparable to that of most vocal recordings, and since gospel music generally evokes an emotional rather than intellectual reaction, most non-churchgoers missed that it was in fact a hymn. Hence, popping fingers and dancing was the physical reaction to it.[11]

The gospel songs that Hawkins arranged and composed for choirs included smooth and sophisticated vocal harmonies and an accompaniment that was solid but possessed an orchestral quality. Some of his melodies were even indistinguishable from those of soul and jazz, and often utilized remote keys such as G flat, E major, and D flat.[12] Choirs around the country quickly began to imitate Hawkins's choral style. Due to the popularity of Edwin Hawkins, James Cleveland, Andre Crouch, Jessy Dixon, and Walter Hawkins (Edwin's brother), the early 1970s was perhaps the pivotal point for contemporary gospel music.

In 1972, Aretha Franklin recorded *Amazing Grace*, one of the most historic gospel albums ever made. It was recorded at the Cornerstone Institutional Baptist Church in Los Angeles under the direction of James Cleveland and the Southern California Community Choir. Franklin's entire repertoire consisted of material from the 1950s from such artists as Clara Ward, her longtime mentor. Cleveland was responsible for arranging music for the live recording. Their collaboration ensured that the music had a contemporary flavor while still maintaining the elements of the 1950s. The varied tracks included secular tunes that were adapted to the sacred idiom. From the song "You Got a Friend," recorded by the pop artists Roberta Flack and Donny Hathaway, Aretha used the tune and changed the lyrics slightly to include a phrase or two of Dorsey's "Precious Lord."

My favorite tune from *Amazing Grace* is a moving rendition of Clara Ward's "Old Landmark," an up-tempo gospel song with a Pentecostal flavor. Instrumentation including piano, organ, bass guitar, and drums enhanced what the soloist and choir were doing. I also discovered that the lyrics to some of these songs possessed many of the Africanisms found in Negro spirituals and jubilee songs of slaves. Most

distinguishable are the elements of call and response, in which the soloist makes a statement and the choir answers in response.

Another choir to gain popularity during the seventies was the Institutional Radio Choir of Brooklyn, New York, directed by J. C. and Alfred White, who also served as pianist, composer, and organist accompanying the group. Together they produced such soloists as Gloria White (J. C.'s wife), Rubesteen McClure, and Carolyn White, who later traveled as an evangelist.[13] The choir's popularity grew even more with its Sunday night radio broadcasts. Many gospel concertgoers jammed the Institutional Church of God in Christ on Adelphi Street to witness the excitement this choir was generating with its music. The choir performed on local and national television and has traveled throughout the United States and Europe; their biggest selling album was *One More Day*.

Still another important choir emerged around the time when Walter and Edwin Hawkins wrote, arranged, and recorded a live album entitled *Love Alive*, which featured excellent choral singing and soloists. The highlight of the recording was two selections featuring the lovely voice of Tramaine Hawkins (Walter's wife); in "Changed" and "Going Up Yonder," she enhanced the choir by utilizing her voice in a manner that blended a gospel and classical vocal style.

Another characteristic of Walter Hawkins's music is the way the soloist and choir line out the music. As in the old Dr. Watts hymns, this process usually occurs at the end or climax of the tune. The beat pattern is free, with much improvisation by instrumentalists and singers. A portion of the verse or chorus is usually repeated with the soloist leading each phrase. Techniques used by soloists include screaming, porta-

Another significant contribution to gospel music was the development of gospel choirs on Black college campuses during the 1970s.

menti, and vibrato. In most instances, the choir sings the finale section in the same manner as earlier sections, but under the strict direction of the conductor. It must be emphasized that the choir may repeat certain lyrics continuously before moving to the next phrase or section of the composition.

Another significant contribution to gospel music was the development of gospel choirs on Black college campuses during the 1970s. Although college officials did not initially recognize many groups, students organized gospel groups secretly. Groups often practiced in dormitories or during late hours in their music departments when college officials, especially music faculty, were not present. Many in the administration and faculty at this time considered gospel music "the devil's music" and felt that these groups practiced bad choral techniques. Some of these beliefs still exist today on campuses and in the Black church.

With the Black Power movement of the 1970s, many student gospel choirs emerged to show to the world that Black Americans needed to cherish their cultural heritage. The result was phenomenal. Students wanted to be a part of a singing organization that expressed the glorification of Jesus Christ in a manner that they understood. Another possible reason for gospel music's popularity is that the music may have symbolized a feeling of security for those students who were away from home: lyrics such as "The race is not given to the swift nor to the strong, but to the one that endureth until the end; there will be problems, and sometimes you'll walk alone, but I know that things, will work out, for the good of them who love the Lord."[14] Many students came to college with a strong religious background. They were taught

at home that when problems emerged, there was a greater force that would see them through their trials and tribulations.

By the late 1970s, more gospel choirs were being accepted on Black campuses because some music educators felt that gospel music was an important entity of the Black experience. On some campuses, choirs were allowed to practice in the music department under the strict supervision of a faculty or staff advisor. In most cases, "legitimate" singers were forbidden to sing with these gospel choirs because many voice instructors believed poor vocal habits would develop.

Regardless, college gospel choirs were gaining momentum. It was also at this time that college gospel workshops and festivals were formed, and this tended to solidify the existence of these choirs. One of the most prestigious workshops to emerge was the National Black Gospel Choir Festival organized in 1972. Usually held in Atlanta, this festival affords gospel choirs the opportunity to sing and hold seminars on various topics in gospel music. One of the highlights of this workshop is a gospel choir competition in which choirs are judged in such areas as diction, tone quality, dynamics, intonation, style, control, and appropriateness of material. They also may be judged on their attire, accompaniment, and choreography.

As with most gospel choirs, much of the musical material is taught by rote memory. However, directors are now using more written arrangements. Rehearsals for many college and university gospel choirs are very similar to those of Black church services. It is not uncommon during rehearsals for singers to become emotional and even break into a religious dance called the "shout." In most Instances, the shout is performed following a hand-clapping, up-tempo song.

By the early 1980s, gospel choirs on Black campuses were common. I cannot explain exactly why Black institutions now readily accept these groups, but I can speculate that this came about because many White colleges and universities allowed gospel groups to form on their campuses without hesitation. Black colleges such as Virginia State University, Howard University, and Norfolk State University now include gospel choirs in their music curriculum.

Many professional singers and musicians have emerged from Black college gospel choirs. The Grammy Award–winner Richard Smallwood of the Richard Smallwood Singers is a graduate of Howard University, and Jackie Ruffin, one of Smallwood's singers, is the founder of the Virginia State University Gospel Choir. Some other professionals include Robert Fryson of Virginia State University and Shirley Ceasar of Shaw University. On many occasions, these artists have come back to their alma maters to perform and give clinics.

Gospel choirs of the 1980s were distinctively different from groups of the 1970s. Technology has played a significant role in these changes. By the 1980s, most choirs were concerned with producing a quality sound in their performances and recordings, resulting in more choirs using state-of-the-art digital recording technology. The advancement of instrumentation such as the use of synthesizers and drum machines improved the sound quality of these groups.

Gospel artists and choirs soon realized that there was big money in the gospel music industry. Groups such as The Clark Sisters, The Winans, Tramaine Hawkins, the New Jersey Mass Choir, Vanessa Bell Armstrong, and BeBe and CeCe Winans all achieved

stardom during this period. The Clark Sisters' tune "You Brought the Sunshine" sparked a new direction in contemporary gospel music. With its steady disco beat, the tune was an instant hit around the world. Although the lyrics were sacred, the word *you* was substituted in many instances for "Christ," "Jesus," or "Lord." I believe that this was done to attract both the non-churchgoer as well as the churchgoer.

Others soon followed the Clark Sisters' lead. Tramaine Hawkins recorded a similar hit entitled "Fall Down," with brassy instrumentation and a choral background. Hawkins was also very cautious with lyrics; in one tune she sings "Spirit, let the spirit fall down on me," and it should be noted that Hawkins never said what type of spirit she was referring to. Hawkins traveled extensively throughout the country singing the song even in discos of major cities like New York, Chicago, and Los Angeles.

In 1986, gospel choirs began to achieve even more attention. "I Want to Know What Love Is" was an instant hit for the New Jersey Mass Choir. With its memorable melody and impeccable vocal tone quality, this medium tempo ballad also featured as guest soloist Jennifer Holiday, the Broadway star of *Dreamgirls*. Soon, many college, church, and community gospel choirs were singing this popular tune.

Quincy Jones was instrumental in organizing a huge choir of famous stars to collaborate on a tune entitled "We Are the World." Singers such as Ray Charles, Diana Ross, Stevie Wonder, Michael Jackson, and the Pointer Sisters all participated in the project. Again, gospel choirs around the world began to sing the tune.

There are many young gospel artists who achieved fame for their choirs during the 1980s. Many

Gospel artists and choirs soon realized that there was big money in the gospel music industry.

The Gospel Choir: The Ideal Gospel Sound

Essay

In my research, I have also found that the ideal sound does not only come from professional performers.

are educated musicians dedicated to achieving a good choral sound. Some conductors train their singers extensively and are very selective in choosing members; music is recorded carefully and arrangements are done professionally. The following artists and their recordings achieved the ideal gospel sound of the 1980s, and will probably set the pace for the 1990s: Richard Smallwood, "I Love the Lord" and "Center of My Joy"; Milton Brunson and the Thompson Community Choir, "Safe in His Arms" and "God's Got It"; Darryl Coley with the Wilmington Mass Choir, "Sovereign"; Keith Pringle, "Perfect Peace" and "When We See Jesus"; Thomas Whitfield, "Oh How I Love Jesus" and "I'm Encouraged"; and finally, Hezekiah Walker, "Spirit" and "The Lord Will Make a Way Somehow."

In my research, I have also found that the ideal sound does not come only from professional performers. There are many outstanding college, church, and community choirs. Some of the best college choirs include Howard University Gospel Choir, Virginia State University Gospel Choir, Florida A & M Gospel Choir, A & T State University Gospel Choir, and Memphis State College Gospel Choir. Among the best church choirs are those from Cornerstone Institutional Baptist Church (Los Angeles), Institutional Church of God in Christ (Brooklyn, New York), Canaan Baptist Church (New York City), and Bibleway Church (Washington, D.C.).

Gospel choir conventions and festivals keep many of these gospel choirs active. The largest Black gospel convention is the annual James Cleveland Workshop, which hosts gospel groups, musicians, soloists, and churches from around the country to perform and exchange ideas about Black gospel music. The Dorsey Gospel Workshop is still very active and attracts a sizable number of participants. In recent years, New York City has hosted the Black College Gospel Competition sponsored by the Black Music Caucus, a group of professional music educators. This competition attracts such colleges and universities as the University of North Carolina, A & T State University, Howard University, Virginia State University, William Patterson College, Alabama State University, Elizabeth City State University, and Delaware State University.

In conclusion, Black gospel choirs have been in existence for more than sixty years. Their music is filled with a rich heritage that exemplifies the struggles that Blacks have endured and continue to endure. My research in the area of the ideal gospel sound has revealed that gospel music and choirs are constantly changing. Directors and musicians of the 1990s are serious about maintaining quality gospel groups, a goal that requires good choral arrangements, good musicians, utilizing good choral techniques, and keeping abreast of the latest recording technology. As long as this type of commitment is maintained, gospel music and gospel choirs will continuously grow and excel as they strive for the ideal gospel sound.

NOTES

1. *The New Grove Dictionary of Music*, vol. II, ed. H. Wiley Hitchcock and Sadie Stanley (New York: MacMillan Press, 1968), 259.
2. Quoted in Tony Heilbut, *The Gospel Sound* (New York: Simon Schuster, 1971), 65.
3. *Roberta Martin and The Roberta Martin Singers*, ed. Bernie Reason, Linn Shapiro (Washington, D.C.: Smithsonian Institution, 1982), 13.
4. Ibid., 14.
5. Ibid., 43.
6. Heilbut, *The Gospel Sound*, 204.
7. Ibid., 234.
8. Ibid., 239.
9. Ibid., 215.
10. Joe Bostic Sr. interview conducted by B. Dexter Allgood, Long Island City, New York, October 19, 1982.
11. Horace Clarence Boyer, "Contemporary Gospel Music," *Black Perspective In Music* 7 (Nov. 1, 1979): 5–58.
12. *New Grove Dictionary of American Music,* vol. II, 258.
13. Heilbut, *The Gospel Sound*, 319.
14. Thompson Community Choir, *For The Good of Them*, Chicago, Illinois: stereo, 33 1/3, 1989.

Celebrating the Blues

20th Annual Black Musicians Conference

May 1 and May 4, 1991

SOCIAL AND POLITICAL PERSPECTIVES ON THE HISTORY OF THE blues was the theme of the 20th Annual Black Musicians Conference. A heated discussion ensued at a panel that brought together three renowned authors who presented both parallel and divergent views on the volatile subject of race and women's issues as they relate to blues.

Featured panelists included Daphne Duval Harrison, the author of *Black Pearls: Blues Queens of the 1920s* and Chair of the Department of African American Studies at the University of Maryland, Baltimore County, who presented, "Aesthetics of Blues Women's Lyrics and Performances." Albert Murray, a novelist and author of *Stompin' the Blues* and *The Omni Americans* spoke on "Stylizations of the Blues." Jeff Todd Titon, a professor

Schedule of Events, May 1 & 4, 1991
CELEBRATING THE BLUES

Wednesday, May 1, 7:30 PM
Cape Cod Lounge/Student Union

Panel Discussion
Perspectives on the Blues
Daphne Duval Harrison, "Aesthetics of Blues
  Women's Lyrics and Performances"
Albert Murray, "Stylizations of the Blues"
Jeff Todd Titon, "The Blues as an Historical
  Phenomenon"
Frederick C. Tillis, moderator

Distinguished Achievement Award Recipients
Jessie Mae Hemphill
Albert Murray

Concert featuring Jessie Mae Hemphill

Saturday, May 4, 8:00 PM
Fine Arts Center Concert Hall
Concert: "The Late Great Ladies of Blues and
Jazz," featuring Sandra Reeves Phillips

The 1991 Black Musicians Conference was a project of the
Fine Arts Center and was funded in part by the UMass Arts
Council, the Chancellor's Office, the Dean of Humanities and
Fine Arts, the Office of Third World Affairs, the Cultural
Enrichment Fund, the Student Government Association, the
Graduate Student Senate, and the (UPC) Union Programming
Council. The concert featuring Sandra Reeves Phillips was co-
sponsored by the Fine Arts Center Performing Arts Series.

of music at Brown University and author of *Early Downhome Blues: A Musical and Cultural Analysis*, presented "The Blues as an Historical Phenomenon." A written transcript of the panel discussion exists as a rough draft, but the material was not publishable because the audiocassette needed for verification purposes is now missing. Daphne Harrison's and Jeff Titon's essays were submitted for publication and appear in this chapter. In 1991, Distinguished Achievement Awards were presented to Albert Murray and to Jessie Mae Hemphill, the blues singer and guitarist. Immediately following the panel discussion and awards ceremony, Hemphill performed a solo concert at the Cape Cod Lounge in the Student Union.

The conference concluded on May 4 in the Fine Arts Center Concert Hall with a concert by Sandra Reeves Phillips. She performed a one-woman show entitled "The Late Great Ladies of Blues and Jazz," recreating the musical stylings of Ma Rainey, Bessie Smith, Ethel Waters, Billie Holiday, Dinah Washington, and Mahalia Jackson.

Introduction by Mark Baszak

LEFT TO RIGHT
Albert Murray,
Jeff Todd Titon,
Daphne Duval Harrison,
Frederick C. Tillis,
Jessie Mae Hemphill
CAPE COD LOUNGE/
STUDENT UNION

Essay

The Blues as an Historical Phenomenon

By Jeff Todd Titon

WHEN THE BLUES LOST ITS BLACK audience in the 1960s, the blues suffered an even greater loss. Black audiences no longer judged what was authentic or not regarding the music. Before the 1960s, except for occasional exceptions, it would have been absurd for a White blues musician to be appreciated by a Black audience.

Authenticity is something that is not inherent in things or people; it is ascribed to things or people by "experts," and is therefore negotiable. The paradox is that people who ascribe authenticity to something or someone believe that person or thing to be inherently authoritative. For instance, the Bible is inherently authoritative to fundamentalist Protestants.

Up to about 1955, the interpretive community who did the ascribing for the blues was primarily Black musicians and audiences. Authenticity was not an issue because there were no White blues singers or players of any significance.

When the blues revival occurred in the 1950s and 1960s, it brought in a new group of experts who would ascribe on the basis of a new expertise. Most were liberal White people who were only too willing to say that blues was a Black art form. But no matter

how much those privileged, rebellious youth might have wanted to identify with Black blues performers, the new White audience was an audience that Black blues musicians couldn't really speak to about shared experiences.

Previously, the blues was authentic in that it was an enacting of certain Black experiences in the United States in this century, just as spirituals had been an enactment of certain Black experiences in the 19th century. Gospel songs are enactments of another kind of Black experience, but that enactment, too, is authentic only for a Black audience. It makes sense only when it's enacted for a Black interpretive community. When enacted for a White audience, it becomes chiefly a form of escape that is acquisitive and exploitative.

It was inevitable that the blues would be "grayed," and that there would be certain White blues musicians who would arise and speak to this new, White audience. In the 1980s, for example, the actor John Belushi took on the persona of a blues "brother" in the film *The Blues Brothers*.

The words *authority* and *authenticity* suggest in themselves ways of understanding the strange path of the blues in recent years. In the 1960s it was clear to me that because blues was a music invented and nurtured by Black Americans, it was obviously a product of Black America. The blues had a forty-year history of recordings made exclusively by and for Black people. It had been sung and played on street corners and in barrelhouses, juke joints, bars, and clubs for at least sixty years, and always by Black Americans for an almost exclusively Black audience. Whether its message was resignation, as some people argued, or protest, as others argued, or freedom, as I came to believe, blues music was clearly an expression of Black America, something that Black Americans were telling one another through music.

Now we have the phenomenon of blues as a tourist attraction, because that is what it was for Whites during the blues revival. Bill Ferris got the idea that Europeans would be interested in a guided tour of blues country, so he arranged tours for various visitors. Tourism transforms the blues into a safe spectacle, an attraction, something that is "in its place" and, like Chartres Cathedral, is splendid and unchanging, which for an art such as blues means embalming and death. Tourism is the "festival" taken to its logical conclusion. At first, blues tourism was for Europeans, who have always found Africans in the New World exotic. Now it's tourism for Whites in this country. At what point will it become tourism for Blacks?

A monument was erected for Robert Johnson in a church near Morgan City, Mississippi, where Johnson was buried. The monument looks like a miniature Washington Monument; it has a photo on one side, historical text on two other sides, and a full discography of Johnson's recordings on the fourth side! Success of the Columbia release of a Robert Johnson recording on CD, which was the result of a great deal of promotion among young White people, resulted in Columbia's fronting money for a publicity event. At the dedication ceremony, the majority of people in attendance were rock musicians, record executives, journalists, and television crews.

Interestingly, the ceremony took place in a small country church. There were about twenty Black people in attendance: the usual congregation at Mt. Zion (near Morgan City). As the Reverend Ratliff preached his sermon, a Springer spaniel ran up the church aisle, hollering and crying as he was led out of the church. Perhaps the dog was the reincarnation of the hellhound that followed Robert Johnson's trail. The dog didn't appear until the Black preacher began his sermon. Johnson is not buried at this church. His body was moved to another small Black church that resisted the publicity stunt, and they refused to honor him because they believed he had sold his soul to the devil.

The changing audience for blues, or blues-based music played by Whites, was arguably present in rock and roll during the 1950s, and accelerated in the 1960s with the advent of groups like the Rolling Stones and heavy metal bands like Led Zeppelin. The few White blues players, like Paul Butterfield and Memphis Charlie Musselwhite, J. Geils, Leon Redbone, and James Montgomery, were inconsequential. Rock musicians like Eric Clapton can be seen in hindsight to have been far more important. Without Eric Clapton, there could never have been a Stevie Ray Vaughan. What was really happening was that urban blues was being transformed into rock and roll. The whole phenomenon of heavy metal is a kind of bad joke about blues. Heavy metal is the result not so much of a co-opting of the blues but rather of a metamorphosis

Whether its message was resignation, as some people argued, or protest, as others argued, or freedom, as I came to believe, blues music was clearly an expression of Black America, something that Black Americans were telling one another through music.

within rock and roll.

Blues has become a static art form that can be performed by Blacks or Whites today, and the audience is primarily White. Blues has achieved a dubious status similar to Dixieland jazz, and has followed pretty much the same route — a minor stream in the musical mosaic.

In this context, the word *authenticity* takes on an interesting meaning. In the 1960s, White blues singers and guitarists were sincere but not authentic, to use the contrasting terms Lionel Trilling wrote about some twenty years ago. They were sincere in that their outward appearance conformed to their inner feelings, but they were not authentic because they were copies rather than originals.

Blues has to be understood as a historical phe-nomenon; its period ended with the blues revival in the 1960s, and it was over at that point. People who are interested in blues as an enactment of Black America will turn to blues only historically. The revival thought it was breathing new life into the blues, but instead, it historicized it.

Blues can be contrasted with the nonrevival aspect of gospel music. In the gospel scene, there has been continuous development, and no new audience made up of young White people. Of course there is a White gospel music movement as well, but it lacks the kind of major institutional backing that the new "gray" blues has. Gospel music still reflects the religious values of an upwardly mobile segment of Black society, and is still a window looking into and out of the world of the African in America.

Essay

Aesthetics of Blues Women's Lyrics and Performances

By Daphne Duval Harrison

BLACK POETRY IS AS MUCH A PERFORMING art as it is a literary art. Rising out of an oral tradition, it is governed by the aesthetic principles of African and African American poetry, folktales, praise songs, and other songs. *Aesthetics* is a term that often arouses controversy in intellectual discourse because of the tendency for discussants to overlook certain salient factors. One in particular is that the definition of aesthetics depends heavily upon a cultural frame of reference. A dialogue on the aesthetic merit of a particular object, or of a certain group's creative acts, will be served well only when those cultural considerations are taken into account.

Although there are certain universals which may be generally agreed upon, they are not useful if cultural variances are ignored. Culture shapes the notions we have of beauty, of the form and mold of the creative act, and of the social, aesthetic, and philosophical values upon which we respond to the artistic object. Cultural perceptions form the basis for the choices of how a creative idea will be presented, where it will be presented, and to whom it will be presented. The content and nature of the art serve as a system of communication for the individual and the group, reinforcing and elaborating upon cultural values.

When these factors guide a discussion on aesthetics, the integrity of artistic efforts and products of any group can be protected from arbitrary interpretation and evaluation. Aesthetic judgment should rely on knowledge and acceptance of the cultural reference system from which art emanates. In our examination of African American women's creative activities — in this instance, their blues songs — the object becomes the definition of itself by reflecting the social, philosophical, and aesthetic values that brought it into existence.

The underlying assumption is that Black aesthetic values derive from a worldview that differs from that of Western cultures. That perspective is grounded in the concept of balance or transcendental equilibrium: in the words of Robert Farris Thompson, "a constant pursuit of an equilibrium which contains a sense of order among all things animate and inanimate."[1] Humans are regarded not as superior beings who can control the forces of nature, but as part and parcel of the entire cosmos, and therefore subject to its vagaries. In turn, good and evil are considered as two sides of a

An examination of the traditional art forms of many African and African Diaspora groups will reveal that their purpose is to communicate with forces in the spirit world.

single coin which, when on balance, provides stability and prosperity for the people; and when disturbed, creates havoc and chaos in the form of pestilence, disease, famine, violent weather, or war.

An examination of the traditional art forms of many African and African Diaspora groups will reveal that their purpose is to communicate with forces in the spirit world. Upon a closer look, this is also evident in popular arts. Such works are not spontaneous abstract creations produced for the individual's satisfaction, but are usually carefully designed according to specifications developed over many generations. They express the political and social values of the group, as well as elements needed for communication with the spirit world. According to Thompson, one of these values is "opposition transformed into affirmation," or the independence of the individual but in cooperation with the group.[2] Stunning examples of this principle can be found in the lyrics of women's blues poetry.

The African American sensibilities from which blues are derived are culturally based and reflect both the African (remote past) and African American (slave/recent past) attitudes toward performance and creation. The constants that are characteristic of the blues contain the major components of the Black aesthetic. According to Carolyn Fowler in *Black Arts and Black Aesthetics*, the blues represents a creative response in African American culture to oppression, repression, coercion, and alienation. Its constants include a preoccupation with stereotypes, a search for authenticity, representativeness/dealing with propaganda, and the tradition of demystifying the superiority of Whites. Major components of Black aesthetics are flexibility and balance, rather than symmetry. Balance is evident in the use of extravagance or exaggeration without losing control, or motion under control.[3] Syncopation and stress off the beat are prime examples in music. Flexibility employs tension yet retains a certain looseness. These characteristics are part of the survival ethos, as well as a core aesthetic concept best described as "grace under pressure."

Playthell Benjamin has described the African American sensibility in our music as having these elements: triumphant spirituality, exuberant emotional expressiveness, unaffected sensuality, earthy humor, grace, and dignity as a counterpoint to life's adversities.[4] I also believe African American music derives its beauty, vitality, and sense of unity with its audience from the following characteristics: spontaneous shifts in mood and dynamics, solo and interactive virtuosity, a rhythmic pulse (whether spoken or sung) that invites movement and dance, repetitiveness to build intensity and to invoke a transcendent state, and descriptive texts and imagery which also invoke images of dance and dancers.

Other writers have discussed the nature and aesthetics of African American music in similar terms. Therese Smith states that "chanted prayers embody many of the aesthetic values of Afro-American culture — a holistic approach to life, an emphasis upon collective consciousness, an expression and sharing of emotions and their expression in improvised, personalized form."[5] It is an apt assessment of a communal reference or framework for an individual creative response to a common experience. Both religious and secular songs in the Black community contain these qualities whose merit may be judged by the artist and the participant/audience.

Several writers view these qualities as the foundation from which the art form of the blues evolved. Ralph Ellison sees the blues as the singer's impulse to keep alive the painful details and episodes of brutal life experiences while transcending them with tragicomedic lyricism.[6] The psychologists Alfred Pasteur and Ivory Toldson express the same view in their discussion of spirituals and the blues:

> The blues... represent a form of social, aesthetic therapy... [and] thus constitute a musical form that allows for the aesthetic and therapeutic expression of one's innermost feelings, ranging from throbbing pain to spirited joy. Often times, these two opposing feelings are conveyed together... The relief gained (through the blues) comes from naturally emitted, African-inspired aesthetic behaviors, intensely expressed while approaching the world of spiritual forces. On return from nearness to metaphysical reality, one suddenly discovers that much, not all, misery is replaced by a sense of ease.[7]

Albert Murray believes that an "art style [in this instance, the blues] reflects... the ultimate synthesis and refinement of a life style."[8]

Sterling Brown addressed the direct honesty and integrity of poetry in his seminal essay, "The Blues." "Although the experiences as expressed in blues lyrics are not unique to Blacks," he says, "the frankness of revelation and language is greater than in the love-poetry of more 'sophisticated' areas." (I question the use of the term *sophisticated* by Brown in this context, because even if the artist is not literate in the technical sense of the term, the use of figures of speech and other forms of mask and symbols in the blues denotes a high level of sophistication.) Brown continues, "The blues have a bitter honesty... [about] the way the blues singers and poets have found life to be. And their audiences agree."[9]

In the above statement, Brown addressed a prime factor in African American aesthetic valuation — the relationship between the performer/artist and the creation and performance of the art because of the intense reciprocal nature of the creative act. Social and cultural values of the group inform the artist who creates the work, presents it, and receives immediate reaction with regard to its quality.

The creative process is continuous. For example, Alberta Hunter sang "I Got a Mind to Ramble" in 1926, and she received reaffirmation in 1982 for a new version of the same blues. The first rendition is jaunty, upbeat, and almost light-hearted. The contemporary version is brassy, a bit arrogant, and self-confident. It is the expression of a mature, wise woman who has weathered eight decades of ups and downs. The transcendence of troubled times is evident in words, music, and performance style. The audience validates

In our examination of African American women's creative activities — in this instance, their blues songs — the object becomes the definition of itself by reflecting the social, philosophical, and aesthetic values that brought it into existence.

the performance with punctuations of "yeah, right-on, speak-on-it," and so on.

> *I got a mind to ramble but I don' t know where to*
> *   go.*
> *Yes, I got a mind to ramble, ooh, but I don' t*
> *   know where to go.*
> *If I' m lucky to leave here,*
> *   I sho' ain' t coming back no mo' !*
> *Folks, I ain' t got a crying penny,*
> *   my poor feet are on the ground.*
> *Folks, I ain' t got a crying penny,*
> *   my poor feet are on the ground.*
> *And if I ever want to be somebody I sho' got to*
> *   leave this town.*[10]

Sippie Wallace sings the following lines, which are very personal but which address a common concern of many Black women, thus linking her to her female listeners.

> *Hey – ey mama, run tell yo' papa, Go tell yo' sis-*
> *   ter, run tell yo' auntie*
> *That I'm goin' up the country, Don' t you wanta*
> *   go-o?*
> *I need another husband to take me on my night-*
> *   time stroll . . .*

> *When I was leaving, I left some folks*
> *   a-grieving, I left my friends a-moaning,*
> *I left my man a-sighing,*
> *' Cause he knew he had mistreat me and torn up*
> *   all my clothes.*
> *He treat me low down and dirty;*
> *He finally reaped just what he done sowed.*

> *I told him to give me that coat I bought him, that*
> *   shirt I bought him,*
> *Those shoes I bought him, those socks I bought*
> *   him,*
> *' Cause he knew he did not want me, he had no*
> *   right to stall,*
> *I told him to pull off that hat I bought him, and*
> *   let his nappy head go bald.*[11]

Her resolution of the dilemma embodies the use of opposing forces as a means of reaffirming her right to joy and therefore, that of all her sisters.

African songs of ridicule, antecedents of this type of blues, allow women to make derisive statements on topics that are otherwise taboo in ordinary discourse. Although overt expressions of anger are frowned upon, singing about the anger is applauded and encouraged. This principle derives from the dialectical role of the Black woman, which is another form of the opposition of forces. This is manifest in artistic, creative expressions such as sweet/tough, smart and cold/naive and warm, vulnerable/ impenetrable, domineered/domineering, strong/weak, mother/child, and nurturer/warrior. An example of this dialectic is found in "Don't Fish in My Sea," written by Ma Rainey and Bessie Smith.

> *If you don' t like my ocean, don' t fish in my sea.*
> *If you don' t like my ocean, don' t fish in my sea.*
> *Get out of my valley and let my mountain be.*

> *I ain' t had no loving, since God knows when.*
> *I ain' t had no loving, since God knows when.*
> *That's the reason I'm through with these no*
> *   good trifling men.*[12]

Because of its evocative power, women's blues have a universal appeal that speaks to the human condition while reflecting the Black woman's response to the American condition.

Obviously, these lyrics are concerned with an unfaithful lover. But more important is the picturesque language used to scathingly denounce the offender and send him packing, to lament the loss of good loving, and to renounce future relationships with men. To pack that much into essentially only four lines is an artistic achievement.

Lovie Austin's "Any Woman's Blues" illustrates the unity of expression and common experience referred to earlier. Bessie Smith's performance empowers the words with a feeling of anguish, coupled with adulation and pride.

> *I feel blue, I don' know what to do.*
> *Every woman in my fix is bound to feel blue too.*
> *'Cause I love my man better than I love myself.*
> *'Lawd, I love my man better than I love myself.*
> *And if he don' have me, he won' t have nobody else.*
>
> *My man's got teeth like a lighthouse on the sea.*
> *My man's got teeth like a lighthouse on the sea.*
> *Everytime he smiles, he throws them lights on me.*
>
> *His voice sound like chimes, I mean the organ kind.*

> *His voice sound like chimes, I mean the organ kind.*
> *And every time he speaks, his music ease my troublin' mind.*[13]

The employment of metaphors in both of these blues demonstrates a sophisticated sense of the value of vivid imagery in depicting intense personal emotion. It gives significant evidence of the level of sophistication of so-called illiterate audiences whose aesthetics belie their lack of formal education.

The use of double entendre allows the blues woman to express emotional exuberance and to be openly sensual without risking direct sanction from the group. All of this is accomplished with a conscious sense of style and grace that is peppered with earthiness, and in some instances, sexual arrogance.

By combining straightforward lyrics with a driving rhythmic pulse which is characteristic of African music, the contemporary blues woman Koko Taylor imbues her lyrics with a torrid sexuality. The movement implied in the following lyrics evokes the imagery of a couple totally immersed in lovemaking. However, Taylor's performance is an expression of sheer joy and ecstasy, not mere erotica.

Come on baby, get wid it,
Get down to the nitty gritty,
'Cause you knows where it's at,
And you knows I likes it like that.

When you hol' me like ya hol' me,
And then squeeze me like ya squeeze me,
And when ya kiss me like ya kiss me, baby,
And tease me like ya tease me . . . [14]

Though limited, the above examples illustrate that the style of performance is just as important as the content. With a very strong reciprocal nature or process, there is indeed a sort of ritual about performance. The ego of the performer is heavily involved, but the performance also requires involvement and verification from the group. When those two separate parts are working well together, they transcend what was there separately, and each part feeds the other to produce something of an even higher order.

The aesthetic principles mentioned above are reflected in the blues of women as participants, observers, and models for creative expression. Within these contexts, blues lyrics can be better understood as an art form, and blues women's poetics more clearly acknowledged as an art style. Because of its evocative power, women's blues have a universal appeal that speaks to the human condition while reflecting the Black woman's response to the American condition. This universality connotes an aesthetic as well as emotional value to the artist and her audience, and serves as a unifying experience for both.

NOTES

1. Robert Farris Thompson, *African Art and Motion* (Washington, D.C., 1974), 23.
2. Ibid., 11.
3. Carolyn Fowler, *Black Arts and Black Aesthetics: A Bibliography* (Atlanta: First World Press, 1982), xvi–xvii.
4. Playthell Benjamin, "Western Culture Revised: The Century of African Music," *Freedomways* (fall 1985), 157.
5. Therese Smith, "Chanted Prayer in Southern Black Churches," *The Southern Quarterly: A Journal of the Arts in the South* 23, no. 3 (spring 1985): 70.
6. Ralph Ellison, *Shadow and Act* (New York: Random House, 1964), 98.
7. Alfred Pasteur and Ivory Toldson, *Roots of Soul: The Psychology of Black Expressiveness* (Garden City, N.Y.: Doubleday, 1982), 128–29.
8. Albert Murray quoted in Benjamin, "Western Culture Revised," 164.
9. Sterling Brown, "The Blues," *Phylon* 4 (1952): 288.
10. Alberta Hunter, "I Got a Mind to Ramble" (Bluesville BVLP 1052, August 1961).
11. Sippie Wallace, "Up the Country Blues," (OKEH 816, 1923).
12. Ma Rainey, "Don't Fish in My Sea," *Ma Rainey's Black Bottom* (Yazoo 1071 reissue of Paramount, 1927).
13. Bessie Smith, "Any Woman's Blues (Columbia CG30126, reissue of Columbia 13001-D, 1923).
14. Koko Taylor, "Nitty Gritty," *Koko Taylor* (Chess CH-9263).

Jessie Mae Hemphill
CAPE COD LOUNGE/
STUDENT UNION

New Trends in Vocal Jazz

21st Annual Black Musicians Conference

February 10 to February 13, 1992

JAZZ SINGING, LIKE JAZZ PLAYING, IS THE EMBODIMENT OF all that is refined and varied in singing. Nuance and shading prevail over volume and power; continuous variation and an unusual turn of phrase predominate over repetition; syncopated and asymmetrical rhythms substitute for predictable four-square movement; unpredictable melodies and harmonies emerge unexpectedly, and virtuosity, both brilliant and subdued, abounds.

First illustrated through the singing of plantation singers in spirituals, work songs, and play songs, and secularized in minstrelsy, the jazz style was developed by the itinerant singers of the blues. It took on new rhythms and melodies in ragtime, borrowed energy and sincerity from gospel, and proclaimed itself independent in the swing era. It incorporated the jagged

Bobby McFerrin and Rhiannon performing from the floor of the Fine Arts Center Concert Hall.

Schedule of Events, February 10–13, 1992
NEW TRENDS IN VOCAL JAZZ

Monday, February 10, 5:00 PM
Augusta Savage Gallery

Art Exhibit & Performance:
Images of Sound
Music by Sonority

Tuesday, February 11, 7:30 PM
Cape Cod Lounge, Student Union

Panel Discussion
New Trends in Vocal Jazz
Phyl Garland, "Eddie Jefferson and Jon Hendricks: Innovators in Modern Vocal Jazz"
Leslie Gourse, "The Unforgettable Nat King Cole: How a Big Legend Grew from a Little Trend"
Jon Hendricks, "The Vocal Jazz Group: A History"
Frederick C. Tillis, moderator

Distinguished Achievement Award Recipients
Phyl Garland
Jon Hendricks

Mini-Concert featuring Just Friends

Thursday, February 13, 8:00 PM ,
Fine Arts Center Concert Hall

Concert featuring Bobby McFerrin with Voicestra

The 1992 Black Musicians Conference was a program of the Fine Arts Center and was funded in part by the UMass Arts Council. *Images of Sound* was cosponsored by Augusta Savage Gallery, and the performance by Bobby McFerrin and Voicestra was cosponsored by the Fine Arts Center Concert Series

melody and rhythms of bop and the eclecticism of cool jazz, progressive jazz, and even third stream. It essayed the elements of abstraction, modality and electronics, and helped to introduce fusion.

From Blind Lemon Jefferson to Ma Rainey, Louis Armstrong to Billie Holiday, Ella Fitzgerald to Sarah Vaughan, Eddie Jefferson to Jon Hendricks, or Cassandra Wilson to Bobby McFerrin, vocal jazz has endured and will surely thrive.

Introduction by Horace Clarence Boyer

THE 1992 CONFERENCE EXPLORED THE DEVELOPMENT OF NEW trends in vocal jazz through the pioneering artistry of Nat King Cole, Eddie Jefferson, Jon Hendricks, Bobby McFerrin, and others in the modern and postmodern era. It opened with "Images of Sound," a group art exhibit in Augusta Savage Gallery that featured works by Nelson Stevens, Dorrance

Jon Hendricks
CAPE COD LOUNGE/
STUDENT UNION

OPPOSITE LEFT
Bobby McFerrin and
Voicestra
FINE ARTS CENTER CONCERT HALL

Distinguished Achievement award
recipients Phyl Garland and Jon
Hendricks, flanked by Horace Clarence
Boyer (LEFT), Leslie Gourse, and
Frederick Tillis (RIGHT)
CAPE COD LOUNGE/STUDENT UNION

Hill, and Adger Cowen.

A Panel Discussion in the Cape Cod Lounge at the Student Union was entitled "New Trends in Vocal Jazz." It included presentations by Phyl Garland ("Eddie Jefferson and Jon Hendricks: Innovators in Modern Vocal Jazz"), Leslie Gourse ("The Unforgettable Nat King Cole: How a Big Legend Grew from a Little Trend"), and Jon Hendricks ("The Vocal Jazz Group: a History"). In this chapter, an edited transcript of panel presentations by Phyl Garland and Jon Hendricks is followed by Leslie Gourse's essay.

Distinguished Achievement Awards were presented to Phyl Garland and Jon Hendricks, and music was supplied by Just Friends, a Boston area group featuring lead vocals by Semenya McCord. It was an exciting mini-concert made even more memorable by an unscheduled and magical performance by the legendary vocalist Jon Hendricks.

The conference concluded with a concert by Bobby McFerrin, an artist who was at the height of his career and enjoying unparalleled success. His Amherst engagement included a performance with Voicestra, McFerrin's all vocal orchestra.

Introduction by Mark Baszak

Just Friends, featuring Semenya McCord
CAPE COD LOUNGE/STUDENT UNION

Tuesday, February 11, 1992
Cape Cod Lounge/Student Union

Panel Discussion Transcript Excerpts

New Trends in Vocal Jazz

Edited Panel Discussion Transcript: Tuesday, February 11, 1992

There's a lot of talk these days about multiculturalism and diversity. People are talking about how to define it, and it's difficult, there's no doubt about it. We can do it, in some ways it can be a very rich and interesting academic exercise to write about it and define all these terms. But it would be interesting to note that some of us have been in the business, and not just writing about it, for about twenty years or so.

INTRODUCTORY REMARKS BY FREDERICK C. TILLIS

LEFT TO RIGHT
Frederick C. Tillis, Phyl Garland,
Jon Hendricks, and Leslie Gourse
CAPE COD LOUNGE/STUDENT UNION

Eddie Jefferson and Jon Hendricks: Innovators in Modern Vocal Jazz

Excerpts from the presentation by Phyl Garland

WE THINK OF INSTRUMENTALISTS as being virtuosos, but a vocal virtuoso is yet another type of being. When everything was getting going at the beginning of time, I'd like to think that the muses of jazz ..., being super hip, decided not to erect barriers separating the domains of vocal and instrumental music. They left it up to us mortals to figure out how the two could be brought together in a highly original art form.

From the earliest days of this music that we call jazz, this concept of duality has fed the flame of creativity. By emulating the human voice, jazz instrumentalists have been able to impose the full force of their own personalities — their thoughts, their lives, and their feelings — and to express these things through their instruments ... and they do so with a level of individuality as distinctive as the name on a calling card. You know who it is when you hear it.

They have even gone beyond speaking or singing, for these instruments can convey a universe of human feelings played in different ways by moaning, shouting, growling, sassing. And sometimes these instruments can even curse you out. Yet it has been left to a few gifted individuals to figure out how this equation should be used in the other direction, with the singer assuming the demands of the instrument, playing his voice like an instrument. This has been a part of jazz, and indeed all African American music, since the beginning. In [early] blues and religious music, the cadences, nuances, and inflections have been there in the instruments, and the singers have also sounded very much like those instruments.

In jazz, this reached a very high level of development. It has remained a staple of the field ever since Louis Armstrong developed the art of vocal improvisation. He perfected the technique of scat singing — singing as brilliantly with his voice as he had played with his horn. But as Louis Armstrong was able to find words, and to create words where none had existed before, there would be others who would take a different direction. They would use existing words and make those words do things that no one had ever thought possible. With tremendous technical virtuosity and intellectual integrity, they would take recorded jazz instrumental solos and transform them into vocal performances of great daring — and they called it "vocalese."

The pioneer in this field was Edgar Jefferson, but he was known as Eddie Jefferson, the man who conceived and developed the art of singing recorded instrumental solos, but adopting them to his own words. Those words often told a story or conveyed a sense of the kind of world the musician lived in. This was a major musical innovation, and very often Jefferson is overlooked. He wasn't a superstar to the general world, but he was a major light in the development of the music . . .

Eddie Jefferson was born in Pittsburgh, Pennsylvania, on August 3, 1918. Many of the reasons why he was willing to accept the challenge of the jazz muses was because he was born in Pittsburgh, and Pittsburgh is a place where the music has always thrived. It has produced many major musical figures including Earl Hines, Marion Williams, Erroll Garner, Ahmad Jamal, and Billy Eckstine, who had the most influential big band of the period. People in that band [included] Dizzy, Charlie Parker, Art Blakey, Roy Eldridge, Maxine Sullivan, Dakota Staton, Billy Strayhorn (Duke Ellington's alter ego), Stanley Turrentine, and George Benson, to name a few.

Eddie Jefferson grew up in "The Burgh." His father was in show business and encouraged him when he showed a passion for music. He studied the tuba, played the guitar and drums; but he also became a dancer. In fact, he made his living as a dancer, and later in life he went back to dancing. When he went out on the road as a professional musician, he took a little portable phonograph along with him, and when he had to stay in these shabby, depressing hotel rooms, he would listen to the music and this would lift his spirits. He fell into the habit of listening to favorite recorded instrumental solos. Back in about 1938, he shared this idea with his dancing partner — a man named Irv Taylor. In 1939 Jefferson wrote words for a Count Basie record called "Taxi War Dance." He set his own lyrics to the solos by Lester Young and Russell Evans, duplicating the nuances, flow, thrust, rhythm, and energy of the solos. This was quite daring. Nothing came of that, and it was going to be a little while before something did come of it.

At first he would write lyrics to these solos, and people often knew the solos from hearing them,

I'd like to think that the muses of jazz, being super hip, decided not to erect barriers separating the domains of vocal and instrumental music.

Where Eddie Jefferson laid the foundation and was rooted very strongly in bebop, . . . Jon Hendricks bridged the various styles from swing through bop to experimental music.

because jazz was a very popular music at that period. Then he began to sing a couple of his creations. One of them was a famous improvisation by tenor saxophonist James Moody, who settled in New York for a while, but in Stockholm recorded a very unusual version of "I'm in the Mood for Love." He borrowed a saxophone from some other musician and played this very eloquent, very original solo. Eddie Jefferson admired this solo very much. He heard the work in the States and wrote some lyrics to this solo. He then began singing it at after-hours sessions, but he sang it a bit too often and was not the first to record this solo. King Pleasure, another vocal innovator, had a great hit with the song back in 1952. It was through this song that Jefferson got an opportunity to begin recording in his own right. He had a very unmistakable voice with a rough, reedy edge to it. It had a grittiness with a touch of the blues in it. The most amazing thing about his voice was the way he really sounded like a horn. His voice had exceptional nimbleness. His lips and tongue could move with great facility in articulating these words, and how anyone could get them out singing that fast, and doing it in tune, was a marvel. All of those solos are quite remarkable. He set many standards to his own lyrics, among them, "A Night in Tunisia" and "Yardbird Suite." One of his hits was "I've Got the Blues."

It seemed that Jefferson's star was beginning to rise again in his later years . . . He was a guest on Dexter Gordon's recording called *Great Encounters* — a remarkable album — and was making more frequent public appearances. I can recall seeing him in 1979 at Carnegie Hall in a concert with Sarah Vaughan. And though I had listened to Eddie Jefferson's recordings for as long as I could remember, I hadn't had a chance to see him in a place like that, and it was a wonderful sight. He didn't stand there as you would expect a singer, he looked more like a prizefighter, leaning into the mike, and leaning toward the audience like someone about to take off on a sprint. It was a very athletic sort of posture, and this sort of athleticism was essential to the music. That was going to be his last major performance in concert.

Within six weeks of that performance, Eddie Jefferson was in Detroit playing a gig at a place called Baker's Keyboard Lounge. After a performance that he mysteriously cut short, Eddie Jefferson walked outside and was sitting in a cab when a car parked near the club pulled up. Four shots were fired. One hit him in the chest, and he died. It was someone he had known, an unemployed factory worker who later was found "not guilty." But he was dead, and it was at a time when he seemed to still be at the peak of his powers . . .

But Eddie Jefferson was not the only person who took up the challenge of the muses. There was another person who took this concept and pushed it further than anybody ever had, developing complex vocal arrangements that are still absolutely astounding. Where Eddie Jefferson laid the foundation and was rooted very strongly in bebop, and inspired those who followed afterwards in bebop, Jon Hendricks bridged the various styles from swing through bop to experimental music. There aren't too many people who can go all the way from Count Basie to John Coltrane to George Russell, and then pause to spend time with everyone in between as well.

What was also quite remarkable about Jon Hendricks was his use of creative and witty lyrics. [The speaker confers with Hendricks regarding his biography at this point in the discussion.] Born on September 16, 1921, Jon Hendricks was the son of a minister. He grew up singing in church, and one of the people he happened to meet in Toledo was a man named Art Tatum, who could do with the piano what Jon could do with the voice. He eventually moved to New York and became a songwriter. At one point, he joined with two other artists to form Lambert, Hendricks and Ross, a group that stands alone in the history of jazz vocals.

What made it so remarkable was that Jon Hendricks wrote lyrics that captured every note and pause of complex instrumental arrangements. Whereas others had done maybe a solo or two, this was the whole arrangement. There is an extraordinary recording called *Sing a Song of Basie*. It was recorded with multitracking before that [recording technique] became popular, and it was innovative in that respect. It is so dazzling, so brilliant, so complex, you wonder how it could all come together as well as it does. I always said that if I ever had to go to a desert island, there are few records that I would take with me, and that recording is one of them.

The extraordinary accomplishment of Jon Hendricks was his ability to use the voice as an instrument — in arrangements that were done by others, solos that were done by others — to create original solos with that level of literacy and articulation. Some have said that he is the poet laureate of modern jazz. His lyrics have little stories in them that you will find most amusing even if you are not concentrating on the music. Listening to what is being said is as much a part of the experience as enjoying the vocal virtuosity. As a solo artist, he has recorded John Coltrane's "Naima," Randy Weston's "Hi-Fly." He has done them all and has an exceptional capacity to bridge different styles, and this is a very high accomplishment. The muses are very, very pleased that someone found out how to make the equation work on both sides...

Tuesday, February 11, 1992
Cape Cod Lounge/Student Union

Panel Discussion Transcript Excerpts

The Vocal Jazz Group: A History

Excerpts from the presentation by Jon Hendricks

Louis Armstrong is the first and the last, the alpha and the omega of jazz singing.

I BECAME A LYRICIST BECAUSE I'VE ALWAYS been somewhat of a poet. I used to write poetry for the high school paper and then for the university paper, and I always tried to put [words] into rhyme. I was singing since I was 7. It was in the middle of the Great Depression, and times were hard. I went to sing in the street for money, and I was an intellectually precocious child. I was always able to gauge people's ethnicity. I would go into bars with a young man in Toledo who played piano, and I would gauge the ethnic clientele of the bar. If it were Italian, I would sing "Torno Sorrento." Then I went to the next bar, and there'd be a bunch of Irish people, so I'd sing "Did Your Mother Come from Ireland?" They all loved me and I made a lot of money that way . . .

I studied under Art Tatum. When I came out of school at 3:00, I would have to go by Art's house and practice with him from 3:30 to 5:30. Then I would go home and I would study from 5:30 to 6:30, then I would sleep until 8:30, because I had to be in the club at 9:30. I got out of the club at 3:00, and I would come home and dump the money that I had made into my mother's apron to wake her up, because she would be asleep by the stove. And then she'd feed me and I would go to bed. I had to get up at 7:00 to be in school at 9:00, and I was maintaining a 3.5 average.

Working with Art, I learned how he substituted chords. Because he had been a violinist, his aim in life was to out-do Jascha Heifetz. He learned all the symphonic pieces very well. Listening to Art Tatum play Grieg's "Elegy" — it's exquisite the way he played it because it's correct, and then when he swung it, it was just incredible . . .

I got a job working in a place called the Chateau France, which was a supper club run by the mob. This was at a time I was working with Art Tatum. There was a room with a piano in back, and we would have to go out into the kitchen area where we had to stand. We could not go into the room with the people to whom we were singing. That was the way it was in those days. Guys were running whiskey back and forth from Michigan down through Ohio, because one state was "dry" and the other one was "wet." They would drive up in these big cars, come in the back door where we were standing, and take out shotguns from under their coats and stack them up in the corner of the room. They would come by and say, "Hi, kid," and give me a pat on the head, which was demeaning in those days. It was considered good luck if you patted a little Negro boy on the head, so they would pat me on the head and put twenty dollars in my hand. Well, twenty dollars could feed my family for two weeks, so I must

I want to point out that jazz music in this country would not exist, and I'm serious about this, if it were not for the gangster element in this country. They are the ones who gave the music a chance to grow. They provided the clubs that became venues for Louis Armstrong and Joe Oliver when they came up from New Orleans after Storyville closed. They gave them the place where they could play the music, because the so-called decent people wanted nothing to do with that music . . .

confess, my anger abated a bit. [Laughter] This is the way that I was to earn a lot of money.

I want to point out that jazz music in this country would not exist, and I'm serious about this, if it were not for the gangster element in this country. They are the ones who gave the music a chance to grow. They provided the clubs that became venues for Louis Armstrong and Joe Oliver when they came up from New Orleans after Storyville closed. They gave them the place where they could play the music, because the so-called decent people wanted nothing to do with that music, and I mean nothing. So we have an anomaly in this country — if it hadn't been for the Mafia, there'd probably be no jazz now . . .

That's the social climate in which the music was engendered, in which it grew. That was also the time the music was becoming the cultural art form that some of us greatly admit it to be today, and a lot of us are very proud that it is acknowledged as such today. It is one of the great cultural art forms existing in the world, and we have to set foot outside the United States to ascertain that. It's a very vital art form, and popular everywhere. Jazz and blues records have sold

in Europe and Japan for thirty-five years, where there's always been a great market for this music and a great deal of an admiration for it. The music is almost non-existent in the United States, but it is very popular all over the world . . .

Jazz singing was done individually at first. Louis Armstrong is the first and the last, the alpha and the omega of jazz singing. This man defined what jazz singing is. The first jazz vocal group was a duo — Noble Sissle and Eubie Blake. Eubie Blake played the piano, Noble Sissle stood up next to the piano, and they sang together and were fantastic. They sang a lot of songs that they wrote themselves and some of the popular songs of the day. They eventually ended up writing a show called *Shuffle Along* in 1922, and they were among the first, if not the first vocal group . . .

It was Duke Ellington's ambition to have an orchestra like Jimmie Lunceford's. Jimmie Lunceford's Orchestra was the coolest, the newest, and best sounding orchestra at that time. The whole band would change clothes three times during one one-hour show. They were sharp, they were cool, and they sounded good, so Duke wanted that kind of a band.

Bing Crosby was very hip. He made a record with Duke Ellington that's really one of the best examples of early scat singing that you will ever hear.

He wanted to do something that would out-do the Lunceford band, so he put together a singing trio amongst his musicians and recorded a tune called "I Want to Be a Rug Cutter" around 1924 or 5. It's a fantastic version of jazz singing of that era . . .

Jimmie Lunceford's orchestra had Sy Oliver in the band at that time. Sy played trumpet and wrote arrangements, Trummy Young was a trombone player, and the alto player was Willie Smith. Those three got together in the band to sing and made some hits — "Four or Five Times," Margie," and "Do What You Do," which was their big hit, a real monster hit for the Lunceford band . . .

Another group that sprang up was called The Spirits of Rhythm, and was composed of three of the wildest jazz singers of all time. The main guy was Leo Watson who was [also] a trombone player, a drummer, and he was probably the funniest character that lived. He was a "Doctor of Philosophy." [Laughter] He did a lot of movies and Broadway shows. I used to listen to these guys when I was 13 or 14 years old, and boy they could swing! They were incredible and very popular for a while.

And then about that time there was an orchestra [Paul Whiteman's] with a vocal group in the band that sang jazz.* They were called The Rhythm Boys, and one of the members, Harry Louis Crosby from Seattle, later became Bing Crosby. He was scatting at that time, and was very hip. Bing Crosby was very hip. He made a record with Duke Ellington that's really one of the best examples of early scat singing that you will ever hear. Bing Crosby was very talented; he loved jazz, loved Louis Armstrong, loved Duke Ellington, loved all the cats . . .

Then came The Mills Brothers from Ohio. They used to rehearse in Toledo and they made vocal jazz singing more popular than perhaps anybody ever has, and they lasted longer than any group. They made everybody very aware of how good four people could sound singing jazz together.

[Vocalists] began to proliferate among the bands. Jan Savitt had a guy singing with him called Bon Bon — like a little chocolate confection — that was his name. Bon Bon was a great scat singer, and if you can find recordings by Jan Savitt with Bon Bon, it's really worth while to get hold of them because he's one of my ancestors. He's one of the ancestors to Eddie Jefferson.

Then you started to get groups like The Merry Macs, . . . who sang with different bands. They had a rhythm section and a vibraphone player, and sang in very interesting harmonic structures at that time — not just third, fourth, fifth, sevenths — they went into ninth and thirteenth [chords]. They went into the [harmonic] area of groups that came out later like The Hi-Lo's, . . . [a group] very popular around the late 1930s. They led to The Modernaires — the vocal group with their own orchestra. They did "Chattanooga Choo Choo" and numbers like that which were very hip.

When that [style of music] got to be popular, Tommy Dorsey, who was always looking for new trends to follow, put strings with his band, as did Artie Shaw. Tommy hired a group called The Pied Pipers — a great vocal jazz group which consisted of Frank Sinatra, who was the band vocalist at that time, and a lady named Jo Stafford, who was one of the best singers ever in the history of the world. This woman hit a note right in the middle and stayed in tune

---

*Hendricks referred to the Jean Goldkette Orchestra in his presentation. However, when the Goldkette organization folded, many of its musicians joined the Paul Whiteman Orchestra, and the Whiteman Band featured The Rhythm Boys.

throughout the song, which is hard to do. They were very good, and did a lot of beautiful numbers that became very popular — "I Will Never Smile Again," with Frank Sinatra. They were called jazz vocalists then because there was no distinction between jazz and pop at that time. Jazz was the popular music of the United States. That distinction didn't come until later, when people stopped swinging.

Tommy Dorsey lured Sy Oliver away from Jimmie Lunceford, and began to write arrangements for Frank Sinatra, and also for The Pied Pipers. They did a masterpiece on a song with strings called "On the Sunny Side of the Street" — and that's one of the great jazz vocal arrangements of all time...

Strangely enough, we come to The Ink Spots. The Ink Spots are not usually mentioned as a jazz vocal group, but if they weren't jazz, I don't know what they were. Although most of the songs for which they are known are lovely ballads, they sang some hip things like [singing] "I love coffee, I love tea, I love the java jive and it loves me." That was a great jazz vocal arrangement. They were a great vocal group and were entertaining. I saw them many times and they swung when they sang those ballads.

After The Spirits of Rhythm broke up, Tiger Haynes organized a group called The Three Flames. These cats do things I still haven't heard anybody [else] do. First, they scatted very fast and coherently on some tunes, and they sounded like instruments.

By that time, the music had begun to undergo a change. Some of the " Young Turks," as they were called, younger musicians like John Birks Gillespie, who was playing trumpet with the Cab Calloway Orchestra, and was threatened with being fired every-day because he was playing what Cab Calloway called

"that Chinese music" [were playing music that] would evolve to be bebop. Bebop was emerging, and it was just a new way of doing an old thing. The rhythm section would play the same chords, but they played a much more sophisticated and hip melodic line. But that new way was very disturbing to a lot of the cats doing the old thing, because it's hard to do. It ain't easy...[Laughter]

I'm going to end now by just mentioning a few of the bebop groups that I used to love to listen to — there was a group called Jackie and Roy. Jackie Cain was a piano player with saxophone player Charlie Ventura [from] the band Bop for the People. Jackie was the vocalist. Roy Kral played piano, and they played nothing but bebop.

Dave Lambert and Buddy Stewart were two cats that I heard in Toledo who did some records on a label called Keynote. I heard these guys and I said, "Wow!" — because that's what I was doing at the time in Toledo in the middle of Ohio. Never having been to New York, I was doing almost exactly what Dave Lambert was doing. Our paths were going in the same direction. So later when I came to New York, and I had written a lyric to Woody Herman's "Four Brothers," I was asked who I wanted to record with, and I said "Dave Lambert." We met and were together for twelve years after that, we just never separated. We thought alike, felt alike, and we were starving alike. And so we thought that before we starve to death, we'd like to leave a work of art on the earth, so that people would know that we had been here. We decided that we would lyricize Count Basie [*Sing a Song of Basie*, 1957], went back to starving, but finally it was number 13 in *Down Beat,* and then we became famous, and it's never stopped. But the reason for the album wasn't

Bebop was emerging, and it was just a new way of doing an old thing.

that we were going to be stars. We just wanted to leave something on the earth.

Babs Gonzales was very important in the development of this kind of singing, not so much in words, but his phraseology that a lot of singers use. Sarah [Vaughan] uses a lot of his phrases, so does Carmen [McRae]. Babs Gonzales was unique in the world. In London, he gave me his card once, and I looked at it, and there was nothing on it except "My Card." He was a funny cat, but he was also fantastically artistic, very hip, and very creative.

Amidst, around, underneath, over, and above, and during all of this there were still the Mills Brothers. Throughout all these years they kept right on going. When everybody thought they were old and passé, they came out with a record with Tommy Dorsey's orchestra called *Opus No. 1*, and it was fantastic. So these guys who were there when it all started, very elderly gentlemen at that time, all grown up and famous, were still here, and they were showing us what we were doing and how to do it . . .

Additional panel discussion comments . . .

Jon Hendricks, responding to a question about why there are not many new jazz vocalists recording today

I think why nobody is singing the music is because the music has now become an industrial economic entity. It's not treated like a culture like it is in the rest of the world. It's a part of a business, and when you get a natural heir to an Ella Fitzgerald, like Whitney Houston and Dianne Reeves certainly are, and they are told by their record companies they can't make a nickel singing that stuff, but they can make money doing "*Oh Baby!*" well, then you have a lot of "*Oh Baby*". . .

Frederick C. Tillis

The real essence of music is that it's another language to communicate your feelings by way of sound, rather than by some literal meaning.

Jon Hendricks

Lester Young said that when you play a ballad, you have to know the lyrics. You can't play a ballad with any degree of feeling unless you know the lyric. Now even though when you play it, no one hears the lyric, if you know the lyric you can subliminally hear the lyric in what the great jazz instrumentalists have played. You know they know the lyric. Music is spiritual, it's as much subliminal as it is overt.

Essay

The Unforgettable Nat King Cole: How a Big Legend Grew from a Little Trend

By Leslie Gourse

THE SOUND OF NAT "KING" COLE'S voice was always haunting and mysterious, tender and romantic. It made him a star recording artist for Capitol Records in the early 1940s. By the time he had a hit in 1946 with "The Christmas Song," most Americans knew his voice very well. Then came "Nature Boy" and "Mona Lisa," and his voice became part of the American psyche. Nobody mistook his mellow baritone and confiding style for anyone else's. He became a legend to the degree that people born after he died recognize his voice when they hear it on the radio today.

When I started to write about Nat in a book called *Unforgettable: The Life and Mystique of Nat King Cole*," the serenity implied by his voice gave me no clue about the turmoil I would discover in his off-stage life. Then I began to interview scores of people who had known and worked with him closely. He was one of the first Black superstars in the country, and in many ways he was a pioneer. He was one of the first balladeers, the first to have his own television show, and the first Black entertainer who tried to overcome discriminatory policies that prevented him from finding a national sponsor. At first NBC sustained his

show, paying twenty thousand dollars a week for production costs until Nat managed to attract several regional sponsors. Their sponsorship wasn't enough, and Nat finally decided to cancel his show. His rise to fame and his stardom never symbolized a life that was as velvety smooth and charmed as his sophisticated musicianship.

Few people really knew much about Cole except for his public image and vocal sound. For one thing, Nat was one of the stars whom gossip columnists protected from any hint of controversy. For another, Nat never lived a flamboyant life. His sister Evelyn Coles, who bears the original family name, and his close friends from his first days in California, painted the picture of a quiet, painfully shy man.

Nearly everyone also portrayed Nat as a very likeable fellow who adored sports, politics, and music. He got along with nearly everybody, and so did his first wife, Nadine, a very attractive dancer, who was about ten years older than her husband.

Nat was also a tireless worker. His fees at first were tiny, but his energy for work was enormous. One Sunday, when he was supposed to pick up the bassist Red Callender and drive to a jam session, a typical Los

His rise to fame and his stardom never symbolized a life that was as velvety smooth and charmed as his sophisticated musicianship.

Angeles-style windstorm knocked a tree across the hood of Nat's battered old Studebaker. The car was badly damaged, but Nat picked up Red and drove to the job anyway. Nat didn't want to miss it, yet it paid just seven dollars.

Some things that happened to him to make him a star were of his choosing. Many were foisted upon him because of the times in which he lived. And sometimes, choice and chance intermingled. If we look at the beginning of Nat's career, we can gain some perspective on how choice and chance made Nat Cole trendy and popular in the first place.

Nat grew up in Chicago, where he led his own small group and a big band. He never wanted to sing. He wanted to become known as a big band leader. Then in 1937, he became the piano player for a show that traveled to a theater in Long Beach, California. The show closed because there wasn't enough money being earned. He decided to stay in California and began to play in every joint he could find just to make a few dollars a night. He also formed a big band, but he was totally unknown and couldn't find bookings for the band. Then the owner of a small club called the Sewanee Inn invited him to put together a trio and perform regularly. Nat did it for the money — seventy-five dollars a week. He also had some day jobs at the time, one for the Parks Department of the City of Los Angeles.

Nat was asked to sing at the Sewanee Inn. When he formed bands in Chicago, he never sang with the groups. He hired singers. Singers in Los Angeles liked his piano playing so much that they hired him to rehearse with them. He taught them phrasing, and as he did that, he also taught himself about singing. Because he was shy and didn't like singing alone, he asked his trio members to sing with him. Their light, swinging sound attracted fans. With all his other qualities, he became a little popular in town. Despite his popularity, the booking agents would not bother with him. They called his work chamber jazz, they thought it was eccentric, and they laughed at him. Big bands were in vogue at the time.

By the early 1940s, the Big Band era began to fade. The government started drafting members of the bands into the military. Nat registered with the draft board, but he was declared 4-F, probably because of flat feet, so he continued working with a trio. He had always known that his trio sounded good. As the big bands were dismantled, small groups were all that was left, and Nat's trio was especially good. Many other musicians formed trios and imitated the King Cole Trio's instrumentation: piano, bass, and guitar, with vocals. Nat's eccentric idea was no longer odd; it was the latest thing, the hot trend. Accidentally, he became an innovator, and he was proud of that for the rest of his life.

By 1944, Nat's trio had a major hit with "Straighten Up and Fly Right," and Nat and his men rode the crest of the trend they had created. He was a very clever man — alert, enterprising, and ambitious, even though he had a very laid-back, affable manner. Jazz critics scolded him when he started to move away from playing jazz piano and to do more singing with orchestras with strings. Although he had been starving as a pianist, Nat rarely showed his anger with critics. Nat pointed out that critics didn't buy records, they got them free. He was keeping his eye on the music business and his ear trained on his own group. He didn't want to become outmoded; he wanted to stay artistically and financially viable.

Backstage at the Apollo Theater one night in 1948, Nat talked about trends in jazz and popular music during an interview with a writer for *Metronome* magazine. He observed that popular music changed every ten years, and he was puzzled about what direction he should go in. He wanted to stay popular so that he could continue to make money and have personal and artistic freedom. He didn't think that his trio's style was written in stone. It couldn't go on forever in the same vein and stay popular and fresh. He wasn't being cynical, and he didn't want to change just for the sake of pleasing the public. He always wanted to try new things — new music and new outlets for his talents.

Nat thought many entertainers were repeating themselves and would have to find new material. He said, "For awhile it was swooners; anybody who could stand up and sing a little was in. Then it was trios, but now all trios sound the same. Back in the old days, every band had its own sound — Benny Goodman, Count Basie, Jimmie Lunceford, and Duke Ellington. Now all the bands sound practically the same except Dizzy Gillespie and Stan Kenton. So now the public sits back and says, 'We don't care what you're going to do, but you've got to do something.' And it if appeals to them, they'll buy it. That's why everyone who has a creative mind should sit down and try to find something new. And that's why I give Stan Kenton credit. He's going his own way. He may not be playing the authentic jazz beat, but he has a new sound. That's something fascinating to me."

He also said at that point that he thought his own trio was stagnant, and he was planning to try to blend strings into his concerts in 1949. He joked, "Maybe if we try the strings, when we go back to the old way with just the trio, they'll appreciate it again."

It turned out that he added a bongo player, and some critics objected because it gave the soft, smooth King Cole Trio a choppy sound. One of his trio members thought the bongo sounded like the clopping feet of a horse. Perhaps the bongo did that at public performances in nightclubs, but on recordings it lent excitement and exoticism to such songs as "Caravan" and "Lush Life." Most of all, it gave Nat a new way to express himself, and that was important to him. The critics wanted him to stay the way he had been.

Nat liked the hard sound of the bongo, and he was convinced that the public taste was also going in that direction. He kept the bongo in his group for a few years. At the same time, he made regular stops and sang with house bands at such places as the Copacabana in New York City, in leading Los Angeles supper clubs, and in Las Vegas casinos. He sang hundreds and hundreds of songs with studio bands for Capitol Records. Sometimes he fitted his trio into the bands, and sometimes he simply sang with strings and incurred the disdain of jazz critics.

Nat King Cole's most popular tunes often had nothing to do with jazz rhythms, and certainly nothing in common with bebop, except that he informed his interpretations with the intimacy of a story-telling jazz singer. He altered the focus of his music, but he didn't

Nat King Cole's most popular tunes often had nothing to do with jazz rhythms, and certainly nothing in common with bebop, except that he informed his interpretations with the intimacy of a story-telling jazz singer.

The Unforgettable Nat King Cole: How a Big Legend Grew from a Little Trend

Essay

alter his quality. He was always a jazz influenced singer, no matter what he was singing or with whom. With the same vocal quality that had enhanced his early hits with his trio, he found fame and fortune as a pop singer recording with studio bands in the era of the late 1940s and early 1950s when that type of music became trendy.

By the late 1950s, however, a new trend that Nat didn't feel open-minded about was afoot in the music business. One night in New York City, he was having dinner with Joe and Noel Sherman, songwriting brothers who had written love ballads for Nat. Nat asked them how they liked rock and roll. He said he didn't think he could ever get into that. He was worried because by the late 1950s he hadn't had a really hot record at the top of the charts for some years. Rock and roll was gaining fast in popularity, so the Sherman brothers wrote a novelty tune for him, with a definite rock and roll beat, called "Mr. Cole Won't Rock and Roll." It was a showstopper with Nat's nightclub audiences, who were made up of well-heeled sophisticates and society types who didn't share the kids' taste for rock and roll. Nat never recorded that song, and Joe Sherman privately owns the only tape known to exist. Perhaps Nat didn't want to have that recording played on the radio because he might not have wanted to offend the people who seemed to be going along with the trend toward rock and roll.

In 1957 Nat recorded his most popular song in a long while: an early rhythm and blues song called "Send for Me." Natalie Cole, who was only 7 years old then, convinced him that he should record it. A music publisher brought the song to Nat's house and asked Nat to sing it. Nat wasn't sure if he liked it, so he asked Natalie what she thought. She began to dance

to it and that pleased Nat so much he decided to let a little child lead him. In 1958 he had a hit with "Looking Back," an early rock and roll song. He knew that he couldn't ignore the inevitable. Then in 1962 he had one of his biggest financial hits with a country and western song, "Rambling Rose," written by the Sherman brothers.

Nat remained primarily a ballad singer, and his late career hits, with which he was testing other waters, presaged a future he wouldn't live to see. Nat King Cole died in 1965. At the time, rock and roll was pushing older singing stars and musicians playing various styles of jazz and other music out of the limelight. By the time Natalie Cole decided to become a professional singer, she wouldn't have dreamed of singing an old style of pop or jazz music to try to establish her career. Other young singers who have tried to sing the music that typified their fathers' eras haven't succeeded very well, at least in terms of commercial success. Yet without commercial success, an artist has little artistic freedom and precious few hours in which to practice and develop. As Nat said, a creative person has to do something new.

Natalie made a wise decision. She became a rhythm and blues singer, and established her own creative style and life. She didn't calculate the decision crassly; she truly loved the style. Unfortunately, she made plenty of trouble for herself in her private life. Luckily, she overcame her problems in recent years, and when she emerged from her battle against drugs, she found herself facing 40. There were new trends in pop music for her to contend with. Analyzing the situation, she began to talk like her father. She told people that she didn't think she could ever get into rap music. She said that some of her parents' conservatism must have rubbed off on her. Cole was gratified that her fans still liked her work and supported her, because she said it was easy to feel old very quickly in the music business.

Natalie began thinking of recording her father's music in 1990 because she knew that her fans liked it. She had been singing duets with his tapes during her performances in theaters for years, and the trick was very effective. I heard an audience cheer for her singing a duet with one of Nat's old records in a New York theater in 1990. When she made the decision in 1990 to record her father's repertoire that following spring, she knew that her fans would like the record to some degree. She had no idea it would become a great hit, selling three million copies to date as the most popular recording of its type in history, according to statistics keepers. She did it without abandoning the soul style that had won fans and Grammys for her in the 1970s, and that is one of the reasons for the great success of her record. She didn't try to mimic her father. The fine quality of the recording job is another reason for its success, and Nat's voice has remained mesmerizing through the decades. His interpretation of "Unforgettable" was a classic and an excellent choice for the duet, because the song had very romantic lyrics set to a simple, touching melody. Natalie was in command of her own voice and could adapt her style to her father's repertoire.

Natalie has since tried to analyze the success of that recording, and has explained that the venture was an idea whose time had come — a trend. She believed that people were eagerly seeking out old-fashioned values in life. The search led them to look back to the natural-sounding, sentimental music of the past, a music that helped them cope with the tensions and complexities in modern life. Perhaps that's what drew her increasingly to the music as she matured.

It's obvious that older music has been undergoing a renaissance in the public's perception for over a decade now. Although the feeling is different in the way young musicians play old standards — Duke's music, bebop, Lambert Hendricks & Ross's music, and all sorts of older, original styles — the polish that the youngsters bring to the music has won over this new generation. Natalie's feeling is different and less haunting than her father's, but her individualistic approach and her decision to try to be true to herself and to the Cole legacy at the same time has refreshed a familiar song and given it new vitality. With an electronic trick on "Unforgettable," she excited Nat's old fans and enticed new ones to appreciate his music and her talent.

If there's a lesson to be learned from this, it's that a trend thrives on something that sounds appealing and sends a message that the public needs to hear. A trendsetter can't begin by calculating exactly, at least not in music or any art. A trendsetter is usually so much a part of the current generation that he or she knows what other people are hungry for. If an artist has a fresh, insouciant viewpoint, can take the pulse of the times, and can communicate with people well enough to start a trend, and if it is good enough, as Nat Cole's music was, that person can also become a legend.

By 1944, Nat's trio had a major hit with "Straighten Up and Fly Right," and Nat and his men rode the crest of the trend they had created.

Great Women of Jazz

22nd Annual Black Musicians Conference

March 22 to March 26, 1993

THE "OLD BOYS NETWORK" DID NOT PREVAIL AT THE 1993 Black Musicians Conference, an ambitious week of programming that celebrated phenomenal achievements of women in jazz. All scheduled activities paid overdue attention to the musical careers of women, and addressed the fact that women who play instrumental jazz in particular are often times marginalized in a world where men make up the majority.

The conference opened with an art exhibit in Hampden Theater and Gallery by the fashion illustrator Gwendolyn Black and entitled, *Beauty and the Beat: Women in Jazz* — a joint presentation with the Residential Arts Program of the Fine Arts Center. Music was provided by Chapter 5, a jazz quintet under the direction of alto saxophonist Corinthia Cromwell.

Cape Cod Lounge in the Student Union was the informal setting for a

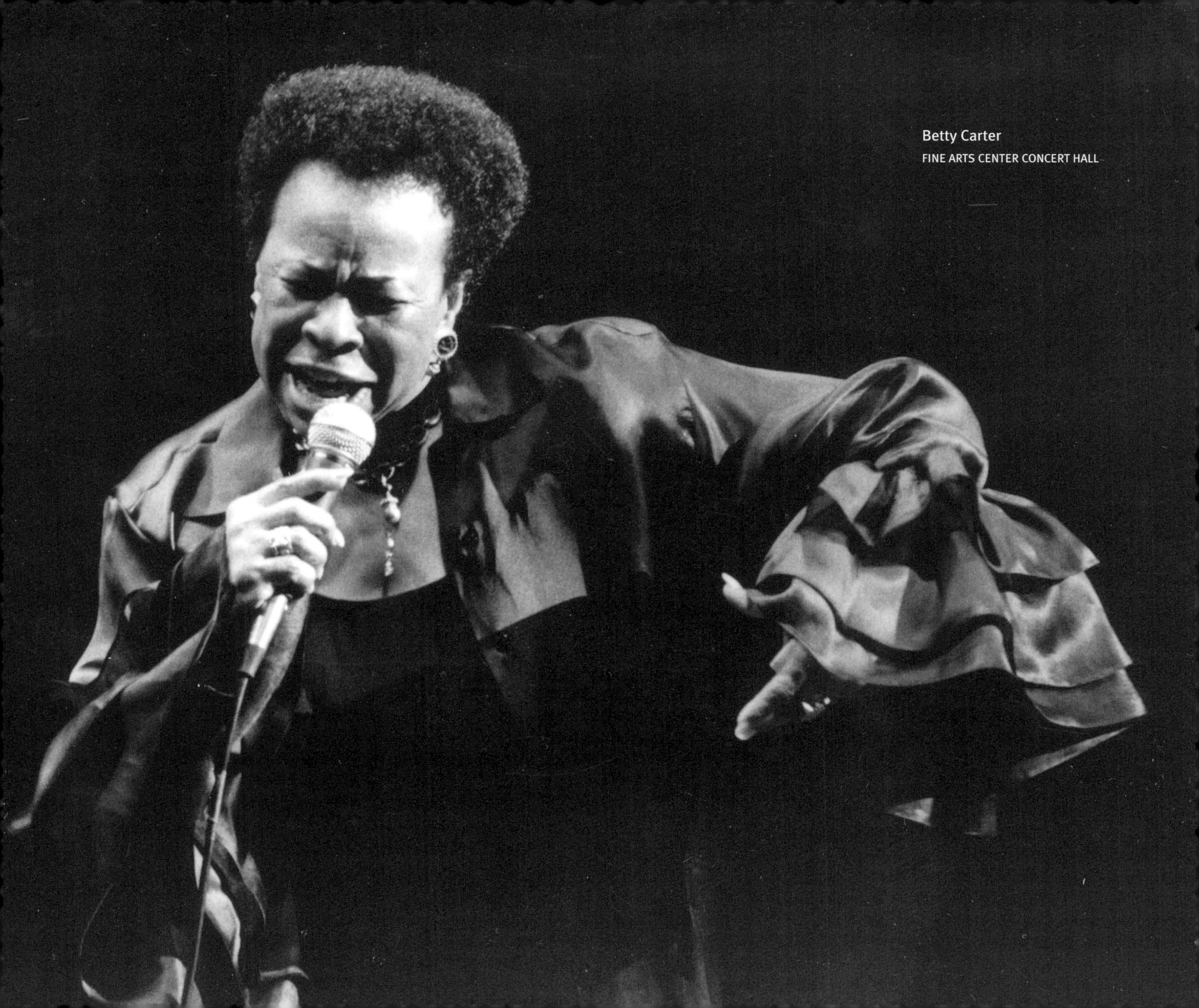

Betty Carter
FINE ARTS CENTER CONCERT HALL

Schedule of Events, March 22–26, 1993
GREAT WOMEN OF JAZZ

Monday, March 22, 7:30 PM, Hampden Gallery & Theater
Art Exhibit and Concert "Beauty and the Beat," Illustrations by Gwendolyn Black. Music by Chapter 5

Tuesday, March 23, 7:00 PM
Cape Cod Lounge/Student Union

Panel Discussion
Malindy Plays as well as Sings: Black Women Instrumentalists in Jazz
Terri Lyne Carrington, "Women, Rhythm, and Horns around the World"
D. Antoinette Handy, "When Women Took To the Bandstand"
Sally Placksin, "The Emergence of Black Women into the Music Marketplace"
Frederick C. Tillis, moderator

Distinguished Achievement Award Recipients
Dorothy Donegan
Clora Bryant

Mini-Concert featuring Nnenna Freelon

Wednesday, March 24, 5:00 PM, University Residence Hall Closed-Circuit Television

Video Screening: *Tiny and Ruby–Hell Diving Women: Black Women Jazz Instrumentalists,*
The International Sweethearts of Rhythm
1:25 PM, Bezanson Recital Hall

Master Class with Nnenna Freelon
7:00 PM, Hampden Theater

Video Screening: *... But Then, She's Betty Carter*

Thursday, March 25

Master Class with Betty Carter and her Trio
2:00 PM, Fine Arts Center Concert Hall

Concert with Betty Carter and her Trio
8:00 PM, Fine Arts Center Concert Hall

Friday, March 26, 5:00 PM
Video Screening: see March 24 event

The 1993 Black Musicians Conference was a project of the Fine Arts Center and was funded in part by the UMass Arts Council, the Chancellor's office, the Dean of Humanities and Fine Arts, the Dean of Students, Everywoman's Center, the Five College Black Studies Department, the Graduate Student Senate, Omega Psi Phi Fraternity, the Pan-Hellenic Council, the Student Enrichment Fund, and the University Women Studies Department. Beauty & The Beat was cosponsored by Residential Arts, and events featuring Betty Carter were cosponsored by the Fine Arts Center Concert Series.

panel discussion that set the tone for the conference: "Malindy Plays as well as Sings: Black Women Instrumentalists in Jazz." Frederick C. Tillis moderated a panel that included presentations by jazz percussionist Terri Lyne Carrington ("Women, Rhythm, and Horns around the World"), Sally Placksin ("The Emergence of Black Women into the Music Marketplace"), and the director of music programs for the National Endowment for the Arts, D. Antoinette Handy ("When Women Took to the Bandstand").

Documentation in the form of written essays or a panel discussion audio transcript did not survive from that night: hence the panel's noticeable absence in print from this book. However, as one well proved dry, another sprang with abundance — the photographer Edward Cohen came to *every* event in 1993 to document a stunning visual history.

That year, pianist Dorothy Donegan and trumpeter Clora Bryant received Distinguished Achievement Awards, while the up-and-coming jazz vocalist Nnenna Freelon, who had recently made her recording debut for Columbia/Sony records, provided musical entertainment. And finally, no one dared to stop Dorothy Donegan and Clora Bryant when they stepped onto the stage to perform a short set, a veritable and impromptu history of music through their

Nnenna Freelon
CAPE COD LOUNGE/
STUDENT UNION

ABOVE
Corinthia Cromwell
HAMPDEN THEATER

ABOVE RIGHT
A dynamic duo: Clora
Bryant on trumpet and
Dorothy Donegan at the
piano
CAPE COD LOUNGE/
STUDENT UNION

unique brands of improvisation. It was a memorable night for jazz at the University.

Other activities included video showings and closed-circuit television screenings of *Tiny and Ruby – Hell Diving Women: Black Women Jazz Instrumentalists*, *The International Sweethearts of Rhythm*, and *. . . But Then, She's Betty Carter*. The undisputed queen of vocal jazz at the time, Betty Carter concluded the 1993 conference with a concert with her trio in the Fine Arts Center Concert Hall. Both Betty Carter and Nnenna Freelon presented master classes during the week. Freelon,

LEFT
Clora Bryant and
Dorothy Donegan

TOP
Dorothy Donegan

ABOVE
Dorothy Donegan, Terri
Lyne Carrington, and
Clora Bryant

CAPE COD LOUNGE/
STUDENT UNION

who is an alumna of the Fine Arts Center's Jazz in July Workshops, also gave a lecture, "On Becoming a Professional Jazz Performer." Betty Carter and her trio worked with vocal students in a presentation called "Participation in Song," in which questions had to be vocalized to fit the trio's chord changes and Carter in turn responded to those "questions" in song.

Introduction by Mark Baszak

Betty Carter at a
reception following her
Concert Hall
performance

Views of Betty Carter, FINE ARTS CENTER CONCERT HALL

World Music and Jazz

23rd Annual Black Musicians Conference

April 11 to April 15, 1994

GLOBAL THEMES IN WORLD MUSIC AND JAZZ WERE DISCUSSED locally over five days in April 1994, when the Black Musicians Conference brought together musicians, educators, scholars, students, and audiences in a celebration that explored the influence of jazz on music around the world and how world music has influenced jazz. The sharing of musical ideas by musicians from around the world continually brings about change. In Jack Wheaton's book *All That Jazz!* the author states: "Jazz, in all its manifestations, grew out of the Afro-American music which preceded it, including spirituals, work songs, minstrelsy, and other forms. These styles, in turn, emerged from the collective experiences of Afro-Americans and the musical traditions of four continents: Africa, Europe, North America, and South America."

Doc Cheatham
BOWKER AUDITORIUM

Schedule of Events, April 11–15, 1994
WORLD MUSIC AND JAZZ

Monday, April 11, 4:00 PM , Student Union Gallery
Art Exhibit: *Music & Other Mysteries*
Sculptures by Dorrance Hill
Opening Reception performance by the Graduate Jazz Quartet

Tuesday, April 12

Panel Discussion
World Music and Jazz
Peter Manuel, "Influence of Jazz on International Popular Music"
Hildred Roach, "Jazz and European Classical Music"
Mark Tucker, "Influence of Duke Ellington on World Music"
Frederick C. Tillis, moderator

Distinguished Achievement Award Recipients
Doc Cheatham
Abdullah Ibrahim

Concert: Abdullah Ibrahim, solo piano

Wednesday, April 13

Video Screening: *Cruisin' J-Town, Nigerian Pop Music: Konkombe,* Campus Center closed-circuit television

Concert: Ernest Boamah, piano
7:00 PM, Augusta Savage Gallery

Thursday, April 14

Master Class with Slide Hampton
2:30 PM, Bezanson Recital Hall

Concert with Jon Hendricks and Company with Slide Hampton and the Jazzmasters
8:00 PM, Fine Arts Center Concert Hall

Friday, April 14

Concert with Papa Susso, Kora
7:00 PM, Augusta Savage Gallery

The 1994 Black Musicians Conference was sponsored by the Fine Arts Center Department of Multicultural Programs and funded in part by the UMass Arts Council, Student Affairs Cultural Enrichment Funds, and the Five College Black Studies Department. Music & Other Mysteries was cosponsored by the Student Union Gallery. Concerts by Ernest Boamah and Papa Susso were cosponsored by Augusta Savage Gallery, and the concert by Jon Hendricks and Company with Slide Hampton and the Jazzmasters was cosponsored by the Fine Arts Center Concert Series.

The conference opened with *Music and Other Mysteries,* an art exhibit in the Student Union Gallery by Dorrance Hill, a sculptor and professor in the University's Afro-American Studies Department. Hill also gave a public lecture about his art. Augusta Savage Gallery presented a solo performance by Ernest Boamah, a pianist from Ghana, and a solo performance by Papa Susso, a Kora player and griot (storyteller) from Gambia. Video screenings of *Cruisin' J-Town* and *Nigerian Pop Music: Konkombe* were scheduled throughout the week on closed-circuit cable television in University residence halls and in the Student Union. The Fine Arts Center Concert Series presented a performance by Jon Hendricks and Friends plus Slide Hampton and the Jazzmasters. Slide Hampton also presented a master class for music students in Bezanson Recital Hall at the Fine Arts Center.

The highlights of the 23rd Annual Black Musicians Conference were a panel discussion, the Distinguished Achievement Awards ceremony, and a mini-concert, which moved its main event location from the intimate and informal Cape Cod Lounge in the Student Union to Bowker Auditorium, a 700-seat performance hall.

A panel discussion moderated by the Director of the Fine Arts Center, Frederick C. Tillis, included "The Influence of Jazz on International Popular Music" by Peter Manuel, "The Influence of Duke Ellington on

Abdullah Ibrahim
BOWKER AUDITORIUM

Backstage with Archie
Shepp, Abdullah
Ibrahim, and Yusef
Lateef
BOWKER AUDITORIUM

World Music" by Mark Tucker, and "Jazz and European Classical Music" by Hildred Roach. Roach's and Manuel's essays appear in this chapter. The renowned trumpeter Doc Cheatham and the South African pianist Abdullah Ibrahim each received a Distinguished Achievement Award that night; and while only Abdullah Ibrahim was contracted to perform a solo concert, Cheatham delighted the audience by taking out his horn for an unscheduled performance.

With an international reputation as one of the world's most distinctive and original concert pianists, Abdullah Ibrahim has composed works that bridge idioms as diverse as jazz, 20th-century classical music, and the rich musical traditions of South Africa. Ibrahim once commented: "In some

Slide Hampton
FINE ARTS CENTER CONCERT HALL

ABOVE
A fan greets pianist Ernest Boamah
AUGUSTA SAVAGE GALLERY

RIGHT
Jon Hendricks and Company
FINE ARTS CENTER CONCERT HALL

ways, we work independently from the whole historical body of music, from the clearest point of our originality. The danger is that if you get locked into that massive body of work, your originality can disappear. This happens a lot in the classical field. In some ways, it restricts the budding young musician because he/she depends almost entirely on an existing body of work in terms of exercise and performance. Improvisation has to do with fearlessness of the unknown."

Introduction by Mark Baszak

Frederick C. Tillis flanked
by Jimmy Heath on
saxophone and Slide
Hampton on trombone
FINE ARTS CENTER CONCERT HALL

Essay

The Influence of Jazz on International Popular Music

By Peter Manuel

IT IS A PARADOX THAT WHILE JAZZ HAS evolved as an expression and product of African American culture and experience, at the same time, it has enjoyed broad international appeal and has been expertly and extensively cultivated around the world. It is well known that there are dynamic jazz scenes in Europe, Japan, and South Africa, as well as pockets of aficionados and performers throughout the developing world.[1]

This would include not only scattered bohemians and students, but also members of the elite. While the American jazz world claims its own Duke, Count, and assorted Kings, an arguably more genuine sort of jazz royalty exists in the form of Cambodia's Prince Sihanouk, a jazz clarinetist, and Thailand's King Bhumibol Adulyadej, a trumpeter.[2]

The field of international jazz is far too vast to address in a short essay. Instead, the focus here will be on the influence of jazz on commercial popular music outside the Euro-American mainstream — a subject only slightly more manageable in scope.

As an international genre, jazz has exerted certain sorts of influences on world popular music. The study of this music may illuminate certain features

not only of those diverse styles of music, but also of the nature of jazz itself. In this regard, it may be equally significant to explore not only such influences, but also the various ways in which jazz has *not* influenced world popular music. Because of space limitations, I can only suggest certain generalizations and questions.

Given the breadth of the topic, let's begin by first clarifying its boundaries. First of all, the mere usage of the word *jazz* in a given popular music does not in itself indicate an affinity with its American namesake. For example, Haitian "mini-jazz" of the 1960s was a subgenre of local *compas (konpa),* which has nothing in particular to do with jazz. Jazz influence was similarly minimal in 1960s Congolese bands named "African Jazz" and "OK Jazz," and the same is true for today's "Acid Jazz."

We must be careful not to automatically infer causality wherever we see similarity. The usage of jazz-type ninth and thirteenth chords in a certain genre might derive from jazz; however, it might also derive from European classical music, since such harmonies were common in the music of Chopin and many others. Similarly, the usage of jazz-type chords by modern flamenco guitarists like Paco de Lucia derives less from jazz than from an extension of traditional sonorities in flamenco, in which tonic sixth chords and other altered harmonies have long been common.

With such qualifications in mind, an inquiry into the impact of jazz on world popular music must clarify which aspects of jazz have been relevant in each case, including but not limited to harmony, instrumentation, rhythm, repertoire, or solo improvisation styles. Without getting bogged down in problematic attempts to define or limit jazz in its various styles, our questions might be inelegantly formulated: Where and when have which aspects of jazz been adopted abroad? And why or why not?

Scanning the global soundscape of world popular music in the 20th century, we can make certain generalizations about which aspects of jazz have been the most influential and for what reasons. While jazz-style ninth chords and the like occasionally crop up in popular music outside Europe and the Americas, what is more remarkable is their rareness. For one thing, such chords evolved within late Romantic classical music and the harmonically related mainstream jazz and Tin Pan Alley music. They do not fit well with types of music which are not based on these harmonic foundations. For example, Greek *rebetika* and Turkish *araabesk* are based on a distinct Mediterranean modal harmony. Jazz chords are not particularly compatible with the numerous international pop styles using rock-derived harmonies (IV-V-I cadences and other blues-derived progressions).

It is in the realm of Latin American urban popular music that jazz harmony has been most widely influential. Sophisticated jazz harmony is one of the trade-marks of Brazilian bossa nova of the 1960s, and an idiosyncratic form of jazz harmony is also used in Cuban dance music and salsa.

In the global perspective, perhaps even less influential than jazz harmony is swing rhythm or the "shuffle beat," which has been one of the trademarks of mainstream, "straight-ahead" jazz from around 1930 until the present. Despite the dynamism of swing rhythm, world popular music styles have generally adhered either to traditional indigenous rhythms, including modified versions, or else to versions of rock or disco-oriented quadratic meters — what jazz musicians might refer to as "straight fours."

Swing rhythm is common in Hawaiian popular song, where it is called "chang-a-lang." That entire genre of music, flourishing from the 1920s on, is perhaps better regarded as a subset of American popular song than a syncretic non-Western style. In its derivative r&b phase, 1950s ska also used a sort of jerky version of swing rhythm, but as Jamaican music came into its own, it forsook swing rhythm for reggae's distinctive beat.

In general, we can hypothesize that during the 1930s, which was the period of jazz's greatest popularity and influence, most of the emerging syncretic popular music of the developing world retained ties to indigenous rhythms. Those rhythms were not easily compatible with the shuffle beat, with its distinctive triplet subdivision of the beat and associated characteristic syncopations. In other cases, traditional folk genres using fast 6/8 meter (which might be compatible with swing) have not evolved into syncretic urban popular genres which could accommodate jazz influences. Such is the case with the Venezuelan joropo and Irish folk music, both of which have remained folk

It is in the realm of Latin American urban popular music that jazz harmony has been most widely influential.

South African Blacks were particularly receptive to influences from African American culture due to their shared experience of racial oppression.

rather than commercial pop genres.

The one realm in which swing rhythm has been adopted was South African urban music of the 1930s–'50s, in particular, township jive and related subgenres. In general, jazz was one of the formative and most important influences on South African popular music of this period. From the 1920s, jazz had become familiar to White and Black South Africans via records and visiting American groups, and swing jazz became widely popular in the thirties. A lively local jazz scene subsequently developed in South Africa, comprising both swing big bands like the Merry Blackbirds, as well as talented keyboard and sax soloists.

What is of greater relevance here is the emergence of jazz-influenced urban popular music, especially the music called "township jive" that flourished in the 1940s and 1950s. Township jive retained the shuffle beat and rhythm section of swing jazz and jump blues, while using vocal harmonies to imitate and effectively replace the big band's horn sections. Typically, the chorus would reiterate harmonized refrains over a I-IV-V ostinato, while a saxophone would loosely improvise in the background.[3]

A related genre was marabi, which emerged from the shebeens or beer halls of migrant workers. Marabi-tinged big bands flourished until the early 1950s, while marabi pianists like Reuben Caluza fashioned their own syntheses of ragtime, jazz, and Shebeen songs. The shuffle beat also pervaded marabi and the related kwela and mbube until the 1960s, when these all shifted to more rock-oriented "straight fours,"

while retaining the characteristic I-IV-I 6/4-V progression typical of so much South African pop music.[4]

The adoption of jazz's shuffle beat, so unusual in world popular music, may have occurred partially because indigenous Black music styles of South Africa lacked strong percussive traditions which might have precluded or inhibited the adoption of such a distinctive and foreign beat. South African traditional music tended to place greater emphasis on vocal choirs than drumming, perhaps because the rarity of trees in the veld limited the availability of wood for drums. On a broader level, South African Blacks were particularly receptive to influences from African American culture due to their shared experience of racial oppression.

Aside from Brazil (in the form of the bossa nova), the other region where jazz has had a profound influence on popular music has been the Caribbean. Although the English-speaking West Indies are less relevant here, where the bouncy, ad-hoc accompaniments to midcentury calypsos reflected a superficial degree of jazz influence, the most characteristic forms of West Indian popular music, reggae and modern calypso/soca, use harmonies and rhythms more akin to rock than jazz. The French- and Spanish-speaking islands, however, are another matter. Jazz itself had established roots in Cuba by the 1920s, and had been introduced elsewhere in the Caribbean by occupying United States Army troops (e.g., Haiti).[5] Since the 1930s, Cuban bands have been playing jazz in hotels and other venues, and Cuba has continued to churn out top jazz artists like Paquito d'Rivera, Arturo Sandoval, and Gonzalo Rubalcaba. Of greater relevance here is that the proximity of the North American jazz world and the existence of a local jazz scene enabled Caribbean dance bands to freely incorporate appropriate jazz elements in fashioning their own syncretic urban genres.

By far the most influential element of jazz was the big band format of the swing era, featuring arrangements for contrasting horn sections (trumpets, saxes, and optional trombones), backed by a rhythm section of piano, bass, and percussion. The use of a large brass ensemble was a logical means of obtaining sufficient volume in a big dance hall, and its adoption in compatible dance music genres in the Caribbean and South Africa was natural. Caribbean precedents to the big band existed in the military-style brass bands popular in the region, the clarinet- and trumpet–dominated *orquesta tipica* of turn-of-the-century Cuba, and the European classical symphony orchestra. Nevertheless, it seems clear that the big band format adopted in Cuba, Haiti, and Puerto Rico derived primarily and directly from the swing jazz model.

In the realm of Cuban dance music, the relevant genre was the mambo, as popularized first by Perez Prado and further refined by such artists as Benny More in Cuba and in New York by the big bands of Tito Puente, Machito (with Mario Bauza), and Tito Rodriguez.[6] Although these bands played both Latin music and jazz when performing in hotels and other venues for Anglo audiences, their forte was the distinctively Latin mambo, whose essence was the combination of big band format with Afro-Cuban rhythms. Song texts, when present, were in Spanish, and the repertoire was predominantly original (although

Machito did record an LP of Irving Berlin songs set to Latin rhythms).

While Cuban fusion was to prove the most durable and fruitful, similar developments occurred in neighboring islands. In the Dominican Republic, Luis Alberti, Antonio Morel, and others adapted a big band format to the salon merengue.[7] In their ensembles, the traditional merengue rhythm was retained, while saxophones played harmonized versions of the fast arpeggios, which, as traditionally rendered on accordion, were basic to the merengue's frenetic pulse. The midcentury merengue then became the primary model for the 1950s konpa of neighboring Haiti, where the competing big bands of Nemours Jean-Baptiste and Weber Sicot adopted big band formats and merengue/meringue rhythms in their own idiosyncratic fashion.

Meanwhile, in Puerto Rico, Cesar Concepcion popularized a big-band version of the traditional plena, combining mambo/swing-style instrumentation with the rhythm, sing-songy melodies and formal structure (alternating verse and chorus) of the plena.

By 1960, all these local adoptions of big-band/mambo formats had declined, just as South African big bands did, and, for that matter, swing jazz itself. Concepcion's plena de salon came to be regarded as stuffy and over-refined, and was replaced by the leaner ensemble and rawer sound of Rafael Cortijo's plena. Dominican merengue bands also shrank in the 1960s, with the smooth, soft sound of massed horns giving way to the crisp, staccato texture of a smaller horn section (typically, two saxes and two trumpets). Similarly, in the realm of Cuban music and the stylistically derivative salsa, big mambo bands were largely replaced by more compact conjuntos, usually

It seems clear that the big band format adopted in Cuba, Haiti, and Puerto Rico derived primarily and directly from the swing jazz model.

Jazz has been able to exert substantial impact on popular music only in places that hosted their own lively local jazz scenes, as did South Africa, Cuba, and Brazil.

having two trumpets and one or two trombones. Jazz-influenced horn and piano solos continue to play important roles in this music, although improvisation styles are quite idiosyncratically Latin.

By the 1950s, Latin jazz had emerged as a genre in its own right, but since it is more a music for aficionados than a commercial popular dance music, I will not discuss it here. However, it does occupy a place in a continuum that would stretch from jazz and Latin jazz, through jazz-informed Latin dance music, to more traditional forms of Latin dance music (son, guaracha, plena, etc.), and to traditional Caribbean folk genres, which have largely resisted commercialization and North American influence. Jazz elements occasionally crop up in the latter genres, but their usage is controversial. The occasional introduction of blues or jazz-type phrasing by cuatro players in Puerto Rican jibaro music is a case in point. When it does occur, purists tend to roll their eyes or disdainfully curl their upper lips.[8]

In conclusion, reiterating a few somewhat obvious generalizations about the influence of jazz on popular music, we see that jazz has been able to exert substantial impact on popular music only in places that hosted their own lively local jazz scenes, as did South Africa, Cuba, and Brazil. Second, the period of jazz's greatest international influence coincided with

the apogee of jazz's popularity in general (the 1930s–'40s), when swing jazz flourished as an accessible, dance-oriented popular music rather than a listening music for aficionados.

With bebop, jazz largely withdrew into its limited, albeit dynamic, world of clubs and aficionados; and it became increasingly difficult to hire big bands, especially when amplification allowed cheaper and smaller groups to be heard. From the 1940s on, the redefinition of jazz as highbrow listening music, now accounting for only around 3 percent of American record sales, partially explains its relatively limited impact on world popular music. Mainstream jazz's isolation has been compounded by the fact that its repertoire and harmonies remain largely rooted in the dated American popular song of the 1930s–'40s.

It is rock music, in its various forms, that has become the new international common denominator. If jazz is to exert any significant influence in the future, it may be via the self-consciously historicizing use of samples by rappers like Heavy D and Digable Planets. However, I consider it questionable whether jazz will again exert significant influence on world popular music, when it has become an almost marginal neoclassical style, however expertly cultivated, in its own homeland.

Notes

1. See. e.g., Pinckney 1989/90.
2. Said a visiting American who sat in with King Adulyadej's group, "He doesn't play too badly, but he takes far too many choruses." Of course he does, he's the king! Off with your head! (In *Downbeat,* Feb. 2, 1968).
3. See, e.g., "Siya Hamba: 1950s South African Country and Small Town Sounds" (Original Music OMCD 003).
4. See, e.g., Stapleton and May 1990:186–212, and Graham 1988:259–60.
5. See Acosta 1993:37; Averill 1989:211–12. It should also be noted that New Orleans jazz was in its origin to some extent a Caribbean genre, with marked affinities to the Cuban da*nzon* and other genres (see Fiehrer 1991).
6. The musicologist Delfin Perez (p.c.) observes that Cuban bands in the thirties, such as the Orquesta Riverside and the band of Armando Romeu, may have been the first to adapt big band format to Latin music.
7. See Austerlitz 1992: ch. 3.
8. This issue was the subject of a heated debate at a panel of Puerto Rican and Nuyorican musicians and aficionados held at New York's Museum of Natural History in June 1992, sponsored by City Lore. Some panelists defended the practice as a legitimate expansion of the genre, while others argued that it cheapened the music and violated its spirit. *Jibaro* is a Puerto Rican peasant (presumably White); the eight- or ten-stringed cuatro is a guitar-like instrument therein.

References

Acosta, Leonardo. *Elige tu, que canto ya.* Havana: Editorial Letras Cubanas, 1993

Austerlitz, Paul "Dominican *Merengue* in Regional, National, and International Perspectives." Ph.D. diss., Wesleyan University.

Averill, Gage. "Haitian Dance Bands, 1915–1970: Class, Race, and Authenticity." *Latin American Music Review* 10(2): 203–5.

Fiehrer, Thomas. "From Quadrill to Stomp: The Creole Origins of Jazz." *Popular Music* 10 (1): 21–38.

Graham, Ronnie. *The Da Capo Guide to Contemporary African Music.* New York: Dutton, 1988.

Manuel, Peter. "Modal Harmony in Andalusian, Eastern European, and Turkish Syncretic Musics." *Yearbook for Traditional Musics* 21: 70–94.

Pinckney, Warren. "Jazz in India: Perspectives on Historical Development and Musical Acculturation." *Asian Music* 21(1): 35–77.

Stapleton, Chris, and Chris May. *African Rock: The Pop Music of a Continent.* New York: Dutton, 1990.

Essay

Jazz and European Classical Music

By Hildred Roach

WHAT IS THIS REMARKABLE THING called jazz? Is it a verb or a noun? Is it just music, or a way of life? Is it, simply the culminating factor of small folk forms from a slave era? Is it instead, a social climber that has advanced to become the "classical music of Blacks," or is it the classical music of all America?

Jazz means a million things to a million people. Jazz has been coupled with a variety of references: from razz and rent to red-light and rowdy; from cooking, cunning, coercive, and classic to jag, jam, and jive; from jubilant Jitterbug and crazy Charleston to hip jargon; from jubilees to holler and blues; from West African rhythms and East African Coptic melismas to Caribbean calypso improvisation; from sacred, secular, standard, scat, scream, shout, slide, smear, stomp, and swing to words like suite, variation, and sonata; from syncopated, spontaneous, sensual, spiritual, soulful, stupendous, and "straight ahead" to — as incredible as it may seem — "snobbish," as recently suggested by the unbelievable shooting of a youth who annoyed another because he was simply "listening to jazz!"

How classical is jazz? *Classical* is defined by Webster's Dictionary as synonymous with "excellent, fine, prime, famous, superior, top-notch, first rank, traditional, authentic, authoritative, and enduring; serving as a standard of excellence; and historically memorable." Whether or not the definitions fit, we have been seemingly more reluctant to discuss direct links between jazz and European classical music than we are to discuss the connections between jazz and small composite folk forms. Among various reasons for this is the association of jazz with disreputable old brothel and saloon settings (versus the high-class palaces of art-music patrons), as well as the inclusion in jazz of the "lowdown" sexy blues and imposing instruments — things considered more aligned with the devil than with the church. After all, it was the church that attempted to shape the thinking of early classical music, thereby making it uncomfortable for classical music to "let its hair down."

But let us look into European associations through the eyes of a jazz forebear, ragtime. This multisectional music, influenced by European jigs, marches, waltzes, quadrilles, and rondos, allowed most European idioms to thrive under its wings. Scott Joplin was certain that he was writing classical music in at least some of his works, and he evidently did not feel as though his talents should be limited as he peddled waltzes, marches, and an opera.

How much additional European classical influence is really in ragtime? Did its anticipated rhythms, which

Both classical and jazz music themes have run the gamut of human emotions from sadness to happiness, from sacred to secular, and from comedy to tragedy. Both have exhibited intellectualism, traditionalism, admirable standards, and historical longevity. They both are tolerant and at peace with one another, and both call themselves "serious as a heart attack."

give jazz its characteristic "before the beat" impetus, take any cue at all from the "over the barline" effects found in the music of Johann Sebastian Bach? Did this highly syncopated music resemble Bach's *Corrente* from *Partita No. 6*? Were Joplin's jumping bass patterns suggested by Chopin's jumping basses as seen in *Etude in A Minor, Op. 25, No. 4*?

What then, of Arthur Tatums's virtuostic runs and stride effects? Listen to Tatum's arrangement of "I Can't Give You Anything but Love." Were they suggested by the music of Chopin, and perhaps inspired by flourishes and cadenzas of the Baroque and Classical periods?

Rhetorical questions about compositional techniques abound. How influential to the left hand of boogie-woogies were such broken basses as those found in Beethoven's *Pathetique* sonata? How fascinated were jazz innovators by the music of Claude Debussy? Some of those harmonies sound suspiciously like jazz of a later time. Conversely, how fascinated with ragtime was Debussy when he wrote *Golliwog's Cakewalk*?

What of categories? Is William Grant Still's *Afro-American Symphony* "nonclassical" just because of its inclusion of a twelve-bar blues in its opening passages? How much less classically oriented than the *Nutcracker Suite* is an excerpt from John Lewis's five-part ballet entitled *Original Sin*?

Consider the merger of Lewis's arrangement of Bach's *C Major Fugue* from *The Well-Tempered Clavier*, Book I. Is Hale Smith's *Nuances For Band* any indication that the two types of music have become "one" at the will of the composer? Who is to say whether those flatted tones in the third movement of Rachmaninoff's *Concerto No. 2 in C Minor* are as "blue"as blue notes of jazz?

Is Ornette Coleman's free-style "Circle with a Hole in the Middle" less twelve-tone sounding than Webern's music, or less serially motivated than original tone rows built by composers like T. J. Anderson? Are George Walker's tetrachords similar to sounds of extended jazz chords? Except for the blues cadence, jazz is governed by the same functional system of harmony as classical music.

In his *New Music*, Aaron Copland stated that jazz had permeated all classical music of the 20th century. Composers have borrowed from each other for centuries, and the modern era is no exception. Darius Milhaud listened and learned from jazz; Debussy, Satie, and Stravinsky copied ragtime; Duke Ellington used concerto, fantasy, and mass in his list of forms and made an arrangement of Grieg's *Peer Gynt Suite*. Oscar Peterson wrote études and minuets, while Charlie Parker wrote musical suites — and the list goes on.

Jazz emphasizes studying through ear training, while classical music attempts to recapture every direction of the composer's printed notes. Classical music prefers pure tones directly in tune with 440 pitch. While jazz tunes to the same 440, jazz then deliberately follows blues rules by bending, breaking, and cramming tones between cracks.

Both classical and jazz music themes have run the gamut of human emotions from sadness to happiness, from sacred to secular, and from comedy to tragedy. Both have exhibited intellectualism, traditionalism, admirable standards, and historical longevity. They both are tolerant and at peace with one another, and both call themselves "serious as a heart attack."

Because of so many similarities and overlappings, one might be tempted to conclude that jazz and classical music are one and the same. Not so, for there are as many differences as there are similarities, from labeling of jazz chords to performance decorum. While classical music is generally founded upon a certain set of rules, jazz aims to break them. Jazz chords are changes, and its scores are charts. Jazz chords are successive sevenths, elevenths, and thirteenths, while classical music usually intersperses extended chords with traditional triads. Jazz emphasizes studying through ear training, while classical music attempts to recapture every direction of the composer's printed notes. Classical music prefers pure tones directly in tune with 440 pitch. While jazz tunes to the same 440, jazz then deliberately follows blues rules by bending, breaking, and cramming tones between cracks.

Most of all, jazz is a communal, participatory art which practically brings the listener onto the stage for spontaneous music making. Members of the audience respond aloud in gleeful communication with the performers, much like the call and response between Protestant singing preachers and congregations, or like a cheering squad. If someone shouts "right on" or "play it, brother!" in the middle of a classical performance, that person has not only spoiled the mood for other listeners and wracked the nerves of the performer but is likely to be ejected from the premises as well. Shout and clap during a jazz performance, and you've "got it going on" or you're "hip."

Perhaps some of the strongest arguments for separateness are that each genre has its own unique sound and therefore declines to abandon its idiomatic peculiarities. But perhaps above all else, jazz has no desire to quit its syncopation, while classical music refuses to swing! Despite their idiosyncrasies, jazz and classical music now enjoy an easier camaraderie than ever before. They go together on many issues, such as maintaining their reputations as influential infiltrators, as immense intimidators, and as instigators of sweat. They go hand-in-hand in a conspiracy of minds over matter. But no matter the materials of which they are made, they are both here to stay!

Recommended Listening
Classical Compositions Influenced by Jazz, and Vice Versa

Anderson, T. J. arr., cond. *Classic Rags & Ragtime Songs.* Columbia.

Anderson, Leroy. *Jazz Legato & Jazz Pizzicato.* Mid-Atl Chamber Orch., 1987–88.

Bach, J. S. *Six Partitas*, Joao Martins, piano. Arabesque Digital Records.

Baker, David. *Concerto for Violin and Jazz Band; Concerto for Flute, Str. Quartet and Jazz Band.* Laurel.

_____. "Le Chat Qui Peche" for Sop., Jazz Quartet, Orch., Mester, dir. Louisville Orch.

Chopin, Frederic. Etude, *Op. 25, No.3.* Dover.

Coleman, Ornette. *Circle With a Hole in the Middle* (Art/Improvisers). Atlantic.

Courlander, Harold, collector. "Go Preach My Gospel" (Folk Songs from Alabama). Folkways.

Debussy, Claude. "Suite Bergamasque"; "Prelude No. 1 (Bk. II)." Reflections/Water (Images).

Dett, R. N. "In a Closed Casement" (Tropic Winter Suite).

Gershwin, George. "Three Preludes."

Hawes, Hampton. *Go Down, Moses.* Northern Windows.

Joplin, Scott. "Maple Leaf Rag." Dover.

Laws, Hubert. "Amazing Grace," arr./flute.

Jazz Piano Greats. Folkways Records.

Lewis, John, arrmts. *J. S. Bach Preludes and Fugues* (WTC, Bk. 1); Phillips, "Original Sin" (mus./ballet); J. Lewis, cond. Atlantic.

Milhaud, Darius. "La Creation." RCA; "Scaramouche for Two Pianos."

Moore, Carman. "Gospel Fuse for Orch.,"soli.

Price, John. "Sonata II for Piano." (Ms., Tuskegee).

Prokofieff, Sergei. "Sonata No.7."

Rachmaninoff, Sergei. Concerto No. 2, in C Minor; Leonard Pennano, pianist; E. Leinsdorf, dir./LA. orch; Seraphim.

Smith, Hale. Faces of Jazz (Belwin); Nuances for Band S. Fox.

Still, William G. "Three Rhythmic Spirituals for Chorus"; "Three Visions for Piano"; "Lenox Avenue for Band." Desto.

Swanson, Howard. "Sonata No. 1 for Piano." 1.; Weintraub.

Tillis, Frederick. "Motherless Child" (Paintings in Sound), sax. P&P Pub., Amherst.

Waller, Thomas (Fats). *Smashing Thirds.* RCA.

Walker, George. "Sonata No. 1" (*Music of Black Composers*, N. Hinderas, piano). Desto.

Williams Mary-Lou. "Zodiac Suite." Verve.

Wilson, Oily. "Piece for Piano and Electronic Sounds" (*Music of Black Composers*, N. Hinderas, piano). Desto.

Recommended Reading

Baker, David. *Jazz Improvisation.* Chicago: Maher, 1969

Copland, Aaron. *The New Music.* New York: W.W. Norton, 1968.

Gershwin, George. "The Relation of Jazz to American Music." *American Composers on American Music.* Stanford: Stanford University Press, 1933.

Gridley, Mark. *Jazz Styles, History and Analysis.* Englewood Cliffs: Prentice-Hall, 1994.

Grout, Donald. *History of Western Music.* New York: W.W. Norton, 1960.

Hare, Maud Cuney. *Negro Musicians and Their Music.* Washington, D.C: Associated, 1936; New York: Da Capo Reprint, 1974

Pleasants, Henry. *Serious Music and All That Jazz.* New York: Simon and Schuster, 1969.

Roach, Hildred. *Black American Music: Past and Present.* 2nd ed. Melbourne: Kneger, 1992.

Roberts, John Storm. *Black Music of Two Worlds.* New York: Praeger, 1972.

Southern, Eileen. *The Music of Black Americans.* New York: W.W. Norton, 1982.

Spencer, Ray, and Arnold Laubich. *Ad Tatum: A Guide to His Recorded Music.* Metuchen: Scarecrow Press, 1982.

Thomas, J. C. *Chasin' the Trane: The Music and Mystique of John Coltrane.* New York: Doubleday, 1975.

Blues-Based Jazz: The Legacy of William "Count" Basie

24th Annual Black Musicians Conference

February 28 to March 2, 1995

ALTHOUGH THE ANNUAL BLACK MUSICIANS CONFERENCE WAS traditionally programmed during the month of April, events in 1995 moved it back a month to the cusp of February and March so that the conference could coincide with a Fine Arts Center Series presentation of "DIVA, No Man's Band" with former Basie vocalist Marlena Shaw.

A panel discussion entitled "Blues-Based Jazz: The Legacy of William 'Count' Basie" was moderated by Frederick C. Tillis. Panelists included Bill Lowe, who presented "The Basie Lineage," and Leonard Goines, who presented "The Basie and Ellington Bands: A Blues Comparison." Edited excerpts from a transcript of their live presentations follow this introduction. Amina Claudine Myers's essay, "Is There Jazz without the Blues?" also

Marlena Shaw
FINE ARTS CENTER CONCERT HALL

The 1995 Black Musicians Conference was sponsored by the
Fine Arts Center Department of Multicultural Programs, and
funded in part by the UMass Arts Council. The concert by
Leroy Jenkins was copresented by Augusta Savage Gallery,
and the concert by DIVA, No Man's Band and Marlena Shaw
was copresented by the Fine Arts Center Series.

appears in this chapter. She was unable to join the discussion as nearly all air flights to the region were canceled from New York City. That year, we were hit with a particularly nasty ice storm on the opening night panel discussion, Distinguished Achievement Awards ceremony, and mini-concert.

Both the vocalist Dakota Staton and the violinist Claude Williams (87 years old at the time) received a 1995 Distinguished Achievement Award. The night ended with a mini-concert featuring Claude Williams performing with locally based rhythm section support: Emery Smith on piano, Avery Sharpe on bass, and Alvin Terry on drums. The inimitable Dakota Staton

Dakota Staton
BOWKER AUDITORIUM

OPPOSITE
LEFT TO RIGHT
Emery Smith, Dakota
Staton, Avery Sharpe,
Claude Williams, and
Alvin Terry
BOWKER AUDITORIUM

ABOVE
Leroy Jenkins
AUGUSTA SAVAGE GALLERY

RIGHT
DIVA, No Man's Band
FINE ARTS CENTER CONCERT HALL

also made an unscheduled appearance with the "house trio," a happening that was becoming the annual trademark for Black Musicians Conference events.

The conference also included a concert by DIVA with Marlena Shaw, a master class with Marlena Shaw, and a solo concert by the violinist Leroy Jenkins.

Introduction by Mark Baszak

Claude Williams
BOWKER AUDITORIUM

Tuesday, February 28, 1995
Bowker Auditorium

Panel Discussion Transcript Excerpts

The Basie and Ellington Bands: A Blues Comparison

Excerpts from the presentation by Leonard Goines

Bill Lowe, Frederick Tillis, Leonard Goines, and Horace Clarence Boyer
BOWKER AUDITORIUM

THE TURN OF THE CENTURY WAS A VERY exciting time for music in the United States — especially for African American music. Count Basie was born in 1904, in Red Bank, New Jersey, and Duke Ellington was born 1899, in Washington, D.C. Ragtime was flourishing, and both Duke and Count are going to play ragtime or its Eastern counterpart — stride piano. Minstrelsy was waning, but for all of the pejorative effects of minstrelsy, there were some positive ones as well. Minstrelsy had attuned White ears to African American music both here and in Europe, and paved the way for its acceptance as a true American music.

At the same time, the spiritual that came out of the antebellum experience changed into concert music with the Fisk Jubilee Singers. Composers were beginning to think in terms of dealing with the Black tradition in two ways — a concert form as well as a folk form. This is going to happen as well in the arena of the Holiness churches, when the spiritual begins to shift into the arena that is going to be called gospel music, which is going to flower fully during the 1920s with a kind of blues-based experience. All of these traditions were converging in various ways, in addition to the syncopated orchestras in New York and Europe... [to become] that music that we are later going to call "jazz." At the same time, Black shows coming out of the minstrelsy experience are going to shed some of the "black face," and are going to lead the way into the true musical, as we're going to find with those like *Shuffle Along*.

Duke Ellington and Count Basie will reflect this environment [in their music]. Count Basie and Duke Ellington have a lot in common, but they are very, very different...

For example, Count Basie and Duke Ellington both came to New York and began to hang out with Fats Waller, James P. Johnson, and all of the other stride pianists who were popular at that time. Sonny Greer, Duke Ellington's drummer in his first band, grew up with Count Basie.

Count Basie thought about being a drummer until he saw all of the things that he was going to have to do even to just catch up with Sonny Greer, so he shifted off into becoming a piano player. Count Basie also said that he just wanted to be an entertainer. He didn't really care too much what he was going to do. Count Basie didn't make a big first impression in New

It was Bubber Miley who shared his [experiences] with "Tricky" Sam Nanton and some of the others who were instrumental in giving Duke Ellington some of that "jungle sound" — what Billy Strayhorn used to refer to as "the Ellington effect."

York, so he began working on the Theater Owners and Bookers Association (TOBA) circuit, and it was then that he found himself in traveling shows going to Kansas City, and having his first real acquaintance with the blues.

Duke Ellington [was not] a blues-based musician at first. His early band was almost a "pop" band, but things are going to happen that will bring that kind of blues flavor into his band. When he gets the job at the Cotton Club, he began listening to and hiring people like Bubber Miley, at a time when both of them were working with Mamie Smith. Bubber Miley had heard King Oliver. He heard the blue notes. He heard the mutes, and he heard the ways of dealing with the colorations and tones. He became very interested in this, he perfected it, and he brought that blues into the Ellington band. It was Bubber Miley who shared his [experiences] with "Tricky" Sam Nanton and some of the others who were instrumental in giving Duke Ellington some of that "jungle sound" — what Billy Strayhorn used to refer to as "the Ellington effect."

Duke Ellington was a visual artist, and there was a time when he thought [about a career in] the visual arts, but he went into music. The way that he dealt with colors in his music is exactly the same way that he would have dealt with them in painting, or any other kind of artistic endeavor. In fact, Duke men-

tioned that he thought of music in colors, as the titles of a lot of his tunes suggest . . .

Once he got to Kansas City, Count Basie began to hear a kind of blues which was not the classic blues of Bessie or Mamie Smith, who were very popular at that time. It was not the earthy blues of Mississippi that had been going on for years, but an urbanized country blues that came out of the Kansas City territory bands. Kansas City was a crossroads, where everybody passing through became part of this big jam session environment. Strangely enough, Count Basie is going to be the prime exponent of this style of blues, and he's going to bring it to New York.

Although he was a bandleader and a pianist, Duke Ellington was basically a composer. He thought like a composer, and his band was his workshop. He wrote for various members of the band rather than writing for instruments. He thought of unusual kinds of combinations. He might have a saxophone, a trumpet, and a flute doing harmonies, rather than the brass or saxophone section. He thought in terms of extended forms, embellishment, and development. He was very different from Count Basie, who kept it very simple, who wanted to distill everything down to its simplest level and to make it swing. Both bands swung, but they swung in different ways.

Count Basie was fortunate enough to have

It was this blues-based riff feeling and this incredible swinging machine that gave us that Count Basie sound that was going to go on forever.

worked with Walter Page and his Blue Devils, and with Moten's band. After Moten died, Basie was able to pull people from both of those bands, and he had one of the greatest rhythm sections ever going — Jo Jones on drums, Walter Page on bass, Basie on piano, and Freddie Green playing acoustic guitar and keeping time. They became known as the "All-American Rhythm Section." That rhythm section, along with the new Kansas City way of approaching the blues with this urban kind of a flavor, was not so much the antiphonal one of New York – where the brass section was against the reed section answering back and forth — but one in which you had a riff, a repetitive figure that was either used in stating the theme, or was there to set fire under the players as they performed. It was this blues-based riff feeling and this incredible swinging machine that gave us that Count Basie sound that was going to go on forever...

Duke Ellington and Count Basie both directed their bands from the piano, and both knew how to anticipate the core that was going to be needed by soloists. They only gave what was needed when comping. Duke Ellington even stopped at times to stand up and conduct with his hands. Piano playing was secondary; it was there to just support the band members when they needed that kind of support...

Duke Ellington played in so many different styles. Even his "mood tunes" — of which "In My Solitude" is one of the prime examples. Without being a blues [song], it has a kind of blues flavor that comes through, and that whole "jungle" sound that came in through Bubber Miley and Tricky Sam Nanton, who infused the music with the blues. Although he was only in the band a short time, Sidney Bechet brought some of his New Orleans experience into the band. Duke Ellington was very eclectic, and he also used other styles of music from around the turn of the century in his music...

Some people are going to begin to say that the Duke Ellington Band is no longer a swinging band because it wasn't playing the "jungle" effects. He was beginning to do things in the arena of "Concerto for Cootie" or "Black, Brown and Beige" which were designed to do more than just swing in a conventional way. Many European critics accused him of trying to be "too European" and not being "Duke Ellington." But Duke Ellington was a complex person who thought in many different kinds of ways, and his music reflected all that he was...

Panel Discussion Transcript Excerpts

The Basie Lineage

Excerpts from the presentation by Bill Lowe

Tuesday, February 28, 1995
Bowker Auditorium

LINEAGE ISN'T JUST ABOUT WHO INFLU-enced whom and who learned from whom. Lineage is about that, but it's also about something I call "webbing" — that the music and the musicians really are about a community, about a family. It's important for all of us to remember that whatever the musical form is, it's people who make the music.

The beauty, ultimately, of Count Basie or Duke Ellington has to do with these people. Duke, Count, and the musicians in their bands were people. That seems like a silly thing to say, but as a person who spends a lot of time working in environments talking about historical aspects of the music, I realize that we can sometimes forget that people make this music, and that it's a music that is about personality. It's a music that's about expression.

I want to focus on Frank Foster as a person whose lineage connects him not only with Count Basie, but also with this larger community. I want to talk about how that connection happens, and share some of my experiences as a card-carrying member of the Loud Minority.

Years ago at one of our gigs, we were bemoaning how few dimes we were getting for the gig, when Frank handed out a contract that basically said: I'm signed up for life; the only way I can get out of this

contract with Foster is to die. That was my only way out. I couldn't buy my way out because there was no money involved anyway. It was a contract of experience and motivation. Frank was joking with us, yet it was also quite serious. One of the main lessons that I learned in Frank's band was this notion of motivation.

Frank Foster is currently the leader of the Count Basie Orchestra; which is really a full circle, because Frank was a part of the Basie Band in the 1950s, the "Two Frank Band," where the two tenor saxophonists were Frank Foster and Frank Wess. When I first joined Frank's band, Frank worked with the Basie Band for many years, and during the late 1960s and early '70s Frank formed his own large band called the Loud Minority.

Frank's reasons for forming his own band had to do with his love for the Count Basie sound, his love of what Basie's band is about, and also his desire to do new things with that same sound. That's the lineage. Where the Count Basie Band would have three trombones, Loud Minority was expanded to have four trombones and a tuba. Frank's Loud Minority was a bigger big band, bigger in ensemble size than the Count Basie Band.

Frank set a challenge for himself. He wanted to have this great big band that could still swing. He want-

Lineage isn't just about who influenced whom and who learned from whom. Lineage is about that, but it's also about something I call "webbing" — that the music and the musicians really are about a community, about a family.

There is this veneration of masters, this love of masters, and at the same time, because of this love, you have a responsibility to carry on. You have a responsibility to do something with this gift that you've been given. You have the responsibility to take it someplace else.

ed to have this great big band that could perform very intricate arrangements and still swing, [yet] where everybody in the band was also a soloist. One of the aspects of the Basie way of doing business ... was that there would be designated people in each instrumental section who were the soloists, folks who would stand up and take an improvised solo. Frank's notion was that everyone should have a chance to do that. In Frank's band, when you performed, you never knew when you might be called upon to solo. On the fifteenth chorus in "Giant Steps," he might point to you and ask you to do your solo, so you had to be ready. It was a purposefully different kind of approach. It was a way of doing business that maintained the sense of swing that he learned from Basie, and maintained the sense that you can really snap your fingers to it.

One of the "accidents of the calendar" is that Frank's birthday is on the same day [September 23] as John Coltrane's, and Frank, being a tenor saxophonist, takes that rather seriously. He sees himself as a person bridging these realities of having grown up with and loving the Count Basie experience, and also being a part of the new set of musical circumstances — the bebop and post-bebop set of circumstances. He grew up in a Coltrane environment.

Frank's place in the lineage of Coltrane's is not the same as his place in the lineage of Basie. For Frank, Basie is a musical father while Coltrane is a musical sibling. These family relationships are really important because it's through your siblings and your parents that you have this connection to both your grandparents, your ancestors, and a connection with what's to come. Much of my experience in Frank's band was about these connections with the past masters. Frank always speaks of Basie and Ellington as masters — masters of form, masters of energy, and masters of motivation. There is this veneration of masters, this love of masters, and at the same time, because of this love, you have a responsibility to carry on. You have a responsibility to do something with this gift that you've been given. You have the responsibility to take it someplace else ...

Frank Foster's idea was to take that notion of swing and put it in contemporary times — mold it with his understanding of his siblings, in this case, the saxophone stylings of John Coltrane. This doesn't mean that what Frank was after was to be like John Coltrane, or to have Loud Minority be another Count Basie Band. Frank used to always say, "Basie already did that. Basie did that very well, thank you very much, and we don't need to do that again. 'Trane already did 'Trane, and that's what that was. We don't need to try to be 'Trane again." What we need to do is listen and learn from [Basie and Coltrane] and then expand and take it someplace else. It's a notion, an idea, a motivation, and it's a reason for being. I learned about this lineage from my experience with Frank.

When Frank was yelling at me for messing up in

section C of his new arrangement, he said, "Man it's got to be tight, it's got to be tight like Basie." The Basie sound becomes a teaching device, it becomes a reason, and it becomes an example. "What's wrong? You guys play the right notes but it doesn't swing like Basie." Or, "Yeah, trombones, do that like Ellington would. Trumpets try to be like 'Trane." Past masters become living examples, so that Foster's big band became for us what the Basie Band had been for him, which was his "university." The whole notion of going into the big band, whether it was Basie's or Ellington's, was that this was an opportunity to really learn. This was an opportunity to be around all [the elements] that the music is about, and your job is to work within that and learn. Foster's notion is that there are other things to learn, and it becomes a question of, "How do you go forward while you still hold on to what's important from before?..."

I'll never forget the night that Woody Shaw came in from out of town. We used to rehearse at a place on St. Nicholas Avenue, uptown in Harlem. The 9:00 P.M. rehearsals would generally start around 11:30, and everybody knew that on certain nights that's where Frank rehearsed. Woody came through one night, and it was at a time later in his life when he had trouble with his eyes. He couldn't see, his sight was failing him, and his pride would not allow him to acknowledge that, but Woody had ears that were as big as this auditorium. Woody would come into the section and say, "Frank, run that again," so that he would hear where his part was. "Let's play it one more time Frank, I think the cats have it now." And then Frank would run it a third time because we all knew what was going on, and Woody played the mess out of it because that's what Woody could do. That was a part of the excitement of that organization.

Emery Smith, piano; Claude Williams, violin; Avery Sharpe, bass; Bill Lowe, trombone; and Alvin Terry, drums
BOWKER AUDITORIUM

ESSAY

Is There Jazz without the Blues?

By Amina Claudine Myers

THE ANSWER IS "NO" TO THE QUESTION, "Is there jazz without the blues?" Jazz has been defined as a fusion of ragtime (composed music that is syncopated) and blues with brass band music and syncopated dance music. Its rhythms came from Africa, its harmonic structure from European classical music, and its melodic and harmonic qualities from 19th-century American folk music, religious music, work songs, and minstrel shows.

Jazz stresses the individualism of the performer and is a vocally oriented music with instruments replacing the voice. The performer uses an original melody within the harmonic structure of a song for improvisation. In this way, the personality of the performer comes through.

No one has been able to say when the blues began; some say "it's always been here." Some musicians heard it back in the late 1800s. Jazz came from the blues, which came from the second generation of slaves, Black work songs, shouts and field hollers, which originated from African call-and-response singing.

The blues developed from social conditions and feelings that the church did not touch upon. Singers in rural areas started accompanying themselves with string instruments: developing sad, slow songs, which at first were called "sorrow songs," just as spirituals were first called, and later called, "the blues."

Although William Christopher Handy, born in 1873 and known as the "Father of the Blues," was the first to popularize the blues when he published "The Memphis Blues" in 1912 and later "The St. Louis Blues," blues singers known as "wanderers" had been traveling from one Black community to another before that time. Singing in railroad stations, street corners, nightspots, eating places, dance social affairs, and even picnics, they sang the blues before Handy's music was published. This music was rejected by the so-called respectable people of its day.

Gertrude "Ma" Rainey, the earliest professional blues artist from Columbus, Georgia, and a fantastic blues singer, heard a woman at a railroad station singing the blues about a man deserting her. She liked the song so much that she started performing it in her own traveling tent shows. Jelly Roll Morton, a pianist/composer from New Orleans, heard Mamie Desdume, a lady with two fingers missing, singing the blues.

Blues had certain traits that were carried over into jazz, characteristics such as slurred notes (also known as blue notes), swoops and scoops, moaning, groaning, whining, shouting, and a special vocal

Amina Claudine Myers

Bessie had a way of communicating with you personally. She would reshape a melody and change the harmonic and rhythmic structure of a song to fit her style. She always did things her own way, and that influenced many jazz players.

device known as falsetto.

There are two types of blues — country and urban blues. Country blues was rural and featured male singers with guitars and later string bands and other instruments. There were quite a few blind singers/musicians during that time. Country blues included the Mississippi Delta Blues and performers such as Leadbelly, Charley Patton, and Blind Lemon Jefferson.

Between 1916 and 1919 Blacks moved north for better jobs, and around 1920, record companies began to release blues recordings. Jazz bands as well as women singers from tent and vaudeville traditions came into the limelight, and blues became more formal. Thus the term "classic blues" was applied.

Two of the most influential artists in the development of jazz from the blues were Bessie Smith and Louis Armstrong. Bessie Smith grew up singing in a church choir, but she also danced and acted in plays. Ma Rainey heard Bessie, and was so impressed with her talent that she hired Bessie for her traveling tent show called "The Rabbit Foot Minstrels." Bessie sang anonymously written blues melodies that were in the public domain, but she also created melodies. Later, she went out on her own as a performer.

Bessie had a way of communicating with you personally. She would reshape a melody and change the harmonic and rhythmic structure of a song to fit her style. She always did things her own way, and that influenced many jazz players. This is how instrumentalists brought individualism to their playing. From Bessie Smith they heard a unique blend of precomposed song structures performed with a Southern blues feeling.

Louis Armstrong, a natural trumpet player, was born in New Orleans. At a very young age he played in riverboat orchestras, marching bands, and funerals. He probably heard and felt the blues from the ragtime and brass bands that played traditional themes in Storyville, a section of New Orleans credited as the birthplace of jazz around the turn of the century. Buddy Bolden played in the ragtime/brass bands of that era, and he also played the blues. I believe blues songs were within the early structure of jazz. Armstrong heard this sound because Louis's playing delved deep into the blues. Soon, jazz was being played all over the South and other parts of America.

Armstrong joined Joe Oliver's band at the age of 14. Later he joined Fletcher Henderson's dance band, and Henderson featured him as an instrumental soloist and vocalist who performed popular music of the day. Armstrong's singing and playing reflected the blues. He was also an accompanist for many blues singers. He loved to sing, and although he would sometimes flub the lyrics of a song, the public loved his voice and the way he performed. I think he may have forgotten the lyrics at times, and would make garbled sounds using nonsense syllables, a vocal technique that later became known as scat singing.

His singing influenced many artists, such as Billie Holiday in the way she phrased her songs. Armstrong's technique developed to the point that he started improvising more creatively. He also explored new ideas in syncopation and rhythm, and his playing is still influencing musicians today.

In the present time, the twelve-bar blues form, for example, "The Saint Louis Blues," is still going strong, and is one of the mainstays of jazz. It was during my freshman year in college, playing with a dance band for a high school prom, that I learned to play the blues. If you could play the blues, you were definitely considered a jazz musician. On occasion, I still may play a standard song such as "Willow Weep for Me," and I perform it in a very, very bluesy and effective way. From my perspective as a performer, there is no jazz without the blues.

References

Collier, Richard Hadlock. *Jazz Makers of the Twenties*. New York: MacMillian, 1965.

Feather, Leonard. *The Book of Jazz*. New York: Dell Publishing Co., 1976.

Jones, Leroi. *Blues People*. New York: William Morris, 1963.

Southern, Eileen. *The Music of Black Americans (A History)*. New York: W.W. Norton & Co., 1971.

The Revolution Returns:
The Next Generation in Jazz

25th Annual Black Musicians Conference

April 1 to April 4, 1996

AN UNPRECEDENTED NUMBER OF CREATIVE MUSICAL GIANTS USH-ered in the new sound of bop when American popular music known as "jazz" underwent a musical revolution during the decade of the 1940s. During that renaissance, 52nd Street in midtown Manhattan was fertile ground for jazz's many innovators. Many believe jazz was experiencing a rebirth of populari-ty and talent in the 1990s, yet others tended to disagree that what was hap-pening then was as revolutionary as what happened to the music in the 1940s.

Have the younger and talented musicians on the scene today tran-scended the musical landscape once again? This was the question posed to three generations of panelists who discussed the conference theme and more. Billy Taylor ('75) is an artist who is well known to Amherst audiences

Christian McBride's master class
for music students
ROOM 150, FINE ARTS CENTER

Schedule of Events, April 1–4, 1996
**THE REVOLUTION RETURNS:
THE NEXT GENERATION IN JAZZ**

Monday, April 1 & 2, 2:00 PM
Fine Arts Center

Master Class with Ethel Ennis

Tuesday, April 2, 7:00 PM, Bowker Auditorium

**Panel Discussion
The Revolution Returns: The Next Generation
in Jazz**
Billy Taylor, "A Participant Recounts the 1940s
   Revolution in American Classical Music"
Teōdrōss Avery, "What We Play and What
   They Call It"
Peter Watrous, "Jazz Revolution or Media Con-
   coction?"
Horace Clarence Boyer, moderator

Distinguished Achievement Award Recipients
Ethel Ennis
Billy Taylor

Mini-Concert
"The Young Cubs" of the Artist Collective,
Hartford, Connecticut

Wednesday, April 3, 4:00 PM
Fine Arts Center
Master Class with Christian McBride

Thursday, April 4, 11:15 AM
Bezanson Recital Hall
Lecture/Demonstration with the Christian
McBride Quartet
8:00 PM, Bowker Auditorium
Concert with the Christian McBride Quartet
and special guest, Nicholas Payton

The 1996 Black Musicians Conference was presented by the
Fine Arts Center Department of Multicultural Programs and
funded in part by the UMass Arts Council. The concert by the
Christian McBride Quartet with Nichols Payton was cosponsored by the Fine Arts Center Series.

because of his numerous area appearances and guest faculty appointments in the Department of Music and Dance and the Fine Arts Center's Jazz in July Summer Music Programs. He presented "A Participant Recounts the 1940s Revolution in American Classical Music." Filling in at the last minute for the trumpeter Nicholas Payton, who had a scheduling conflict on the day he was to appear on the panel, was saxophonist Teōdrōss Avery, a rising young star in this era of accomplished and ever-younger jazz musicians. Avery presented "What We Play and What They Call It." In addition to having the distinction (along with Billy Taylor) of holding an academic degree from the University of Massachusetts, Peter Watrous ('82) is a distinguished journalist who covers jazz and other topics for the *New York Times* (among many other publications). He presented "Jazz Revolution or Media Concoction?" on his academic home turf. Excerpts from that panel discussion appear in this chapter.

Receiving the year's Distinguished Achievement Awards were the phenomenal Baltimore-based jazz singer Ethel Ennis and the one and only Billy Taylor. Ennis also performed a benefit concert later that week at American International College in Springfield for the Community Music School of Springfield, a copresenter of the area's Ennis events. The evening culminated with a mini-performance by the Young Cubs from the Artist Collective

The Young Cubs of the Artist Collective
BOWKER AUDITORIUM

Billy Taylor and Ethel Ennis, with Fine
Arts Center Director Frederick C. Tillis
BOWKER AUDITORIUM

based in Hartford, Connecticut, and coached by the jazz saxophonist Jackie McLean. Other activities during the conference included master classes
with Ethel Ennis and Christian McBride, and a finale performance by the
Christian McBride Quartet with Nicholas Payton as special guest trumpeter.

Introduction by Mark Baszak

Back stage
with Ethel Ennis and
Horace Clarence Boyer
BOWKER AUDITORIUM

Tuesday, April 2, 1996
Bowker Auditorium

Panel Discussion Transcript Excerpts

A musician who was nearing 40 once said to me, "I don't think it's a revolution because when there is a revolution you must charter a new territory." Are the young musicians today chartering new territories, or are they becoming perfectionists at what was chartered many years ago?

HORACE CLARENCE BOYER

A Participant Recounts the 1940s Revolution in American Classical Music

Excerpts from the presentation by Billy Taylor

LEFT TO RIGHT

Horace Clarence Boyer, Teōdrōss Avery, Peter Watrous, and Billy Taylor

BOWKER AUDITORIUM

WHEN I WAS GROWING UP IN Washington, D.C., jazz was the popular music. As a matter of fact, jazz was the popular music in 1944 when I moved to New York City from Washington, D.C. Everywhere I went jazz was being played. I heard it on the radio, in theaters, dance halls, nightclubs, movies, and private homes. It seems everyone had a favorite style of jazz and really enjoyed the playing of specific jazz artists. Fans danced to big band jazz in dance halls like the Savoy Ballroom, [to] small band jazz in clubs like Small's Paradise and Minton's Playhouse...

In the 1940s, many nightclubs and restaurants featured well-known and not so well-known jazz artists, who played for dances as well as for listening. During this period, I played in dance bands led by Coleman Hawkins, Lester Young, Lucky Millinder, and

Noble Sissle. It was a real thrill for me to play in the same band with musicians I only knew from recordings. I had met many of them when I worked on 52nd Street with Ben Webster. Many well-known jazz musicians were featured on the radio every day. They were on a variety of shows...

Many well-known jazz musicians were heard regularly from clubs, theaters, and dance halls. They called those "remotes" because they set up a mike wherever you were working. Musicians were rarely paid for those nonstudio broadcasts. It was considered good publicity and viewed as part of the job. That still goes on. Even though World War II was being fought and there were restrictions on travel and food was being rationed, there was no lack of entertainment on the homefront.

There was a jazz scene in Harlem, another one in

The most concentrated assemblage of celebrated jazz musicians was in midtown Manhattan on West 52nd Street. In the two blocks between Fifth Avenue and Seventh Avenue, it was possible to trace the entire history of jazz, from early New Orleans right up to bebop, by listening to the artists who had helped create that repertoire, vocabulary, and the traditions.

Greenwich Village, and several smaller scenes in the Bronx, Brooklyn, and across the Hudson River in Newark, New Jersey. However, the most concentrated assemblage of celebrated jazz musicians was in midtown Manhattan on West 52nd Street. In the two blocks between Fifth Avenue and Seventh Avenue, it was possible to trace the entire history of jazz, from early New Orleans right up to bebop, by listening to the artists who had helped create that repertoire, vocabulary, and the traditions.

Jamming was very much in vogue. Frequently the audience got much more than it paid for — like a trumpet duo between Roy Eldridge and Charlie Shavers, or Coleman Hawkins, Don Byas, and Ben Webster trading fours. Though the 52nd Street clubs were very small and inexpensive, they featured two and sometimes three groups. They were tiny rooms, about the size of your basement if you lived in a house, because that's what they were in — those were brownstone houses on 52nd Street. They used to be [called] "speakeasies," and the basement was turned into a nightclub. On either side of the street you had clubs that featured Billie Holiday, Art Tatum, and Erroll Garner. Name [anyone] and they were playing on 52nd Street.

Despite the fact that there were so many musicians, the atmosphere among musicians was friendly and supportive. I was luckier than most musicians. I had met "Papa" Jo Jones, the wonderful drummer with Count Basie. I met him when I was in college, and he had talked Count Basie into letting me sit in with the band. Now if you can imagine a rhythm section with Jo Jones and Freddie Green and Walter Page — you don't have to do anything, just sit there. I thought I had died and gone to heaven. Anyway, he liked the way I

played. When I came to New York, he was delighted to find me working with two of his friends, Big Sid Catlett, a wonderful drummer, and Ben Webster.

Ben Webster was my all-time favorite tenor saxophone player. I love Coleman Hawkins, I love many other people, but Ben Webster had a quality in his playing that was unlike any horn player that I had ever heard. He could play a ballad like no one else I ever heard. The sound, the feeling, everything was just perfect in my view. To work with him was just a dream which came true.

Jo Jones appointed himself my guardian and introduced me to all his friends who were working on the street at that time. Because of this, I was able to meet, socialize with, and play with many of the legendary artists who would help shape and define the music I was trying to learn to play. I found them accessible, articulate, and supportive. When they realized how much I respected them as creative artists, they shared many of their insights and experiences with me. The information they gave me in casual conversation started me on a lifelong quest of gathering historical, cultural, and musical information about jazz.

Fifty-second Street was my postgraduate school. I was playing piano with Ben Webster's quartet at The Three Deuces, opposite the Art Tatum Trio. That was a wonderful job, but while I was doing that, Dizzy Gillespie brought the first bebop band to 52nd Street. This was an exciting event, and musicians who played in every jazz style came to the Onyx Club to check out the new concepts Dizzy was introducing. The band featured Dizzy on trumpet, Don Byas on tenor, Oscar Pettiford on bass, and Max Roach on drums. Bud Powell was supposed to play piano, but he was working with the Cootie Williams Big Band. The rumor was that

The experiments which had been started in Harlem at Minton's Playhouse were being formalized and codified in the compositions of Thelonious Monk, Benny Harris, Dizzy Gillespie, Charlie Parker, Kenny Clarke, and many others. The excitement of new discoveries began to take over, and different approaches to melodic articulation led to different ways of breaking the tyranny of the swing approach to accompaniment. New harmonic devices gave rise to more adventurous melodies.

Cootie, who was his guardian at that time, would not allow him to leave the band. Trumpeter Benny Harris, who is not as well known as he should be, was a very fine trumpet player who was a part of the Earl Hines Band for a long time. He had introduced me to Dizzy and Charlie Parker much earlier, when they were all with the Earl "Fatha" Hines Band. I reintroduced myself to Diz, and he immediately invited me to sit in, because he didn't have a piano player at that moment. He liked the way I voiced chords, so I showed him some of the voicings that I learned from Art Tatum. He showed me how he was using sequences, cycle of fourths, altered chords, and a whole lot of other stuff that I had never heard before.

These were new harmonic devices to me, and this is when I realized that bebop was evolutionary, not revolutionary. Bebop was the logical extension and expansion of earlier jazz styles. Roy Eldridge, Coleman Hawkins, Benny Carter, Don Byas, Charlie Shavers, and others were already improvising six- and eight-bar phrases which crossed over bar lines and started and stopped in unexpected places. Duke Ellington, Billy Strayhorn, and Art Tatum were expand-

ing the jazz harmonic vocabulary. Jo Jones, Sid Catlett, Kenny Clarke and many others were exploring new rhythmic approaches to jazz. Many of them were tired of just beating 1,2,3,4, 1,2,3,4 as they had to do it with most of the swing bands at the time. They wanted to do a little more.

The experiments which had been started in Harlem at Minton's Playhouse were being formalized and codified in the compositions of Thelonious Monk, Benny Harris, Dizzy Gillespie, Charlie Parker, Kenny Clarke, and many others. The excitement of new discoveries began to take over, and different approaches to melodic articulation led to different ways of breaking the tyranny of the swing approach to accompaniment. New harmonic devices gave rise to more adventurous melodies.

Contrary to some reports in the media at that time, there was considerable exchange of ideas between musicians of different generations. I remember seeing Charlie Parker sit in with Sidney Bechet. Sidney was working in a place called Jimmy Ryans, and they were playing the New Orleans repertoire. Obviously "Bird" knew him. He went in and they had a conversation, and when the band went on, he went and played some tunes with him. He played bebop with what they were doing, but he played it so that it worked in that context. Contrary to what a lot of folks seem to think, there seemed to be lot of camaraderie between that particular group and Charlie Parker.

Coleman Hawkins was one of the first major jazz artists to embrace the new music, but he was one of many, and there were many others not so well known as far as the public is concerned. One has only to study the records which were made during the 1940s to realize to what extent this change was taking place. If you listen to the first records of Dizzy, they had Clyde Hart playing piano, and Clyde was never a bebop player. He was a swing player who was in that kind of transition era that I call "prebop." He was one of the people who harmonically laid the foundation, along with Tatum and others, for what the bebopers were doing.

Listen to how Jo Jones displaced the beat using his bass drum for accents, using his cymbols to create a new kind of swinging feeling, and thus setting the stage for Kenny Clarke, Max Roach, Roy Haynes, and many others. Listen to the Duke Ellington Band, the way that Tatum's piano prepared the musicians and the public's ear for more challenging harmonies, making way for Thelonious Monk and Bud Powell. Listen to the way Ellington, Nat King Cole, Count Basie, and many others changed the way pianists accompanied other instruments. Listen to the way Jimmy Blanton and Slam Stewart changed the jazz bassist concept of playing melodies and accompanying other artists, and the way Django Reinhardt and Charlie Christian did the same for guitarists. Listen to the technical virtuosity of Art Tatum and reflect on what lessons Dizzy and

"Bird" learned from him. They always said that they listened very carefully to Art Tatum.

All the musicians that I just mentioned came up through the big bands, worked in the swing period, and were a part of the forging ahead, the changing of direction, the exploration of other things and other concepts, other ways to present jazz ideas. They were the people that made it possible for those of us who wanted to play bebop. The music had very firm roots in the tradition, and it's because of its firm roots in the tradition that bebop has earned its place in the mainstream of jazz. Like the jazz styles which proceeded it, bebop owes much of its development to the spirit and ingenuity of the jazz musicians of the 1940s who considered improvisation the best way to express the essence of a given composition in an unrestricted yet creative way.

In this context, the player was expected to alter or revise the composition, to expand it rhythmically, harmonically, or melodically, without losing the feeling of spontaneity and immediacy. All these people did just that. Our principal models in those days were Dizzy Gillespie and "Bird" — but we also learned a lot from Fats Navarro, Bud Powell, Howard McGhee, Kenny Dorham, Tadd Dameron, and many others. Buddy DeFranco, who was thought to be a great swing player, was one of the better bebop players very early on. He was the only one in the early days who would really play bebop on the clarinet. He kind of got lost in the shuffle when people started counting noses as to who was doing what.

Charlie Parker epitomized the jazz composer/performer of the 1940s — a truly brilliant improviser with a unique melodic gift. His collaborations with Dizzy, both as a player and as a composer, established the

I realized that bebop was evolutionary, not revolutionary. Bebop was the logical extension and expansion of earlier jazz styles.

guidelines for the bebop style very clearly. Dizzy Gillespie was the organizer. He wrote out melodies, riffs, interludes, and complete arrangements for others to learn. He often dictated what each instrument should play, even the rhythm section. He gave me the first lead sheet I ever saw. I didn't know what it was because I had not seen chord symbols written out like that, so he had to explain what that meant.

Both Dizzy and Parker taught by giving examples of what could be done with the material at hand. But the vocabulary they developed was so useful that it was fully explored and expanded by the musicians they influenced. Like Dizzy, I was fascinated with Latin jazz. I played with Machito's band in 1945, and learned a lot about that style from Mario Bauza, Dizzy's Latin jazz mentor. There was a close relationship established between New York musicians who played bebop and musicians who played Latin jazz. Their musical exchanges set the stage for what's going on right now in jazz.

Latin jazz has been a very important part of my music ever since the 1940s. In 1949 I was asked by music publisher Charlie Hansen to write a book which would help pianists play bebop. I did, and that was the beginning of my interest in writing about jazz and presenting it on radio and television. I also wrote a book on Latin jazz which was published during the same period. Since that time many excellent books have been written on both styles and transcriptions of jazz compositions, and they have both become com-

mon property. *The Real Book* and many other books contain a lot of information that one can just look at and say, "here's what it sounds like and this is the way I can play it."

Jazz concepts that were developed in the 1940s are basic concepts of mainstream jazz [instruction] and playing today. No one plays or writes effectively in a contemporary jazz style without paying homage in some way to the bebop pioneers. One of the things that I learned when I was house pianist at Birdland for two years between 1949 and 1951 was that everybody at that time was really trying to assimilate the things that bebop players were playing — even Louis Armstrong, who at one point was quoted as saying he didn't like the music. We have a television clip of [Armstrong] and Dizzy as they played together on a television show. He's fitting right in to Dizzy's band, and you could see the compatible way that this very early pioneer of jazz could fit the things that he did with one of the people who was looking forward and was very contemporary in those days.

There are many examples of how the music became a part of mainstream jazz, how it became the "lingua franca," I guess you could say, of today. In order to play jazz, everybody has to make reference to those tunes and people who were the pioneers. I guess the biggest lesson that I learned was that there is one big family as far as jazz is concerned, and as time goes on everyone seems to find his or her place in that family circle.

Tuesday, April 2, 1996
Bowker Auditorium

Panel Discussion Transcript Excerpts

Jazz Revolution or Media Concoction?

Excerpts from the presentation by Peter Watrous

RUMORS OF WYNTON MARSALIS'S EXIS-tence were already heard down the musician's wire in the late 1970s. He was supposed to be a brilliant young trumpeter from New Orleans who was playing in the tradition and really burning. What was notable was that he was swinging, and that everybody was taking note that he was playing in the tradition and playing it well. People were shocked by his virtuosity, and this is really important — they were also shocked about how rare he was.

At the time, few young musicians entered that particular arena — gravitating instead to the avant-garde, to fusion, or pop music. At the time, New York was an extraordinary, thrilling place musically. Henry Threadgill, the World Saxophone Quartet, Arthur Blythe, Craig Harris, and David Murray were playing places like The Tin Palace and Sweet Basil's. Sun Ra was performing in an underground theater on 14th Street.

Wynton Marsalis quickly became a famous oddity. In 1982 he released two albums simultaneously, a jazz record and a classical record, and that right there secured his public image. Wynton dressed well, played well, and thought well. The combination gave him access to media venues that had really been closed to the average jazz musician for decades...

At the same time, there was a technical revolution happening. Record companies began reissuing their back catalogs on CD and making a lot of money. Jazz reissues were a big portion of the releases, and combined with an increased interest in the media for younger jazz musicians, a handful of labels that had been inactive or mostly dormant sprang back to life.

Blue Note, Verve, and along the way Atlantic and RCA started recording again. Many record companies had to find something to sell. An obvious paradigm was what was then disgracefully called "the neo-conservative movement" — headed by Wynton.

During the early and middle 1980s, young musicians were being signed regularly with record companies milking the novelty of this young talent. Without the media, it is debatable whether any of this would have continued in the way that we know it now. Record companies packaged performers in a way that was both easy to write about and easy to get contentious about.

The CD revolution made much of the history of the music available. In New York, rumors of the next hot player finally burned out. There were just simply too many good young musicians addressing the same issues of swing, blues, and harmony — what it takes to be a consistent, solid, good jazz musician...

From the fifteen years since Wynton arrived, there has been a series of fragile, sometimes dubious successes — an apparently unstoppable onslaught. There are far too many young players to be absorbed by the major record companies, and if a revolution is judged by its number of participants, then the revolution has been successful. I've asked older musicians and critics on the scene, and they don't remember seeing as fertile a period since the late 1950s.

I would like to divide the revolution, if that is what it is going to be called, in half. Two extremely important things have happened during the last fifteen years. The first is a general aesthetic change and desire on the part of younger musicians to reconnect to the jazz tradition by learning about rhythm, harmony, and blues, and that in itself is a victory. But beyond that, the important younger musicians are gaining individual voices. Younger musicians are amplifying achievements of their elders, which is exactly what they are supposed to be doing. Specifically, I hear a radical change in the working of the average rhythm section, with the way that players have absorbed innovations of the rhythm sections of Herbie Hancock, Ron Carter, Tony Williams, or of Charles Mingus and Danny Richmond. There is an improvisatory approach to tempo and feel that simply didn't exist before, and it's becoming standard.

But I also hear a historicism in many young musicians, coupled with the real ability to reproduce older styles. It hasn't always been standard practice in jazz. Manifestations of that are heard in soloists breaking away from the music school form of "technocracy" – embracing instead, a more melodic form of improvising.

The second example of what has happened in the last fifteen years isn't musical; it's jazz's larger cultural reception. Jazz is in the most visible state it's been in since the fusion movement in the late 1960s and early 1970s, if we're to even agree that fusion is to be considered jazz. Just look at its public profile – jazz is found regularly on television as the background to advertising in a sophisticated market. It can be found visually in magazine advertisements. There are regular jazz concerts, at least in New York. Major labels are spending record amounts of money signing younger musicians, and the companies are marketing them like pop stars.

Jazz contests like the Thelonious Monk Institute in Washington, D.C., have garnered all sorts of attention and helped launch careers. Look at its reception in places that were previously the halls of European upper-middle-class culture. At Lincoln Center and Carnegie Hall, jazz programs regularly sell out, and those institutions have bands that tour the country and the world. The Smithsonian has its own jazz orchestra . . .

A recent article in the *New York Times* on the graying of audiences for high culture quoted a National Endowment for the Arts study that said that only art museums and jazz concerts were attracting a younger, larger audience. Another NEA study documented a strong growth and interest of jazz over a ten-year period between 1983 and 1993. Clubs in Manhattan are doing 30 to 100 percent better business now than they were doing even a year ago. So clearly, something is happening out there.

I would like to [address] the critical backlash of the whole movement of young musicians. The reception they have received by some jazz fans and plenty of older, established critics has been extraordinarily

If a revolution is judged by its number of participants, then the revolution has been successful.

In the late 1970s and early 1980s, it was quite possible to think that jazz was either dying or dead. Few young musicians were coming up who could actually play in a manner that would have passed muster with a majority of jazz musicians over history.

harsh. They feel let down by the work of younger musicians — "disappointment," to paraphrase some — [stemming] from the fact that young musicians haven't in any way absorbed procedures of the avant-garde of the 1960s. They seem less adventurous, less obviously radical. It seems to those critics that the younger musicians, in their search for a connection to the jazz tradition, have abdicated a jazz musician's task of moving forward.

What critics have overlooked is the simple fact that cultural information can be lost, and that practices and abilities can vanish. It is completely possible to break the line of a tradition and be left with nothing except memories of a golden age.

In the late 1970s and early 1980s, it was quite possible to think that jazz was either dying or dead. Few young musicians were coming up who could actually play in a manner that would have passed muster with a majority of jazz musicians over history. There were few record companies documenting the music, and audiences were old. A trip into the Village Vanguard for a 21-year-old was a trip into a crowd several

generations grayer. There were fewer jazz concerts, and there was virtually no public attention available for the music. The notion of excellent institutional jazz orchestras at Lincoln Center and Carnegie Hall would have been ludicrous. The present was an unthinkable future.

Race is essential in this discussion. What this racially integrated movement has done has recuperated great Black art from being lost. Swinging in a blues sensibility and improvisation are some of the great contributions that Black culture have given to the world, and innovation within those parameters is by no means exhausted.

The music is flowering again and being received by a wide audience, from mobs of college-age kids at the club Smalls at 2 o'clock in the morning in Manhattan, to wealthy elders at Lincoln Center, and it is a cause for rejoicing. All that knowledge could have vanished just like mist at noon on a hot summer day. It's not simply on recordings, it's here in the hands of 20–30-year-olds, and they're figuring out what to do with the riches that they've been bequeathed.

Panel Discussion Transcript Excerpts

Tuesday, April 2, 1996
Bowker Auditorium

What We Play and What They Call It

Excerpts from the presentation by Teōdrōss Avery

A LOT OF RAP ARTISTS WANT TO KNOW about jazz, but some of them don't care — some just want to find different sounds to sample. I collaborate with rappers, and I find that some really know what's going on. They listen to [jazz] records because their parents have Dizzy Gillespie, Charlie Parker, and Coltrane records.

On my second record, I collaborated with Black Thought [Tarik Trotter], a rapper from a group called The Roots — musicians who have played jazz and funk music. He has experience playing with improvisational music, and I would not have been able to collaborate with him if he didn't have any knowledge about what I do. It would make it very difficult if he didn't know where I'm coming from with my saxophone, or when I write music. I like to collaborate with people who know what I'm doing, whether it's a rapper or it's a percussionist. I spent a lot of time, and I still do, studying the masters of jazz . . .

I started playing the saxophone when I was in junior high. My father gave me a guitar when I was 5, I started lessons when I was 10, and then switched to saxophone at 13. My father had records by Yusef Lateef and Eddie Harris. My saxophone teacher played John Coltrane's "Giant Steps" for me. When I heard "Giant Steps," there was so much power — Paul Chambers playing the bass with so much conviction, and when I heard Coltrane start to play, it just cap-

tured my ear. I couldn't speak during the whole song. I just had to stay in tune to it, and from that point on, I really took jazz seriously. I started buying a lot of records. I would listen to them and try to learn some of the solos . . .

Living in Oakland, California, I was able to hear Art Blakey, Freddie Hubbard, and Donald Byrd. These people would let me sit in with them. I realized that people my age weren't really listening to jazz because they really didn't understand it. Unfortunately, in this country people don't really educate young people about jazz and about culturally aesthetic art in general.

I would always go and listen to these musicians on weekends, and I would study the way they were playing, study their personalities, because the music was an extension of their personality. When I would go to hear Art Blakey, I saw how much of a commanding presence he had on stage. All the musicians were so much taller than he was, but when they looked at him, you could see they respected him so much . . .

It was important for me to hear the masters of the music, and also hear local musicians who came up in those times. I noticed that when they played the music, they had a natural feeling, it wasn't preconceived. When they played, they would sing through those ballads in a way that musicians my age weren't doing.

This is the disadvantage that a lot of younger

> I learn from the tradition, use it to carry it on, but while I have one foot in the tradition, I've got one foot in the future.

I want to play jazz from my perspective — embrace the tradition but also bring [to the music] some of the other influences that I've had over the years. My generation should be able to represent ourselves with our own music.

musicians have right now. There aren't many working bands out there for musicians like myself to join. A lot of my friends who grew up playing jazz and who were very talented musicians ended up doing something else because there was a lack of playing opportunities for musicians. Either they've gone on and played another form of music, or they just stopped playing music altogether.

You get most of your education from listening to the records. All my friends traded records, transcribed the solos, transcribed the melodies. You get more education from listening to the records and also from going to hear the masters play live. I was one of those musicians who said, "I want to play this music regardless if there is an opportunity out there, or if there's a band out there that needs a tenor player. I still want to play the music." I got my own group together and I started writing my own music. I would work between Boston and New York — wherever we could play. I just love the music, and it was important to me to present it in the best way I could.

A drummer by the name of Carl Allen heard me while I was [a student] at Berklee. I was featured on his first record, *The Pursuer*, which was released in 1993. That record gave me some exposure. [Later on] I got a phone call while I was in school in Boston from this guy at GRP Records who said, "We want you to join us" — that's how my recording career started . . .

I had to think about my options. Did I want to graduate from college, or did I want to take this opportunity to record? I had to take the opportunity that was there for me. I was very serious about playing the music, and I continue to be serious about playing the music. What I wanted to do was to give my contribution to the music the best way I could, and I'm still doing that.

I learn from the tradition, use it to carry it on, but while I have one foot in the tradition, I've got one foot in the future. I have to be true to myself as a musician, and also to the public about my musical contribution and about what I want to bring to the music. I think that every musician along the way has to do that. You can't go around saying, "I'm the next 'Trane," or "I'm the next Sonny Rollins." Musicians today have to create their own scene, and do the best that they can, and be honest and be true to what they are doing.

There are people out there who want to mold you into being somebody else. They want to mold you into being the next Joe Henderson, for example. I prefer people to say, "Hey, that's Teōdrōss Avery." My second record is a better representation of me because I embraced the tradition, but I add some contemporary elements as well.

I've played in funk and reggae bands. I've been [performing] with rappers since I was in high school. Rapping is something that's social for young people. It really doesn't make me feel good when I read about people bashing rap. Usually these are people who don't have any connection to rap. They're sitting on the sidelines trying to judge something that's going on in the game, but they haven't experienced what [rappers] were experiencing. Anybody who tries to say that rappers shouldn't comment on what they see or how they live should really reevaluate what they are saying, because you can't censor someone's mind or what they feel.

I want to play jazz from my perspective — embrace the tradition but also bring [to the music] some of the other influences that I've had over the years. My generation should be able to represent ourselves with our own music . . .

Final Words by Billy Taylor

I THINK MILES [DAVIS] WAS 18 WHEN HE JOINED CHARLIE PARKER. DIZZY WAS 18 when he was working with his first big band, so there's nothing magical about starting at a young age. Too many of the great artists died much too young, and did a lot in a very short time. I guess the thing that we search for in today's age, and Teōdrōss has a good handle on it, is someone who is really following the tradition and is doing exactly what the elders in the 1940s were telling everyone to do.

They said, "Don't do what I do, find your own way of saying it." Lester Young said to tell your own story. I was with Art Tatum at an after-hours place one night, and a guy came in and he had transcribed Tatum's version of "Elegy." For someone to do this was astounding. This is tremendous virtuosity, and this guy had not only transcribed the notes, but also had everything exactly the way Tatum had recorded it.

I looked at Art and said, "Wow!" and he said, "He knows what I do, but he doesn't know why I do it." He wasn't impressed at all. He would much rather go and hear a guy playing some funky blues,... playing his own thing, so you're absolutely on target in your direction in finding your own voice...

The economics of jazz are treacherous, as are the economics of many businesses. It's very heartening to me to find that most of the people in this generation that's come along in the last 15 years are much more economically aware of what they're doing. They don't sign away the composition; they don't do a whole lot of things that we did in the forties, fifties, sixties, and seventies. They're protecting themselves as much as they can...

The other problem in the business is one of race. Race has always been an enigma in this country. In the 1940s, one of the highly publicized reasons that Dizzy Gillespie and many other musicians tried to create a music that was difficult, something of their own, was so that people couldn't steal it from them. They were reacting to the popularity of the big swing bands. The most popular bands were Benny Goodman and Artie Shaw, and they were all-White bands. This was at a time when Duke Ellington and Count Basie were at their [artistic] height, and they had great bands — man for man, better bands then at other times in their careers...

Gospel in the 1990s:
The Reason Why We Sing

26th Annual Black Musicians Conference

April 7 to April 10, 1997

ALTHOUGH GOSPEL IS A DISTINCTIVE STYLE OF MUSIC FIRMLY rooted in African American tradition and Christian spirituality, it's also an influential music that transcends racial and religious boundaries. If imitation is any indication of flattery, then gospel music has been flattered indeed. Regardless of one's spiritual beliefs or skin color, gospel music continues to thrive, evolve, and influence the secular music industry worldwide. According to Horace Clarence Boyer, one of the country's foremost gospel scholars, "Without a doubt, the 1997 Black Musicians Conference was the closest to the cutting edge of contemporary Black music that the Fine Arts Center has addressed in several years. Black gospel is the driving force behind all styles of American popular music; but Black gospel itself is in the throes of radical

Pastor Marvin L. Winans
BOWKER AUDITORIUM

The 1997 Black Musicians Conference was presented by the
Fine Arts Center Department of Multicultural Programs and
was funded in part by the UMass Arts Council. The screening
of *Say Amen, Somebody* was also a presentation of the 4th
Annual Multicultural Film Festival. Kenanyah was copresented by Augusta Savage Gallery and The Fairfield Four was copresented by the Fine Arts Center Series.

change. The sound that influenced American popular music is rapidly becoming indistinguishable from popular music, and could very well become one and the same. The goal of the 1997 conference was to assess the present state of Black gospel and its direction at the beginning of the 21st century, and to discuss the influence it has and will continue to have on popular music."

The Conference began with a film screening of *Say Amen, Somebody* – a 1983 documentary directed by George T. Nierenberg. Horace Clarence Boyer introduced the film, which includes footage of legendary gospel artists in performance: Willie Mae Ford Smith, Thomas A. Dorsey, and the Barrett Sisters among others. Highlights included Mother Smith's performance of "Never Turn Back" accompanied by a family quartet; an impromptu duet of "If You See My Savior" by Dorsey and Sallie Martin, performed as they listen to his 1932 recording of the tune; and the O'Neal Twins' rousing "Jesus Dropped the Charges."

A panel discussion titled "The State of Gospel Music in the 1990s" was moderated by Horace Clarence Boyer and included a discussion with two of the most important figures in gospel music. Marvin Winans of The Winans (the major crossover group before the appearance of Take 6) spoke on the topic, "The New Direction of Black Gospel." The Reverend Milton Biggham,

Willa Ward
BOWKER AUDITORIUM

Deacon Randy Green
BOWKER AUDITORIUM

director of the popular Georgia Mass Choir, presented "Where Does Gospel Music Stand Today?" Both Biggham's and Winans's remarks, which are printed in this chapter, were presented in a style that Horace Boyer referred to at the panel discussion as "that wonderful Black preacher's delivery."

The Distinguished Achievement Awards for 1997 were presented to the legendary gospel performer Willa Ward of the famous Ward Family Singers, and Deacon Randy Green from Boston. The program concluded with a mini-performance by Saints and Friends Fellowship Choir, a contemporary gospel ensemble based in Springfield, Massachusetts, directed by Elder Zachary Reynolds.

Other conference events included a jazz/gospel performance by Kenanya and the New Hope Ensemble at Augusta Savage Gallery. The conference culminated in Bowker Auditorium with a performance by The Fairfield Four, "gospel music's grand ambassadors" and Nashville's foremost emissaries of the proud heritage of Black gospel harmony singing.

Introduction by Mark Baszak

The *five* members of The Fairfield Four
BOWKER AUDITORIUM

Essay

Where Does Gospel Music Stand Today?

By The Reverend Milton Biggham

We cannot afford to be flirtatious with commercialism. We cannot let the dollar dictate our destiny. Yes, we all dream of having a hit that crosses over, but what good is it to cross over without the cross? Jesus must remain the subject of our song!

I CONSIDER IT AN HONOR AND A PRIVILEGE to be asked to stand up and speak on behalf of gospel music, the music that I grew up with. Actually, it's the music that grew me up! The question being posed is, "Where does gospel music stand today?" The good news is that gospel music is alive and well. Yes! This music that was created by God and fathered by the late Thomas A. Dorsey, this gospel music, which for many generations has been analyzed, criticized, scandalized, and even prostituted, remains a source of inspiration to millions all over the world.

The life and well-being of gospel music today first can be seen in its uniqueness. Gospel music, unlike any other music, is a musical expression that is based on divine truth. That truth is the good news of Jesus Christ that sets every man free. "For God so loved the world that he gave his only begotten son that whosoever believeth in him should not perish but shall have everlasting life."

There are, of course, many contributing factors that are causing gospel music to be as viable as it is today. Technology has increased the creative base of gospel music. More creative power has been given to the individual. Sampling has virtually made every instrument accessible to the fingertips by just plugging in a keyboard and turning on a computer. This

has resulted in more polished productions which also bring about better reproduction for the listener.

The "live" gospel recording, which was first done by the Reverend Lawrence Roberts and the Angelic Choir, has virtually taken the church experience to the ears of the listener. The results – the gospel music buyer likes it. The possibility is that two out of every three recordings today are "recorded live."

Video and television have increased the commercial base of gospel music by allowing the listener to experience the added dimension of sight. This by far has resulted in a higher consumption of gospel music — not just by church folks, not just by African Americans, but by an ever-growing number of people from other races. Because of television and video, many more can now enjoy gospel music in the confines of their homes. Under normal circumstances, these same individuals would never visit a Black church or even drive to a Black neighborhood to purchase the product.

Radio still remains the single most powerful media through which the public is exposed to gospel music. The creation of hundreds of 24-hour and day-time gospel music stations over the last five to ten years has filled the void that once existed when gospel was heard only during early-morning and late-

The Reverend
Milton Biggham
BOWKER AUDITORIUM

Our greatest challenge is keeping the gospel in the music. You see, the message is where the ministry is, and we somehow must learn to major in the ministry and minor in the music.

night programming.

Hollywood is playing an important role in the exposure of gospel music to a broader audience. Movies such as *A Leap of Faith* and *The Preacher's Wife* brought gospel music into the hearts of millions for the first time, and for many, it won't be the last time.

Many gospel music record labels have discovered the benefits of promotion and marketing. More attention is now given to cover designs, so we look better. More attention is now given to the print media, so the public, as well as music distributors, are more informed about the gospel artist. As a result, gospel music can now be purchased from the shelves of major chain stores throughout America, such as HMV, Coconuts, and Sam Goody's.

We must not forget the incredible contribution that has been made by gospel music artists. Not only do we have more new artists than ever before, but they are also so incredibly gifted. With all of this in mind, I think it's fair to say that more people are listening to gospel music today than ever before. But there's another all-important reason for that, and that is because of the times we live in. These are difficult times. People are faced with dysfunctional families, social problems, financial problems, and people are looking for real answers to real problems that they have to deal with from day to day. Gospel music offers an antidote for the poisonous negativity that we are forced to digest into our minds from day to day.

People are hurting and they need healing — gospel music does that! People are down and need lifting — gospel music does that! People are giving up and they need to be holding on — gospel music gives you a reason to hold on! People are feeling defeated and need deliverance and hope, and gospel music offers that!

Finally, even though gospel music is alive and well, we currently are standing at the crossroads. One road will lead us to more life and longevity; the other road will certainly lead to destruction. Our greatest challenge is keeping the gospel in the music. You see, the message is where the ministry is, and we somehow must learn to major in the ministry and minor in the music.

We cannot afford to be flirtatious with commercialism. We cannot let the dollar dictate our destiny. Yes, we all dream of having a hit that crosses over, but what good is it to cross over without the cross? Jesus must remain the subject of our song!

Tonight I can proudly say I love gospel music for what it is and for who its stands for. You see, gospel music will stand because when we stand up, we stand out. The message has been sung in Jerusalem, the message has been sung in Judea, and we are now getting that message to the outermost parts of the world. We cannot ever forget who it is that we are standing up for – Jesus!

Saints and Friends Fellowship Choir
BOWKER AUDITORIUM

Essay

The New Direction of Black Gospel

By Pastor Marvin L. Winans*

WHEN THE WINANS FAMILY FIRST started singing, my great grandfather was a pastor in Detroit. He started a church of God In Christ in 1917, built the church from the ground up, and was one of the first overseers of a church that sat fifteen hundred people in 1929. Our parents met singing; my mother and father married when she was 17 and he was 19 years old. My father was an only child, and my mother only had one sister, so I guess they made up for it by having kids. They met in a gospel choir called the Lucille Lemon Gospel Chorus. My mother was also a member of Lemon Special — which was a group within a group. She played the piano, and [though] she took lessons, she never had the time to teach any of us how to play; she was busy having children!

The first name of our group was Elder Winans' Great Grandchildren. My mother taught us just the melody of the songs that we sang. I must have been 4 years old when we first sang together; it was "the big four" as my father called us — David, Ronald, my twin brother, Carmen, and myself. At a church convocation where we first sang as a group, we were such a smashing hit that my father took over and started teaching us how to sing. This was torture at the time, but it really proved to be an [excellent] education.

My father loved quartet singing. He was a friend of Sam Cooke's, The Soulsters, Flying Clouds, The Trumpelettes, and just about everybody. We had to learn all those songs, and we sang all sorts of things we heard on AM radio. We would be right in the middle of watching a Western on television, and he would come in with his guitar and say, "Turn that foolishness off." We would have to turn off the television and go sing.

When I was 11, we were doing this new version of "Jesus Be a Fence All Around Me" at the annual church convocation. David was playing bass, and we told our father, "Okay Dad, you can sing backup." We were trying to tell Dad that we wanted to spread our musical wings, but he didn't like the way we were singing. It wasn't going over like he thought it should, so he bust right in the middle of a tune and took the music another way. We had to stop singing and follow what he was doing! After that moment we "retired."

I started writing songs when I was 12 years old, and it was a defining moment in my life. We grabbed some young people from around the church and started singing. I discovered that there were other young people in the church who could identify with what we were doing. It was very difficult for me to sing "Sometimes I Feel like a Motherless Child," because I had

* Pastor Marvin Winans's essay is a composite of notes he submitted for publication and excerpts from a transcription of his live presentation in Bowker Auditorium on Tuesday, April 8, 1997.

We would go to school and change the lyrics of Gladys Knight's song, "Midnight Train to Georgia" to "First Trumpet Sound of Glory." One of the first songs we did was a tune by Sly and the Family Stone! We changed their song "Hot Fun in the Summertime" to "High Time in My Jesus' Name.

my mother, my grandmother, and my great grand-mother around. We did not cater to that style of music because we couldn't relate to it, so we started making up our own songs.

I was born at a very strategic time when all of Motown was just at our fingertips. I grew up on the northwest side of Detroit, and all the Motown greats lived in our neighborhood. When I went to elementary school, I had to pass Smokey Robinson's house, Marvin Gaye's house, and Barry Gordon Jr.'s house. I was on the phone one time with Smokey Robinson and told him, "We used to shovel your snow!" He lived on the block in front of us. Stevie Wonder lived on the block behind us. The Four Tops lived two blocks away.

Growing up in Motown, we would hear all the popular melodies, but we came from a strict Pentecostal sanctified church background. Never in the history of the Winans family was there an r&b recording in our home. My eldest brother tried to play an r&b record at home and almost lost his life doing it. We heard the music when we went to the malls and to school, but we couldn't sing those songs. We had to change the lyrical content. We would go to school and change the lyrics of Gladys Knight's song, "Midnight Train to Georgia" to "First Trumpet Sound of Glory." One of the first songs we did was a tune by Sly and the Family Stone! We changed their song "Hot Fun in

the Summertime" to "High Time in My Jesus' Name." We would teach our versions to classmates in school who would sing the songs with us, and we discovered that our peers identified with what we were doing.

Mumford High School is the name of the school I attended, and Mumford just oozed with talent; it was the most talented school and was tremendous even in gospel music. We went to the same school as the Clarke Sisters and Fred Hammond. A bunch of well-known people went to Mumford High School.

Entering the Mumford High Talent Show was a defining moment in the making of The Winans. One thing you didn't want to do was to enter a Mumford talent show and not be good. The audience would immediately let you know their reaction. It was like New York's Apollo Theater in Detroit. We were ready to go on stage one night, when the announcer, who was just about ready to introduce us (we were known as The Testimonial Singers then) asked, "Are you really going to go out there and sing gospel?" It was like we were frozen in time. We realized that we could get booed and might have to come back to school the next Monday embarrassed.

All of a sudden it just clicked, and we knew we had something to say. We said, "Yes!" and we went out there and sang "J-E-S-U-S." We were the only group that was applauded, so we had to come back

We are not going to sing acid rock or hard rock, but we are going to sing about a rock, and that rock is Jesus.

and sing another song. It taught us something, and I remember so vividly what I said from the piano that night. I looked at the audience and said, "We are not going to sing acid rock or hard rock, but we are going to sing about a rock, and that rock is Jesus." We made them cheer Jesus. The experience let us know that young people could relate to what we had to say if we made it palatable, if we sang in a style where they could reach it and identify with it.

I can speak on behalf of The Winans because I did 95 percent of the writing for the group then. We never sat down and said, "Let's write a song that is purposely camouflaged; let's write a song that can go both ways." That wasn't our interest. I was 12 when I started writing, so I wrote songs that I felt 12-year-olds to 18-year-olds could relate to. As I grew up, I wrote about what I was experiencing, and discovered that Jesus can relate to you on whatever level you are on!

Early in our recording career, I met Andrae Crouch and sang a few of my songs for him. He liked our music, and invited us to perform at the dedication of a new church his father had just built. At the dedication service, he asked us to sing two songs and said, "You have to sing 'Are We Doing Your Will?'" We recorded that song on our first album for Lite Records. The congregation responded with this wonderful reception. I then just looked at my twin brother, Carmen, and said, "What do we do for the second one?" I was playing the piano and he said, "Do 'The Question Is.'"

"The Question Is" was a song that we discovered was being played on secular radio, which was not our intention. You have to understand that at that time, we had no church body that represented us. We didn't belong to the National Baptist Convention. We didn't

belong to the Church of God in Christ and PAW (Pentacostal Association of the World). The song was too worldly for gospel stations and too religious for secular stations. We were just out there, and our music started to be played on secular radio. Ever since then we sort of had a fix in secular radio.

We discovered some years later that everywhere we went, people would say they enjoyed our music. The amazing thing was that people would pay to come see The Winans, and the day after a concert they could come to our church and hear us for absolutely nothing at all. We once did a performance with Nancy Wilson and she said, "I listen to your music every day." We were getting calls from everyone from Patti Labelle to Stevie Wonder to Oprah Winfrey. Oprah called us and asked us to come on her show. That was when she was a reporter in Baltimore. We had just done a television concert in town, and she came backstage to meet us. She was just a news anchor at the time, but then she went to Chicago and the rest is history.

Where is gospel music going next? As long as we stay relevant, there is no limit to what gospel music can achieve. As Brother Milton Biggham so eloquently states, "People are people, and wherever you have people, you have problems that need to be solved." Not only do I think Jesus is an answer, I think Jesus is *the* answer. I think that wherever people are hurting, they are going to need healing — that is the purpose of gospel music. As I was preparing to come to Amherst, a scripture from the psalms just kept jumping out to me — "Sing unto the Lord a new song." I think that as long as we have people who are willing to open themselves up, there will be a new song.

There have been two questions that I have been

The amazing thing was that people would pay to come see The Winans, and the day after a concert they could come to our church and hear us for absolutely nothing at all.

asked many times. Ever since The Winans began, I've been asked, "With the success of The Winans in r&b and in gospel music, was it just a step?" They cite all of the other r&b stars and celebrities who have their base and foundation in gospel music but have gone on to other forms of music. When asked if that was our intent, the answer has always been a resounding "No!" It's not because I am just loyal to a particular genre of music; it's because I am loyal to "the message" before I am a Grammy-winner.

I believe what I am singing. I believe that gospel music is the greatest music in the world. I think that I am singing because I am not limited to what goes on here; I'll be singing in the next world. How many artists can say that? How many folks can say they have a spot reserved for them in the next world singing the songs that they sang in this world? How many people can say that they have a spot in a heavenly choir?

If everybody believed what they sang, and sang what they believed, they wouldn't have to worry about "getting hoarse," and wouldn't have to worry about getting tired. I believe that, and because I believe that, I am excited about where I am going.

Gospel music must always be true to its lyrical content. We had a saying when The Winans first started that, "It is not what you are playing, it is what you are saying." I remember when Take 6 (their name was Alliance then) came to my house. I got a call from

them asking if they could come over to the house, but before that, I had never heard of them. They were in town from the suburbs of Detroit for a convention of barbershop quartets. They were in my den, and they started singing "Get Away Jordan." My sons Skeeter and Marvin Jr. were sitting in the room and I was almost in tears when they finished. I was so blown away by their music. I looked at Take 6 and said, "Gospel music is in great shape. You guys are going to change gospel music, and you're going to open it up to a whole new audience." And they did exactly that.

Gospel music will move in a new direction as long as singers are true to what it is we have to do, and true to the message that we have to sing. Once gospel radio stations understand the necessity of consolidation, once there is a format and a congealing of radio stations, and they understand that all of them have to play the same record at the same time, gospel music will explode. Because gospel radio play is isolated, you can have a hit in Boston, but people in New York have never heard of the group. You can have a hit in Los Angeles, but the folks in Detroit have never heard of the group. There has to be a consensus throughout the gospel radio stations in the country. Once that happens, you're going to see gospel music take off like you would never believe, and if that happens, the future of gospel music will be even brighter than its past.

A Great Day in Harlem:
A Tribute to Dr. Frederick C. Tillis

27th Annual Black Musicians Festival

April 14 to 16, 1998

WITHOUT A DOUBT IT WAS A GREAT DAY IN HARLEM IN 1958, but for those who experienced Black Musicians Festival events forty years later in 1998, it was three great days in Amherst. The Black Musicians Conference also officially had its name changed to Black Musicians Festival to reflect the true nature of activities. The decision to increase the accessibility of the Fine Arts Center's annual series of programs celebrating Black music was a secondary priority as a "conference" underwent a subtle transformation to "festival."

Horace Clarence Boyer explained his motivation to change the program's name in the Spring 1998 issue of *Diversity*, the newsletter of the Fine Arts Center Department of Multicultural Programs: "For the past twenty-six years the University of Massachusetts has presented a series of musical and

Jean Bach speaking about the musicians and film, *A Great Day in Harlem*, with Horace Boyer's assistance.
BEZANSON RECITAL HALL

Schedule of Events, April 14–16, 1998
**A GREAT DAY IN HARLEM:
A TRIBUTE TO DR. FREDERICK C. TILLIS**

Tuesday, April 14, 8:00 PM
Bezanson Recital Hall

**Panel Discussion
The Music of Harlem in 1958**
Jean Bach, "A Great Day in Harlem: The Musicians and the Film"
Milton and Mona Hinton, "Jazz in the 1950s"
Horace Clarence Boyer, moderator

Distinguished Achievement Award Recipients
Frederick C. Tillis
Milton J. Hinton

Mini-Concert
Featuring: Steve Turre, trombone and conch, with Jeff Holmes, piano, Avery Sharpe, bass, Alvin Terry, drums

Wednesday, April 15, 8:00 PM
Augusta Savage Gallery

A Tribute to Dr. Frederick C. Tillis
Performances by the University Jazz Ensemble and the Vocal Jazz Ensemble
Poetry readings by Ingrid Askew, Terry Jenoure, Ann Maggs, and Ron Welburn

Thursday, April 16, 8:00 PM
Bowker Auditorium

Film Screening: *A Great Day in Harlem*
Introduction by Horace Clarence Boyer and Catherine Portuges

Concert: Art Farmer and his ensemble playing the music of their colleagues featured in the film

The 1998 Black Musicians Festival was presented by the Fine Arts Center Department of Multicultural Programs and was funded in part by the UMass Arts Council and the Massachusetts Cultural Council. The screening of *A Great Day in Harlem* was also a presentation of the Fine Arts Center Series and the 5th Annual Multicultural Film Festival.

related activities celebrating Black American Music and its complementary arts. These activities have been festive, celebratory, and joyous. Unlike conferences that are often bogged down in ponderous minutiae, our activities highlight the music, biography, and influences of those persons who gave American music its integrity. It's high time that we call this series of activities by its proper name — a festive celebration. With its new and correct name, the Black Musicians Festival will continue to present events related to this great American music and hope that the new name will influence us in planning future activities for this festival-like celebration."

The three-day Black Musicians Festival opened with its annual panel discussion, Distinguished Achievement Awards ceremony, and mini-concert. Festival staff moved the "main event" proceedings from last season's 700-seat Bowker Auditorium to Bezanson Recital Hall, an intimate 200-seat hall within the Music Department. Moderated by Horace Boyer, "The Music of Harlem in 1958" was a panel discussion that included a presentation by the Academy Award–nominated filmmaker Jean Bach (*A Great Day in Harlem*) and bassist/photographer Milt Hinton's personal recollections from that historic gathering of jazz greats. Mona Hinton joined her husband on stage to provide commentary on a special black-and-white slide presentation of Milt Hinton's photo-documentation of that impressive era in jazz history.

Yusef Lateef presents
the Distinguished Achievement
Award to Milt Hinton

Jeff Holmes presents
the Disinguished Achivement
Award to Frederick C. Tillis

Milt Hinton flanked by
Avery Sharpe and Steve Turre

BEZANSON RECITAL HALL

Avery Sharpe
BEZANSON RECITAL HALL

Although the audio recording of the evening's presentations proved to be of such poor quality that it was indecipherable, Bach's dynamic talk (delivered up tempo for those present that night!) follows this introduction.

Milt Hinton and Fine Arts Center Director Frederick C. Tillis received the year's Distinguished Achievement Awards in a ceremony later that evening. The opening-night event concluded with a mini-concert by a renowned quartet of University-affiliated musicians. The group featured Steve Turre ('80) on trombone and conch, Prof. Jeff Holmes (Department of Music) on piano, Avery Sharpe ('76) on bass, and Alvin Terry on drums performing in homage to some of the legends featured in the photograph and film, *A Great Day in Harlem.*

The following evening's presentation in Augusta Savage Gallery was a tribute to Frederick C. Tillis, musician, composer, poet, and visionary director of the Fine Arts Center, who retired from the University of Massachusetts later in 1998. Students in the University Jazz Ensemble and Vocal Jazz Ensemble performed a selection of Tillis compositions, while local performer and poet friends (Terry Jenoure, Ron Welburn, Ingrid Askew, and Ann Maggs) gave dramatic readings of their favorite Tillis poems. A sampling of Frederick Tillis's poetry has been reprinted in this chapter, along with photographs from his tenure as director of the Fine Arts Center.

The festival culminated in Bowker Auditorium the next day with a sold-out 16mm screening of Jean Bach's 1995 Academy Award-nominated documentary, *A Great Day in Harlem*, followed by a live film-related performance by trumpeter Art Farmer and his ensemble. Horace Clarence Boyer and Catherine Portuges, professor of comparative literature and director of the annual Multicultural Film Festival at the University, shared the honor of introducing the film, a documentary inspired by Art Kane's historic photograph, which also provided inspiration for programmers of this year's Black Musicians Festival.

Introduction by Mark Baszak

Steve Turre
BEZANSON RECITAL HALL

Essay

A Great Day in Harlem: The Musicians and the Film

By Jean Bach

IN MY LATE 30S, I BEGAN CELEBRATING MY birthday each year with a phone call to my mother, to thank her for getting me to the planet when she did — early enough in the century for me to have known Duke Ellington, to have known the members of the John Kirby band, and to have known Jimmy Blanton, Billy Strayhorn, J. C. Higginbotham, and Ivie Anderson.

I heard Louis Jordan at the Elks Rendevous, Fats Waller at the Panther Room, Horace Henderson when he had Ray Nance in the band, and Lil Armstrong singing "Brown Gal." In other words, although I'm older than anyone on this campus, you will not hear me complaining about my age.

I treasure the memory of Chick Webb playing for dancers at the Savoy, and Jimmie Lunceford playing the aptly named "For Dancers Only." Dancers responded to those great swinging sounds, and the musicians always said they played better when the lindy-hopping was good.

Back in my formative years, you could actually tell Black players from Whites just by listening. I'm not even a musician and I could tell. In the mid-1930s you could be tuned in to Benny Goodman's broadcast from the Congress in Chicago, and it was very nice.

Then, a half-hour later, from another part of town, you could hear a Fletcher Henderson remote from the Grand Terrace playing the same arrangements, but man, what a difference. You heard Chu Berry's tenor gliding gorgeously, and Roy Eldridge's trumpet careening wildly. Oh my Lord — what bliss!

All this color-coding was fairly easy, but only up until the arrival of bebop and cool. I couldn't pass that blindfold test today. But since we're pegging this festival on *A Great Day in Harlem*, let me turn the spotlight on some of my then and now favorites in the famous photograph that inspired the movie.

Among the pre-boppers, there's Stuff Smith — standing front and center next to that other magnificent giant, Coleman Hawkins. Jazz history boasts only a few violinists, all terrific by the way, but Stuff swung like mad — good night, did he go! It had to get to you; he was a wild man.

In my movie, *The Spitball Story*, Jonah Jones explains why he had to quit his job with Stuff to join the orchestra of the more sensible Cab Calloway. It seems that Stuff was an epic drinker, and he expected as much from his men. When one night Cozy Cole decided to switch to club soda, some of the others fol-

Whenever I make appearances in connection with the movie, I'm invariably asked, as I should be, "Where is Duke Ellington?" This towering figure that continues to affect so many of us decades after his death certainly loomed supreme when the subjects were being rounded up. I can only conclude that the band must have been on tour when the picture was taken.

lowed suit. Stuff listened to them playing, then announced, "Something don't sound right. It just don't sound right. Cozy, are you high?" Cozy shook his head no. "Jonah, you high?" Another negative. "Listen," Stuff announced, "anybody ain't high by the next set, it's a ten-dollar fine." So they all trooped out to the alley and knocked back a few before returning to the stand.

All this took its toll, and the upshot was a warning from Jonah's doctor, following a quite scary attack, that he might not last another six months at this rate. In Jonah's words, "I was just 28 years old." Thus, he moved to the more disciplined Calloway orchestra, where alcohol on your breath got you an even bigger fine.

Color lines began to blur soundwise with the advent of the newer styles of playing, the frenetic bebop and laid-back cool. Newer guys with younger ears picked up everything instantly. The more established jazzmen with older ears had to revise their musical reflexes. The late trumpet player Shorty Sherock, my first husband, began as a Dixieland star with such bands as Jimmy Dorsey, Ben Pollack, and Bob Crosby; but then he heard the siren sound of Roy Eldridge, and he fell in love. It was not hard to do; so did Dizzy Gillespie and dozens more of us who listened to the radio. Shorty managed to retool his brain

so successfully that some of his recordings have fooled more than a few jazz mavens. Incidentally, that blows my Black/White theory out of the water!

Shorty's music got an overhaul and his wardrobe did too. He even got a LaSalle convertible just like the one Roy drove. One day this blue-eyed, blond chap in his unlikely zoot suit stood lounging against his sharp-looking convertible when a fellow trumpet man walked by. He spotted Shorty, and he asked, "Hey, what happened?" Then came the deathless answer, "When I change, I change all the way!"

All of this probably gave Gene Krupa, his then boss, the idea to replace this "fake" Roy with the real thing, and Shorty was out of a job. Shorty took himself over to 52nd Street to sit in with an old friend, Coleman Hawkins. Charlie Parker was on the stand that night, calling out strange new tunes with unfamiliar chord changes that had poor Shorty scuffling to keep up.

Still sorting out ethnic identity, Shorty got himself a mixed band, and they were dressed by a Chicago tailor who was a jazz musician manqué who claimed to have invented the zoot suit. His quite extensive obituary in the *New York Times* acknowledged as much. The tenor star of this sextette was Paul Quinichette — later to be featured in Basie's band as the "Vice Prez" after his idol — Lester Young.

You would have thought that by the time this picture was taken, in the summer of 1958, there would have been more than three females in the assemblage. But there they are, left to right, Maxine Sullivan, Marian McPartland, and the brilliant Mary Lou Williams, just two pianists and one wonderful singer.

Lester, Count Basie, and Coleman Hawkins all appear in the legendary photograph. But whenever I make appearances in connection with the movie, I'm invariably asked, as I should be, "Where is Duke Ellington?" This towering figure who continues to affect so many of us decades after his death certainly loomed supreme when the subjects were being rounded up. I can only conclude that the band must have been on tour when the picture was taken. It never occurred to me to ask him how he missed out, but there is a full-page portrait of him elsewhere in that issue of *Esquire* magazine, the all-jazz issue that produced this historic picture.

At the annual International Ellington Conference, I expect to be quite a curiosity. I'm the only "member" still breathing who caught the "famous orchestra" during the two weeks they played the Congress Hotel in June of 1936 and for the balance of that decade. I was on hand whenever the band came to town. I took to asking questions about music whenever I got a chance, and I remember especially an exchange that took place when boogie-woogie came into vogue. Duke dismissed it. "Listen, any janitor can play that way. I prefer music that is more technically interesting like the Lion and James P." All of this is evident in Ellington's own piano playing.

While the maestro is AWOL from that famous photo, some former Ellingtonians are pictured, including three who contributed to that musical tapestry of colors and sounds that held us all spellbound: drummer Sonny Greer, trumpet pixie Rex Stewart, and the glorious Lawrence Brown. Sonny did not read music, but neither did some other great percussion masters — Art Blakey and Buddy Rich, to name but two. Sonny got the essence of that exquisite Ellington repertoire back when it was advertised as "jungle music." I hesitate to guess why.

Sonny's light touch, so hip, so fly, simply completed the mosaic in a perfect way. Graceful as a Balinese dancer as he wove around all that percussion equipment, he made a dazzling picture. Surrounded by the chimes of "Ring Dem Bells," the great gong of "The Mooche," and assorted cymbals, snares, and probably more stuff than he was ever going to need, it certainly made an exciting tableau.

Another early addition to the Ellington Band was that original thinker, Rex Stewart, from whom we learned all about the possibilities of the half-valve and the tricks you could do with it. Ivie Anderson and Rex conducted a spirited dialogue at the beginning of "I'm Checkin' Out, Good-Bye," with Rex speaking his lines through the half-valve trumpet. When Ivie answered "the phone" and asked, "Hello, hello, is this you?" — one could actually hear Rex pronouncing the words, "Well, who the hell do you think it is?"

When I decided to make the movie, *A Great Day in Harlem*, two of my oldest and closest friends in the photograph, Roy Eldridge and Lawrence Brown, had died just months earlier. Brown was the handsome, beautiful trombone soloist you see standing between Marian McPartland and Mary Lou Williams. His appearance was always suave and self-possessed, but his music betrayed an inner sadness, and the overall effect was quite moving. When he died, he was buried in his native California, but since he had so many admirers back east, I decided to arrange a special memorial service for him in New York.

The interesting thing about the Ellington band (one of the interesting things) was the way each person's personality helped shape the ultimate product, and surely Lawrence Brown's romantic voice was an important component. I always said I thought he looked like Rudolph Valentino, and that if Valentino had played the trombone, it would have had to sound like Lawrence.

You would have thought that by the time this picture was taken, in the summer of 1958, there would have been more than three females in the assemblage. But there they are, left to right, Maxine Sullivan, Marian McPartland, and the brilliant Mary Lou Williams, just two pianists and one wonderful singer.

Mary Lou Williams's story continues to amaze me: a kid in her teens, playing piano and writing absolutely swinging arrangements for Andy Kirk's Clouds of Joy. Sammy Cahn wrote a song about her, and I use a bit of it in the movie; it's called "The Lady Who Swings the Band" — and that title is no lie, I can

assure you.

Mary Lou knew music up one side and down the other. She was continually exploring, advancing, and she had a kind of salon up in Morningside Heights where all the great progressives would gather — Art Blakey, Thelonious Monk, and Bud Powell. They showed each other new ways to approach a musical problem, knocked each other out with crazy chords, just gorged on music, music, music.

One night some years later, I dragged Artie Shaw in to hear Mary Lou at a place near where I live, the Cookery, run by Barney Josephson. "Who are you seeing now, Mary Lou?" Artie asked coyly. "Who's the man in your life?" "Well," she said, "I'm too caught up in my composing right now. Don't have that kind of time anymore." "Aw," he persisted, "there must be somebody." "Artie," she said, a shade impatiently, "if you can't understand that, probably nobody can."

But I did. She was deep into her writing at that point, and turned out all manner of serious work — suites, cantatas, and a "Mary Lou's Mass" that's stunning. It was played at her funeral in St. Patrick's Cathedral, with a choir of marvelous children and Dizzy's splendid trumpet. Benny Goodman came with my husband, Bob Bach, and they both were crying. What got to me was Rose Murphy, if you can believe it, the baby-voice who sang "Chee Chee Chee." She sang so sweetly, "Mary Lou, I love you" — and I cried.

A lovely priest who was a devoted fan managed to get permission from Rome to travel with Mary Lou as a kind of road manager, and I guess, as a spiritual advisor. When she became artist-in-residence at Duke University, he joined her down there and frequently took over her classes in music appreciation when she couldn't make it. He said she preferred to focus on

I don't recall if Whitney Balliett said that "tap dancers were drummers standing up" or "drummers were tap dancers sitting down," but since Eddie Locke has been both, I guess he qualifies either way.

Mary Lou knew music up one side and down the other. She was continually exploring, advancing, and she had a kind of salon up in Morningside Heights where all the great progressives would gather—Art Blakey, Thelonious Monk, and Bud Powell. They showed each other new ways to approach a musical problem, knocked each other out with crazy chords, just gorged on music, music, music.

joyous, upbeat stuff. When the subject was something more atmospheric, it was [the priest] Peter's turn. Her length of stay there was supposed to be two years, but Mary Lou's classes were so popular she remained for at least eight.

Williams would get the whole classroom rocking, and these weren't musicians, just "civilians" who wanted to know something about jazz. "All right," she'd say, "I'm going to play the blues; and then I'll give you something simple to sing against the background." And they'd get grooving. "One time," she said, "I just told them to go for themselves — a whole roomful just scatting." "Ye gods," I said. "What did it sound like?" "Terrible," she laughed. "It sounded like Cecil Taylor."

That was an in-joke based on a true experience. Cecil Taylor is a major exponent of what they call "Free Jazz," no preordained structure, no time, no nothin'. But Mary Lou was old-fashioned enough to believe that "God is Love" and somehow they would find a way to play duets. A concert was scheduled on the stage of Town Hall, and the Taylor claque seated themselves down front, on their man's side of the hall. Before Mary Lou could call the tune and key (what key?), Cecil was off on his own thing, elbows and ankles flying, and Mary Lou struggled gamely to play

some noncontroversial blues. They released a commercial recording of this historic train wreck, but to tell you the truth, I've never had nerve enough to hear it again. I was there and that was more than enough.

I mentioned Mary Lou as a serious composer, but you should also consider the fellow on the extreme left of the photograph, Gigi Gryce. Here's a talented genius who actually studied in Paris with Honegger and with the famed Nadia Boulanger. He died much too young, having spent much of his brief life coleading a group with Art Farmer. This brings us to that illustrious dual-national, Art Farmer. While he's currently on tour in the States, appearing with the movie in which he stars, *A Great Day In Harlem*, he's also at home in Vienna, where he settled years ago.

Art has been admired by his peers since the early 1950s as a consummate artist, capable of playing anything, and praised, particularly by Dizzy Gillespie, when I was doing interviews for the movie. "Oh, Art Farmer," Dizzy began, launching into a story about his being dragged into a recording studio by Duke Ellington to do an impromptu reading of "UMMG" (Upper Manhattan Medical Group). Dizzy wasn't all that pleased with the results, claiming it was too "spur of the moment." But then he said, "Art Farmer made a record of it the way it should be played." Dizzy was rhapsodic.

As Art mentions toward the end of the film, so many of these magnificent beacons have left us [Art Farmer died in 1999], so it's good to be talking about those still with us. I think particularly of Horace Silver, whose purity and goodness seem to shine through his music. Like the late Art Blakey, Horace inspirits the men who play his compositions, and it must be heaven to play that fascinating stuff. Art Farmer told me how much he appreciated the time he worked with Horace, how forceful he was at the piano leading the group along. When Art joined Gerry Mulligan's celebrated pianoless quartet, Art said it was like one of those dreams where you're walking down the street with no clothes on.

The leaders do pull you along. Benny Golson, top left, surrounded by Art Farmer and Blakey, said that when he joined Blakey, he noticed the great drummer played louder whenever he got a solo. Finally he figured it out — he was too tentative in his playing. Blakey was just trying to bring Benny out of his shell.

Two survivors, both stars of the tenor sax, are enormous favorites wherever they appear. Johnny Griffin makes his home in France, so I had to wait till he hit New York to film a conversation with him. He was wonderfully interesting on the subject of Thelonious Monk, whom he knew well. The other celebrated tenor, Sonny Rollins, revealed some marvelously sensitive insights during our conversation, and I often think of his, "What's the use of living to 100 if you don't accomplish something?" He's an interesting guy, a very interesting player, and a superstar as well.

We are lucky to still have with us, and playing so attractively, Hank Jones, of the celebrated Jones family of Detroit, and Eddie Locke, a favorite drummer of a million local groups. Hank never seems to age, he's a perennial favorite of other pianists. I don't recall if

Whitney Balliett said that "tap dancers were drummers standing up" or "drummers were tap dancers sitting down," but since Eddie Locke has been both, I guess he qualifies either way.

And now for my most favorite survivor of all, America's sweetheart — Milt Hinton. He starred in both *A Great Day* and *The Spitball Story*, and besides being one of the all-time leading bass players of the world, he's a distinguished photographer, and he's responsible for my meager career as a filmmaker. It all began when he brought his movie camera to the spot where they were going to take that group shot for *Esquire*. At that point, a movie by me seemed the logical next step because I had known probably nine-tenths of all the people in the photograph, and Milt had this glorious home movie footage, shot by his darling wife, Mona. Knowing nothing at all about movie-making, I plunged in. Without Milt, I probably wouldn't be here tonight, so I thank him for everything, including his fine playing.

I've said nothing about social matters in discussing Black music makers; you may have noticed. I don't fancy dwelling on painful subjects. So many jazz movies made today are such downers; it's always raining and the guys are always strung out on dope. Don't forget, I lived through the period when Blacks couldn't find places to stay on the road, and worse.

I'll just close with one of the frequent conversations I used to have with Miles Davis when he'd phone me at work. "Miles! Good to hear from you. How are you doing?" . . . (Pause) "Oh, Jean, I'm a Black man in a White man's world." "That's true enough," I had to agree. Miles continued. "You White people find a way to take credit for everything. You treated us terribly on the plantations, so we had to invent the blues. Now you're taking credit for getting the blues invented!"

So many jazz movies made today are such downers; it's always raining and the guys are always strung out on dope.

Words and Images:
A Tribute to Frederick C. Tillis

Such Sweet Thunder: Views on Black American Music would not have been possible without the artistry, humanity, and leadership of Frederick C. Tillis. He was director of the Fine Arts Center from 1976 to 1999, and in the fifteen years that I have known him, Fred often said that he "wore many hats." A musician, composer, educator, administrator, poet, author, mentor, and life-long supporter of the arts, Tillis was unwavering in his belief that the arts are essential to life and understanding the world in which we live.

Fred Tillis thought outside the box and epitomized the true meaning of that expression decades before it became a cliché. He continually challenged the status quo and helped to create a multicultural and diverse movement in arts and education long before the practice became fashionable. He brought many innovative programs into the Fine Arts Center family, including the Black Musicians Conference and Augusta Savage Gallery. He founded the Jazz in July Summer Music Programs and the Department of Multicultural Programs. He encouraged my colleagues at the center to launch the Bright Moments Festival, New WORLD Theater, and the Asian Dance and Music Program. Tillis established the Afro-American Music and Jazz Studies Program within the Department of Music and Dance at a time in the early 1970s when very few academic institutions offered even a course on the subject.

For many years, Fred Tillis led the way to many "Great Days in Amherst." Within the tenure of his twenty-three years as Director of the Fine Arts Center, most of the celebrated Black musicians of the 20th century performed at the University of Massachusetts. A few images of those great artists by the photographer Edward Cohen have been selected to appear in this tribute. Poems that appear alongside those photographs were chosen by Fred (from his seven books of poetry) for inclusion in this chapter, and are reprinted here with his permission. The power of Fred's words and Ed's accompanying images combine in a unique way to speak volumes more about the man whom we hold in such high regard.

Mark Baszak,
November, 2002

Frederick Tillis on saxophone
FINE ARTS CENTER CONCERT HALL
CIRCA 1989

ABOVE, LEFT TO RIGHT
The 1999 Jazz in July Summer Music
Programs Faculty
(FRONT ROW) Billy Taylor, Genevieve Rose,
Frederick Tillis. (SECOND ROW) Sheila Jordan,
Chip Jackson. (THIRD ROW) Jeff Holmes,
Charles Ellison, Yusef Lateef. (BACK ROW) Evan
Price, Winard Harper, Mark Summer, Rick
Stone, Chris Lightcap, Danny Seidenberg,
Mark Holovnia, Jonathan Nathan, Horace
Boyer, David Balakrishnan
GARDEN PATIO OF THE LORD JEFFERY INN, AMHERST
JULY 14, 1999

Visions of the Muse

Something the poet must not abuse
Is the power of the goddesses of the muse.
These charming and mysterious goddesses
Are the sources of the poet's inspiration.
Without their grace and blessings
His verses would be void of valuable sensations.

The goddess of music and poetry
Is endowed with the warm milk of humanity.
Regardless of the wind or shade of the season
There will always be a need and reason
For her to be near... and dear.
I need the resonance of her vibrant voice
To make soothing rhythms and melodies of choice.
The flowing imagery of the poet would be diminished
Without at least one goddess
By whom his creativity could be replenished.

I wish not to lose
  The visions, myths, and moods
    Of the healing powers
      During the darkest hours
        When dreams and fantasies
          Join the magic and enter the veil
            Of the reigning goddess and bearer of new views
              Queen of the heavenly earth and muse.

from *Of Moons, Moods, Myths, and the Muse*, 1993

The Tender Years

Too much is enough
When you already have plenty.
Too little is too much less
If you don't have any.

The face of a little child
Is like the face of the moon
Open, full, and smiling at times
Withdrawn, brooding, and hiding
Behind sour moods of silence
And a veil of clouds, myths, and treason
Seemingly, without rhyme or reason.

Indeed, if you don't have any
Too little is much too less.
But when you already have plenty
Too much can be a holy mess.

Holding on to dreams and fantasies
Is a special blessing for children
And a special gift for grownups
Who can recall the playful joys and cheers
Of happy days and the tender years.

from *Of Moons, Moods, Myths, and the Muse*, 1993

Art Blakey (A Salute to Art Blakey)
FINE ARTS CENTER CONCERT HALL
OCTOBER 18, 1975

Blakey later appeared at the Fine Arts Center
on the bill with The Jazz Messengers on
November 6, 1987

The Spirit of X

There were those who considered him militant
he considered himself Malcolm
strong, volatile, and virulent
like the music of Parker and Coltrane.

A major theme of his text
was "make it plain" — make it plain
the potent phrase of three words
with resonance still proclaimed.

Tension, turmoil, and toil
were crosses he would bear
time, temperance, and endurance
are legacies we now all share.

No one could have predicted
in the soul of one so complex
how the pain upon him so inflicted
could sustain the spirit of Malcolm X.

from *Harlem Echoes*, 1995

For Langston Hughes

Jesse B. Semple
smiled a lot,
had big dimples

Humor was his pallet
a canvas of politics and persuasion
pimps and prostitutes, no evasion

Preachers and teachers
were painted too
nothing escaped the black and blue

Night clubs and music
fights at the bar
everything he saw, up to par

Playing blues and dancing
through early morning hours
good times rolled to highest powers

Semple's core like the apple
had no evil pit
his essence was charm, humor,
and Jesse's down-home wit.

from *Harlem Echoes*, 1995

Archie Shepp, Ella Fitzgerald, and Max Roach
BACKSTAGE AT THE FINE ARTS CENTER, DECEMBER 4, 1975

The Future

The future
is the distant past
and what the prophets see
when they look at time
in the hour glass.

The sun does not kiss its own shadow
nor eat the fire of its soul
it has no fear of winter
nor does the moon's night-wine matter
the warmth of its flame lingers.

While progress moves in a circle
its beginning or end does not render
a profound truth or curse
to which we should surrender
for time is the keeper of faith
and the provider of peace and the purse.

from *Harlem Echoes*, 1995

Mother and Child
(for Elizabeth Catlett)

The artist who made wood cry
by the swelling reign of tenderness
born in the shadows and shapes
of forms deeper than vision's eye.

An artist whose valiant passion
was burned through prints on paper
bearing a soul of mature compassion
leaving images I embrace and savor.

Her wood, bronze, and marble sculptures
of beloved mother-and-child
echo the warmth of human flesh
with a soft heart's lingering smile.

Though declared an undesirable alien
a citizen of both the U.S. and Mexico
she created art reflecting her African-American heritage
maintaining pride and a universal visual language.

Figurative forms used symbolically
gracefully expressing abstract ideas
powerful portions of intuitive and intellectual energy
are catalysts for her magic over the years.

She draws from the earth
elements of life's fiber and core
while inspiration gives new birth
to a lasting spirit, now and here-to-fore.

*Nduma Eagleview**
from *Harlem Echoes*, 1995

*Nduma Eagleview is another voice, an alter ego, that draws on the poet's African and Native American roots.

Dizzy Gillespie and Bill Cosby
FINE ARTS CENTER CONCERT HALL
DECEMBER 11, 1976

This photograph was taken at a program
called "An Evening of Giants" featuring Jo
Jones, Mary Lou Williams, Dizzy Gillespie,
Charles Mingus, and James Moody. Mary Lou
Williams was seated at the piano behind
Gillespie and Cosby!

Yoruba and Beaded Crowns

Between the Niger and Dahomey rivers
along the West African coast
lies a land of rich artistic heritage
trading and crafts allowing southwest Nigeria to boast.

As early as the 13th century
masterpieces of bronze casting and wood carving
were produced in Yoruba lands by fertile artists
along with mysteries and other secrets of the dark continent.

Multicolored layers of beaded crowns
treated inside with secret medicinal herbs
to enhance the king's ase (or life force)
symbolizes spiritual links with his royal ancestors.

Crowns with long-hanging beaded strands
concealed the faces of the wearers
like curtains or blinds over doors or windows
to keep the eyes and thoughts of strangers in secrecy.

Coda: Beaded crowns — babalawo olodu
    beaded gourds — old and new
  priests, rattles, and shakers
    secrets and earthquake makers.

Nduma Eagleview
from *Children's Corner: from A to Z,* 1997

The Tree of Life

The tree of life is a woman.
She is wise, mature, and towering symbol
with roots that grow deep and firmly in the land.
She filters the air and sets our breath free
giving a sense of gravity
to the heart of earth, sky, and sea.

Her curved branches and limbs
embrace us with kindness and gentleness
drawing us closely to her breast
as we cringe from the heat of anger and war
looking to her for shelter, comfort and rest
knowing that sustained peace comes from her arms.

She preserves the soul and soil of the earth
holding the land and hands firmly from birth
so that rains, storms, rivers, and the wind
do not blow or wash us into the sea
nurturing forces of time and eternity.

Life on earth could not be
without her grace and fertility.
Legends and myths of her powers and charm
are the changing moons and myths
that have kept us alive
preventing self-destruction and the ultimate harm.

from *Seasons, Symbols & Stones,* 1999

Sarah Vaughan, FINE ARTS CENTER DRESSING ROOM, DECEMBER 1, 1984

Sarah Vaughan's first appearance at the Fine Arts Center was on September 29, 1977

The River's Prize
(A Sonnet)

When the sun dries the ocean and wind
There is an ancient rite and prize
As the river cries
And weeps beyond its banks.
Time seeps through the hour glass and realizes
Why we should give thanks
When the bending waters smile
And roll gently like a calm breeze
Nurturing the land and its people for miles
Sustaining the life of grasses, animals, and trees.
Accountable to the heavens and rains
It is a main artery of the earth's veins
An even-handed source of pleasure and pain
An ultimate blessing in which the whole world gains.

Nduma Eagleview
from *Seasons, Symbols, & Stones*, 1999

Silence

Late in autumn
through window panes
in the corner room
I watched a silent rain.

A triangle-stream
of falling waters
passed through rain spouts
silently dancing on pebbles and stones.

Leaves are not restless
in this daunting mourning
when winds only whisper
and time is a chorus of silence.

Nduma Eagleview
from *Akiyoshidai Diary*, 2000

LEFT
Max Roach
FINE ARTS CENTER CONCERT HALL
CIRCA 1985

Beginning in 1982, Roach performed regularly at the Fine Arts Center. For many years, he taught in the Afro-American Music and Jazz Studies Program and the Jazz in July Workshops in Improvisation, and he was a featured performer at the Bright Moments Festivals

ABOVE, LEFT TO RIGHT
The Jazz All Stars: Frederick Tillis, Max Roach, Hank Jones, Stanley Turrentine, Ray Brown, and Milt Jackson
DECEMBER 7, 1985

Daybreak

This morning
instead of rain
  longer green stems
in the rice fields.

  More birds singing
songs of the valley.
  With dry feathers today,
rain no longer fills the silence.

  In the rice fields
the loud "pop-gun" shatters the air.
  Still, more crows are talking
and other feathered friends follow.

  Fish in the moat
are harder to see
  soil and roots washed from mountain
made dark gray-chocolate-red water.

  Under blue sky
with silver clouds and sunshine,
  daybreak's chill is crisp
like the dagger's edge.

Nduma Eagleview
from Akiyoshidai Diary, 2000

Gotham City: 9/11

Raging flames of fury!
Melting steel, dust and gray ash!
Burned flesh, charred bones, and broken glass
Debris, human misery, and suffering
Crushed bodies and buildings, hauled off in dump trucks like trash.

A dreadful day of horrors and sorrows
Phantoms – Ghost Phantoms
Avengers wrath – for pent-up grievances
of the past, present, and future.
Wayward clonings of Robin Hoods.
Aggrieved souls, sowing bad deeds in the name of good.

Dreams of twin Towers of Babel are cursed!
Ways of reaching heaven through marketed commerce
are lost in schemes and entanglements of greed reversed.
Lost notions of who owns vengeance (other than God)
are no more sacred than musings of ancient bards.

Not only Gotham City – lost some luster and desire
But a deep gash of fire – pierced a side of the Pentagon.
Virtue and wisdoms are lost in these fruitless battles.
Nevertheless, heaven and hell linger on.
While cradles of ghouls and tormented souls are rattled.

unpublished, 2001

1975–1999

A sampling of all the artists associated with the Black Musicians Conference and Festival as well as the prominent Black artists who have appeared at the Fine Arts Center under the leadership of Frederick C. Tillis.

Frederick C. Tillis
JULY 10. 2002
BOWKER AUDITORIUM

Teodross Avery
Pearl Bailey
Kenny Barron
Count Basie
Mario Bauza
Harry Belafonte
Louie Bellson
Milton Biggham
Ed Blackwell
John Blake
Art Blakey
Patti Bown
Clarence Brown
Jeri Brown
Ray Brown
Clora Bryant
Freddie Bryant
Donald Byrd
Cab Calloway
Terri Lyne Carrington
Benny Carter
Betty Carter
James Carter
Ray Charles
Doc Cheatham
Ray Copeland
Roberta Davis
Dorothy Donegan
Ted Dunbar
Mercer Ellington
Charles Ellison
Ethel Ennis
The Fairfield Four
Art Farmer
Ella Fitzgerald
Roberta Flack
Nnenna Freelon
Chico Freeman
Tia Fuller
Victor Gaskin
Dizzy Gillespie
Leonard Goines
Dexter Gordon
Randy Green

Johnny Griffin
D. Antoinette Handy
Slide Hampton
Winard Harper
Jimmy Heath
Jessie Mae Hemphill
Jon Hendricks
Al Hibbler
Milt Hinton
Harold Holt
Freddie Hubbard
Abdullah Ibrahim
Milt Jackson
Illinois Jacquet
Leroy Jenkins
Claude Jeter
Steve Johns
Luther Johnson
Hank Jones
Jo Jones
Thad Jones
Yusef Lateef
Ramsey Lewis
Abbey Lincoln
Melba Liston
Bill Lowe
Kevin Mahogany
Ladysmith Black Mambazo
Ellis Marsalis
Wynton Marsalis
Christian McBride
Semenya McCord
Bobby McFerrin
Jackie McLean
Carmen McRae
Mighty Clouds of Joy
Charles Mingus
Dwike Mitchell
Amina Claudine Myers
James Moody
Stephen Newby
Odetta
Jimmy Owens
Nicholas Payton

Oscar Peterson
Awadagin Pratt
Leontyne Price
Tito Puente
Sandra Reaves-Phillips
Dewey Redman
Joshua Redman
Dianne Reeves
Vernon Reid
Max Roach
Marcus Roberts
Sonny Rollins
Willie Ruff
Mongo Santamaria
Avery Sharpe
Marlena Shaw
Archie Shepp
Bobby Short
Richard Smallwood
Emery Smith
Dakota Staton
Bob Stewart
Slam Stewart
Maxine Sullivan
Stanley Turrentine
Billy Taylor
Alvin Terry
Clark Terry
Lesa Terry
Bob Thomas
Leon Thomas
Steve Turre
Uptown String Quartet
Sarah Vaughan
Hezekiah Walker
Willa Ward
Mark Whitfield
Claude Williams
Marion Williams
Mary Lou Williams
Cassandra Wilson
Nancy Wilson
Marvin Winans
Reggie Workman

The Blues Lives On

28th Annual Black Musicians Festival

April 13 and 14, 1999

ALTHOUGH INSTITUTIONS OF SLAVERY MAY HAVE BEEN ABOLISHED in post–Civil War America, the ugly faces of racism remained behind. Despite this alleged new-found freedom for all Black Americans, subtle and not-so-subtle varieties of discrimination and oppression grew and stayed firmly rooted within the cultural soil of American society, a condition that gave rise to a new and glorious form of expression, a music called "the blues."

"Freedom was our birthright. But in fact, slavery was still in place in the form of sharecropping and exploitive industrial practices — the unending debt and humiliation of continuing to work for the same master they were supposed to be free from. Hard times and difficult situations gave birth to the blues. This feeling came forth in the form of talent, one element of

Clarence Brown and Luther Johnson, BEZANSON RECITAL HALL

Schedule of Events, April 13 & 14, 1999
THE BLUES LIVES ON

Tuesday, April 13, 1999
8:00 PM, Bezanson Recital Hall

Panel Discussion
The Blues Lives On: Personal Reflections
Clarence "Gatemouth" Brown, performer
Luther "Guitar Junior" Johnson, performer
Paul Kahn, artist manager, Concerted Efforts
Steven C. Tracy, moderator

Distinguished Achievement Award Recipients
Luther "Guitar Junior" Johnson
Clarence "Gatemouth" Brown

Mini-Concert
Solo acoustic sets by
Clarence "Gatemouth" Brown and
Luther "Guitar Junior" Johnson

Wednesday, April 14, 7:00 PM
Augusta Savage Gallery
Film: premiere of *Blues Stories,* about
the history and roots of American music of
the 1920s and 1930s. Introduction by Larry
Banks, director

The 1999 Black Musicians Festival was a presentation of the
Fine Arts Center Department of Multicultural Programs, fund-
ed in part by the UMass Arts Council and the Massachusetts
Cultural Council, and sponsored in part by WMUA91.1FM and
WRNX100.9FM. The screening of *Blues Stories* was also a
presentation of Augusta Savage Gallery and the 6th Annual
Multicultural Film Festival.

which is the inherent self-expression found in the power of music. Many could not read or write, but they felt the blues which could be expressed with harmonica, guitar, and voice." So begins *Blues Stories,* a documentary film by Larry Banks and narrated by the (University alumnus) Taj Mahal, which chronicles the history and roots of American music of the 1920s and 1930s. A rough-cut screening of *Blues Stories* was cosponsored by Augusta Savage Gallery and the 6th Annual Multicultural Film Festival.

Horace Clarence Boyer explained his motivation for selecting the year's theme — "The Blues Lives On": "As we enter the 21st century it seems not only fair, but also proper, to set aside some time to pay homage to that indispensable element that serves as the basis of African American secular music and the foundation of American popular music — the blues. What started out as a crude commentary on work, love, travel, disappointment, and the hard times of a lone and disenfranchised singer became a vehicle that transported every type of American song. Whether it is the music of Count Basie, the Beatles, B. B. King, Bonnie Raitt, or Nirvana, the blues is the element that holds the music up and together. The blues comes in such varied shapes and colors that it is often unrecognizable as the blues. It has become so subtle that many people today have no idea that most of the music produced throughout this century is the blues, imitates and projects the blues, or is

Clarence
"Gatemouth" Brown
BEZANSON RECITAL HALL

Frederick Tillis and Luther Johnson
BEZANSON RECITAL HALL

Clarence Brown and Paul Kahn
BEZANSON RECITAL HALL

inspired by the blues."

The festival opened with a panel discussion, Distinguished Achievement Awards ceremony, and mini-concert in Bezanson Recital Hall. This year the festival honored two living blues legends — Clarence "Gatemouth" Brown and Luther "Guitar Junior" Johnson. Each shared his personal reflections on the past and current state of the blues and received a Distinguished Achievement Award for his work, and they took turns on stage to perform a solo acoustic mini-set for a standing-room-only crowd. Steven Tracy of the Afro-American Studies Department was the panel discussion moderator. Joining Tracy on the panel was Paul Kahn, Brown's and Johnson's manager. An excerpt from the panel discussion transcript follows this introduction. Just as a recording cannot capture fully the excitement of a live performance, a written transcript, no matter how accurate it is, never captures fully the nuances of body language, audience reaction, and the thrill of being there when it all happened.

Introduction by Mark Baszak

Luther "Guitar
Junior" Johnson
BEZANSON RECITAL HALL

Tuesday, April 13, 1999
Bezanson Recital Hall

Panel Discussion Transcript Excerpts

The Blues Lives On: Personal Reflections

With Clarence "Gatemouth" Brown, Luther "Guitar Junior" Johnson, and Paul Kahn
Steve Tracy, Moderator

Horace Clarence Boyer made the following introductory remarks
prior to "The Blues Lives On" panel discussion

Steve Tracy and Clarence Brown
BEZANSON RECITAL HALL

ON JANUARY 1, 1863, THE EMANCIPATION PROCLAMATION WENT INTO EFFECT, AND IN 1865, the thirteenth Amendment was ratified, which finally said that all slaves in the United States, regardless of color, were to be free. Now this promoted a very interesting musical activity, because as you probably know, previous to that time in 1865, Black people lived in groups, large groups of twenty-five, and fifty, and one hundred, and a music was produced which was a choral music, because it was communal music. The Negro spiritual was the major part of this music. After 1865, we have in the United States for the first time, what is called, dig this, the nuclear Black family – a husband, a wife, and 2.5 children, working on a plantation. Well this promoted something very interesting. For the first time on these shores, Black people worked singularly, and music was such a part of the culture brought from Africa that they sang even one person at a time. There was no overseer who had to be watched. As a matter of fact, there was a belief that you would get paid according to your worth. It was during this time that people began to sing about love, about travel, about work, and about longing. By 1905, Gertrude Ma Rainey, the first female Blues singer, said that she heard a young woman in St. Louis singing a kind of music that she picked up on and was among the first to introduce to the world. This music was first done by sharecroppers, and long before the juke box came along, we had what we called juke joints, even little tents, sometimes, with sawdust on the ground, where a single person played the banjo, or harmonica, or a guitar when they could afford one, and sang. This music then went from singers to instruments, from guitars to saxophones. And around 1940 this music became the music that undergirded all American music, whether we know it or not. The blues is the foundation of American music.

Steve Tracy (ST): *The [first] question I would like to throw out has to do with the various influences that you bring together in your work. You're known as eclectic, multidimensional artists. Can you talk a little bit about how you feel about the label of "blues performer"? When you are called a blues performer, do you feel that this adequately addresses the kind of thing you do in your music?*

Clarence "Gatemouth" Brown (CGB): I reject the label of being a blues player because I play all styles of music — country, cajun, bluegrass, jazz, blues, calypso, bossa nova, semiclassical, and whatever else I try and play. I don't want no one to call me no blues player, 'cause I know what the audience thinks when they call it blues. They think of the blues that really makes them feel down, but I don't, 'cause blues is played in many forms. It can be happiness — positive — or it can be negative — sadness. I try to stay away from the sad part of it.

Luther "Guitar Junior" Johnson (LJ): I'm considered a blues player, but I'm like Gate, I play a variety of music — country & western, hard rock, soft rock, r&b, spirituals. Music is to me what you got your heart into when you're playing it. Some people think it's a sad music, but my blues is happy. It makes people want to get up and dance, and shout,... makes you want to love. My music makes you want to do everything and I love it.

Paul Kahn (PK): These guys both know a few tricks, and that's one of the things they have in common. They're the best at what they do, and are really incredible, articulate purveyors of their art forms.

They're also both great entertainers as well as being great musicians.

ST: *Over your careers, you have been labeled "blues singers." Do you think that has held you back in any kind of way?*

CGB: Well in a way. I'm not a prejudiced person because I love all of it, because you're my friends and my brothers and my sisters. But you know, the White society wants to keep you in this category — a Black man, a great athlete, a great jazz player, a great blues player. But I've fooled the world, I play everything, so they have to back off and say I'm a musician rather than what they want me to be.

ST: *I know you've played with some people in genres other than blues. Is your style influenced by other kinds of music, or do you simply play lots of different kinds of music?*

CGB: I play different types of music. I promised my father before he passed, I was going to be the best that I could make of myself. I didn't want to be stuck in one style of music. I couldn't sit up and listen to myself all night doing one thing. I don't like to listen to nobody else doing one thing. Be creative, man. If you're not going to be creative, that would put you in a bag of copying, and I don't like a copier. I'll take your song, I'll use your identification, but I'll put myself in it, and I'll completely turn it around, so that it's not a copy.

ST: *Some people think of blues and jazz performers as performers who are playing on emotion — that you*

When I'm performing, I'm trying to hit somebody on the first note. If I get someone on the first note I hit, I ain't worried about the rest of them.

LUTHER JOHNSON

In my music,
everybody in my band
knows exactly what I
am going to do, period.
It's together — it's not
everybody going his
own way trying to
impress the audience.
It's not all out-of-sync.
It's played where
everybody is tight as
beeswax, and that's
pretty tight.

CLARENCE "GATEMOUTH" BROWN

*just let go and let things flow out... Can you
describe what you do, what you're thinking about
when you're on the stage, and what kind of apprenticeship you went through that allows you to make
the magic that you make when you play?*

CGB: In my music, everybody in my band knows exactly
what I am going to do, period. It's together — it's not
everybody going his own way trying to impress the
audience. It's not all out-of-sync. It's played where
everybody is tight as beeswax, and that's pretty tight.
Nobody is on his own. When you're on the bandstand
with me you're going to play what you're supposed to
play. It should sound like music and not noise.

ST: *How about you Luther, when you're playing, what
are you thinking about when you perform?*

LJ: When I'm performing, I'm trying to hit somebody
on the first note. If I get someone on the first note I
hit, I ain't worried about the rest of them. It's like
going to church — it's like a preacher preaching in a
pulpit. It's the same thing we're doing... When I'm
performing I'm watching people sitting out there.
When I've got my guitar in my hand, I'm a different
man, because I change when I get my instrument. I'm
Luther now, but I don't know what I become when I
get my guitar... I just want to make you happy. And
once I get you going I'm going to keep you there. But I
like for you to sit when I start playing to you, and talking to you — singing easy. I want you to watch me for
awhile. Then when I get tired of that, I want you to get
up and dance. And then when I hit ya, you got to go.
You get stung by my music, buddy, you get stung.

CGB: See that's what makes a musician, ladies and
gentlemen. What he's saying is true. He likes for [his
audience] to dance, I like for them to sit and watch
and learn and listen. We're different that way, because
I've played places where people are jumping up and
you're sitting there trying to watch the show, and
they're all in your face, kicking you on the heel. You
ask them, "What did you hear?" and they say, "I don't
know." No, I consider myself a teacher... of my work
of art. And if you're jumping around and screaming
and hollering and whistling and beating on each
other, you don't know what I am doing. You can't
explain nothing to your friends.

PK: I admire the fact that you're standing up for your
art form and rejecting and rebelling when people try
to put you in a straitjacket of any kind. And some people I guess have commended you, or criticized you, for
being politically incorrect and pointing out what you
thought was the truth. But I think the truth is what
you are a purveyor of in your art. And that's what really moves people, and the same thing [is true] for
Luther... When Luther plays with his band, he can
achieve more with fewer notes than a whole busload
of guitar slingers... Both of these guys can really
swing, but they do it each in their own way. Their
musical definition of what they do is their own personalities, and they're very different.

ST: *Both of you have played many different places
over the years, and been in the music for such a long
time that you played a number of famous nightspots
— clubs and concert halls around the world. Do you
have any kind of special memories that you want to
share about any of those places, some particularly
nice or funny things?*

LJ: I played in Chicago one night with a three-piece band, and this guy in the club who had a wife named Louise thought his wife wanted me, and I'm singing "Shotgun, Shoot 'em 'fore He Runs." I look around and [see that] this guy had a double barrel shotgun behind the bar pointed at me. I was drinking during the time and I got sober as a judge. [Laughs] My drummer tried to hide behind his drums. That's the worst thing that ever happened to me playing music because I didn't know what was going to happen . . . So I don't play there no more. [More laughter]

CGB: I was about 19 years old and I had just started out in my hometown in Texas, and we had this little band called Gay Swingsters . . . We were up in a little town in Texas called Silsby, just playing, when all of a sudden I heard "POW, POW." I thought it was firecrackers. All of a sudden this guy was running toward the bandstand and his eyes were dancing. My piano player jumped under the piano and I froze. He came right by the bandstand and made a complete circle around us like a chicken does when they get shocked. He grabbed the banister, rolled, and fell and hit his head on the ground. The coroner wouldn't get out of bed, so we had to stay the whole night and wait until he came, with this guy laying there . . . I didn't play there no more. [Laughs]

PK: Thinking about some of the gigs that I've seen you guys do, some of the highlights, I remember when Eric Clapton had you come to Royal Albert Hall for twelve nights in a row. It was really great because it was a 6,000-seat circular venue. Gate came on with his band and had exactly thirty minutes to do the history of American music à la Gatemouth Brown. People

didn't know who the opening act was. They didn't know what to expect, even though Eric Clapton had a nice color photo of Gate in his program. At the end of that thirty minutes, Gate said to Eric to his face, "I feel sorry for you!" [Laughs]

CGB: We did nineteen days at Albert Hall, and then [Clapton's] manager said, "Gate, will you do a month in Europe with Clapton?" . . . [On that tour] I said, "Hey Clapton . . . I understand through the grapevine that you're coming to my country." He said, "Yeah Gate." I said, "Well, I tell you what, I'm going to be on this show, now I helped you in yours, can you help me in mine." Clapton says, "I'll let you know in thirty minutes." Fifteen minutes later he said, "It's a deal." So we played all over the United States.

PK: They played in sports arenas [like] Nassau Coliseum and the Meadowlands—two nights in each place. The worst place to see music is a sports arena. But Gatemouth actually can turn a sports arena into one of those chicken coop barrooms that we all remember so well. And Luther here, I remember the night I got a call and Stevie Ray Vaughan was playing at E. M. Loews in Worcester, and they needed an opening act. Luther got out there with his band, the same kind of thing, nobody knew who the opening act was and all these kids were there, and Stevie Ray was really at the peak of his popularity, and Luther just got out there and totally tore up the house.

CGB: Clapton once trapped me on the bandstand. I walked into the House of Blues with Jim Bateman, my manager, who I've been partners with for about twenty years. Called me at my house and said, "Gate, Clap-

LEFT TO RIGHT
Clarence "Gatemouth" Brown, Esther Terry, and Luther "Guitar Junior" Johnson
BEZANSON RECITAL HALL

When Luther plays
with his band, he can
achieve more with
fewer notes than a
whole busload of
guitar slingers

PAUL KAHN

ton is playing at the House of Blues," and said, "want to go see him?" . . . So I dressed and got in my car and went on down there, and we met there. I went up in the VIP [area] and sat down, and I listened to him. And he was playing them hard blues, boy, and he had a guitar to match every tune. All of a sudden somebody touched me and said, "Gate your amp is set up . . . and Clapton wants you to sit in with him." I said, "Oh man!" But I went on down there and sat in, and then an hour later, Jim Bateman came back to me and said "Gate, how would you like to go to London, England, and open for Clapton for nineteen days?" . . . It started there and that's what happened.

ST: *Do African American and White audiences respond differently to your music?*

CGB: I don't have a Black audience anymore, because honest, no offense friends, I don't have a Black audience because it was once said that I sold them out. I said, "How did I sell out?" "You're playing cowboy music." And I said, "Oh, you got to come listen and you'll know what I'm playing." But my audience is all over planet Earth. Now the only time I have a big Black audience would be like in Houston at the Juneteenth Festival and the Jazz Festival in New Orleans, but other than that, no. I play big venues, big clubs, big theaters, and you can count my people on your hand. They're not there . . . All the youngsters in the White race are there.

There is a reason for that. The news media, radio and television, have brainwashed all the youngsters they could on this rap crap, disco crap, and all the stuff that don't make sense that's causing our kids to go berserk and kill each other, and kill others, and I

don't care for it. Have you read in the papers about how they killed them rappers out there in California? And you ought to hear how they do their performance. Don't have nothing to do with music — it's all vulgarity, and sex, and stuff that we don't want our children to be listening to. So I don't care if I don't get that type of people around me, man. [Applause from the audience]

ST: *People have said those types of things about the blues in the past.*

CGB: Well, I'm not a blues player as I've told you [laughs], and yet my blues is positive. You pick up one of my CDs: I'm telling every youngster out there how to take his life and do something worthwhile rather than going out there speeding, wrecking, tearing up other people's property. I tell them that in my songs . . .

ST: *Has the mainstreaming of the kind of music that you play, in a sense the commercialization of it, detracted from the music? We hear the blues in TV and radio commercials. Has anything been lost or sacrificed?*

CGB: Yes, a bunch of it, and I'm here to prove it . . . Decency for one thing, and that means a lot. Self-respect is another thing. That starts from yourself. A certain artist, and I won't ever call his name because I wouldn't do that, got on the bandstand at the House of Blues and I went to listen to him. He was a friend of mine — I said *was*. He got up there and used vulgar language, used the worst of words, and I got up and walked out.

Because we have children sitting out there, and every artist is a role model, good or bad. Every artist got an audience. A lot of people say, "Well that's what makes the world go 'round." I don't want to go 'round with it, not that way, where you got to be vulgar and get on the bandstand and do all kinds of vulgar acts. That's nothing to be doing around people, and I just won't do it.

What's lost right now, and I've been watching this come in, [is that] people got no identity. It's horrible to see where our music has gone, everybody's snatching from each other, stealing one another's music, putting their names on it and claiming it . . . Big lawsuits everywhere. It happened to me but they couldn't really play what I play, but they were trying. That's the way music's gone. It's lost its merit — it's lost its pureness.

PK: Yes, sometimes there are compromises that are made when something gets commercialized and it's usually a double-edged sword. Not too long ago, Luther did a TV commercial for Kentucky Fried Chicken that was for KFC everywhere outside of the United States. He came in with his band and recorded a song, and the deal was supposed to be "we want you to do a song in your style, your kind of song." And they had ad execs come in from New York with a song that they thought was what a blues artist style was, or what their idea of a song was. I was involved in producing the session and the song was about as far from Luther's style as anybody could imagine. After a couple of hours the thing just wasn't working, so we approached it from a different direction. I had to say, "We've got to throw out this song that you wrote," and [asked] Luther, "Don't sing, just talk." And he

started playing the guitar and just talking and making stuff up, and that's what they ended up using. But that was a very good payday and even though it could have been a disaster, it worked out in the end. Those opportunities are important for artists to have, to do commercials, like when the House of Blues had a thing, and the new Blues Brothers had a TV show in Atlanta on VH1. They invited Luther to come down and do a guest appearance. That's a great bit of exposure.

CGB: I've turned down three movies in the past four years. Because in the first place I'm not going to be an Uncle Tom to nobody. I'm not going to get vulgar for nobody. And if it's a part that they want me to do . . . I will not do it. I turned down [a movie offer] in New York just this year. They wanted me to act like one of them old honky-tonk people. I'm not going to do that. I won't lower myself, nor my people, nor you by doing such.

PK: And it's true that because of his principles and integrity, Gate turned down projects that he just didn't feel were right for him as an artist. Alligator Records had this idea a few years back of doing a guitar showdown, a Texas guitar shootout . . . Gate just didn't feel that musically it was a good move for him. Because what his band was doing, and musically what he was doing, he thought was in a different direction, so Robert Cray ended up doing it . . . Robert Cray was at his peak at that point, and Gatemouth turned it down . . . and that album [*Showdown*, A. Collins and J. Copeland, released in 1985] won a Grammy. It was Alligator's biggest seller. So in certain ways, sometimes you take the long way home, but you get there, and the cream rises eventually.

Well, I'm not a blues player as I've told you [laughs], and yet my blues is positive. You pick up one of my CDs, I'm telling every youngster out there how to take his life and do something worthwhile.

CLARENCE "GATEMOUTH" BROWN

It's horrible to see where our music has gone, everybody's snatching from each other, stealing one another's music, putting their names on it and claiming it. Big lawsuits everywhere. It happened to me, but they couldn't really play what I play, but they were trying. That's the way music's gone. It's lost its merit — it's lost its pureness.

CLARENCE "GATEMOUTH" BROWN

Steve Tracy on harmonica joins Clarence Brown and Luther Johnson
BEZANSON RECITAL HALL

A question from the audience:
I'd like to know how you got into music as a youngster, and maybe how you got from your very beginning roots to where you are now?

CGB: Before I was born, my mom said that as my daddy was playing fiddle, singing cajun, country, and bluegrass, I was trying to get out of her stomach . . . kicking all over the place [laughs], and she knew right then I was going to be a musician. Five years from that moment when I was born, I picked up an old guitar that we had lying around the house and I started playing behind my dad. Didn't know what I was doing — I was making noise. But when it got to where I would sound like what he was doing, I just started developing. And when I got to be 10, I picked up his fiddle and I started tinkering with it while he was at work, and I learned how to play fiddle. My father was my greatest influence, the biggest influence in my life. I just kept on developing and learning different things that I thought nobody else could do, and that's why I'm where I am today.

LJ: When I started, an uncle who played an acoustic guitar around the house [took me along to] what we used to call "Saturday night fish fries" down South. He played at those and people gave him fifty cents, quarters, nickels, dimes. I was a little boy with him, eating fish and [listening to him play]. I said that when I grow up, I want to be able to play some kind of instrument.

But mostly [my influences] came out of church, because in Mississippi I had to go to church and Sunday school every Sunday. I used to have my own spiritual singing group . . . When I got up in age I wanted to do something else besides singing with the choir and leading the choir.

When my older sister had taken sick in Chicago, I went to Chicago to babysit for her for a couple weeks. I was something like $17\frac{1}{2}$ years old. When I went to Chicago, Muddy and all of them were playing in Chicago, Jimmy Reed, all the big guys, Sonny Boy Williamson. I was a little boy putting on a false mustache and a big hat, going in the bar ordering a shot of hundred-pound granddaddy, drinking, and listening to that old blues. The bartender would look at me and say, "Is you old enough to be in here? — Let me see your identification." I said, "Well I ain't got no identification." "Then you got to get out of here."

My sister was living three doors from a club

called The Rock 'n Roll Inn in Chicago on Roosevelt Row. They had a band in there on Friday, Saturday, Sunday, a rock and roll band. My sister had told them about me, that I could sing. I went in there with her and we were told, "He can't have nothing to drink, but if he wants to sing... If the guys want him to sing, he can sing." The place was packed on Sunday; I never will forget it. So [the band] called me up to the stage, said, "Ladies and gentlemen, we got a guy just came from Mississippi, and we want to get him up here and sing some for you all." Everybody was looking, 'cause in Chicago they want to see what I'm gonna do from down South up there. So I got on stage and they started playing. I was young and I was full of it. I just started dancing, and singing, and jumping over the chairs. The people went for it so they hired me. [Laughs]

Another question from the audience:
Paul touched on a point I'd like to hear more about. He said Luther could say more than a lot of guitar players in just a few notes, and I'm wondering if Luther could say something about the editing process. Did you study a lot of other types of music, or guitar players, how you expunged the chromatic notes from stuff that everybody else does, so that it has meaning in your leads or whatever you're playing. In other words, how do you keep from being too notey as a guitar player?

LJ: I always like the shortest cut. Of anything, I always take the shortest cut. Anything you do, it's the way you do it. It ain't what you do; it's how you do it. You've got a million notes on the guitar, but you don't need all those notes. I don't. I can take two notes and run everybody out of here. Run everybody out of here with two notes, just two notes, but they're strong. I can hardly explain to you what I'm doing, but there's something in you that's got to come out of you... and that's what happens. Everybody plays differently, every musician in the world don't play alike. I got my style, Gate got his style. That's what makes music so good...

ST: *There was an LP that came out a number of years ago by Count Basie and Oscar Peterson, where you have Basie playing this very concise, compact style. And Peterson was all over the piano, and in fact both the styles work, but so many people seem to get so much involved in playing lots of notes, as if that's somehow superior.*

CGB: No it's not superior. Look man, I've heard [many] guitar players and I don't know what them guys are playing. They're playing a million notes and not making any sense. You've got to stay in the pocket. You've got to be consistent on what you're doing... I play hard lines with my guitar... [in which] I can breathe, space, and I'm not up there trying to do all them solos, 'cause there are only so many solos you can do. Let somebody else solo, and you can think about the next thing you're going to do. I'm not going to play a tune no twenty minutes long — it's not necessary because everybody is gonna forget what you're doing, including you. I make my music short, sweet, and snappy.

> I always like the shortest cut. Of anything, I always take the shortest cut. Anything you do, it's the way you do it. It ain't what you do; it's how you do it. You've got a million notes on the guitar, but you don't need all those notes.
>
> LUTHER JOHNSON

Biographies

Allgood, B. Dexter

(b. 1935) At the time of his 1990 Amherst appearance, Dexter Allgood was an associate professor of music at Elizabeth City State College in New Jersey, where he also directed the school's gospel choir. He later went on to chair the Department of Music at Norfolk State University, and currently teaches at Seton Hall University and in the New York City public schools.

Allgood's specialty is commercial music, gospel, and jazz. He received his Ph.D. from New York University. His dissertation, entitled *A Study of Selected Black Gospel Choirs in the Metropolitan New York Area*, was the first study to address the topic.

1990: The Time Has Come: Gospel Music, panelist

Avery, Teōdrōss

(b. 1973) A young and talented tenor saxophonist who made his recording debut as a leader on GRP records in 1994 (*In Other Words*), Avery was just 21 at the time. His next release on Impulse! (*My Generation*) in 1995 firmly established his musical reputation. Avery studied with Joe Henderson, attended Berklee College of Music, and was lured away from academia when he was offered a recording contract after appearing on Carl Allen's 1993 recording, *Pursuer*.

After a six-year recording sabbatical, Avery released *New Day, New Groove* in 2001 on Orchard. In addition to his work with Carl Allen, Avery has appeared on recordings featuring Ann Hampton Callaway, Dee Dee Bridgewater, and Talib Kweli and Hi Tek among others.

1996: The Revolution Returns: The Next Generation in Jazz, panelist

Bach, Jean

(b. 1918) The award-winning documentary *A Great Day in Harlem* was Jean Bach's debut as a filmmaker. It premiered in Los Angeles in September 1994 and soon went on to win a Gold Hugo Award at the Chicago International Film Festival, major acclaim at the London Film Festival, and an Academy Award nomination in 1995. In 1997 Bach directed *The Spitball Story*, about Dizzy Gillespie's days with Cab Calloway.

Growing up in Milwaukee and Chicago exposed Bach to African American music at an early age. She was a young enthusiast of the music and attended performances of all its early contributors, including Duke Ellington, Billie Holiday, and Earl Hines. She began her career as a society column writer for the *Chicago Times*. Eventually she earned the position of jazz columnist — a job that granted her access to all of her favorite musicians when they visited Chicago.

In the early 1940s, Bach moved to New York and began a successful career in television and radio. Before pursuing her latest career as a filmmaker, she enjoyed a range of employment, most notably a 24-year stint as producer of the syndicated *Arlene Francis Program* — New York's top-rated talk show.

1998: A Great Day in Harlem: A Tribute to Dr. Frederick C. Tillis, panelist

Baraka, Amiri

(b. 1934) With numerous plays and works of fiction, nonfiction, and poetry to his credit, Amiri Baraka (LeRoi Jones) is a celebrated writer and specialist in American music and social history. He has received many awards and honors, including a Whitney Fellowship, a Guggenheim Fellowship, a Rockefeller Foundation Fellowship in Drama, and an Obie Award for the 1964 production of his play *Dutchman*. He has taught at Yale and Columbia, and most recently at the State University of New York, Stony Brook, from which he retired in 1999. Baraka is still active as an artist and lives with his wife, Amina, in Newark, New Jersey.

1989: Black Music and Social Change, panelist

Benjamin, Playthell

(b. 1942) A founding member of the W.E.B. Du Bois Department of Afro-American Studies at the University of Massachusetts, Playthell Benjamin taught on the Amherst campus in the early 1970s before establishing his prolific writing career in New York. A journalist, novelist, cultural critic, and former columnist for the *Village Voice* and the *New York Daily News*, Benjamin's articles appear in major newspapers and magazines in the United States and abroad.

1989: Black Music and Social Change, panelist

Biggham, Milton

(b. 1945) One of the most prominent contributors to the advancement of the industry and art of sacred music, the Rev. Milton Biggham is an active performer and composer of gospel music, leader of the standout Georgia Mass Choir, and a gifted vocalist and motivator. He is also producer for and executive director of Savoy Records, one of the most important recording labels for Black gospel music.

As a young man in Tampa, Florida, Biggham began a musical career through his involvement with church and as a singer. He formed the Tampa Mass Choir which became, through an association with the Rev. Art Jones, the Florida Mass Choir. Big-

gham later formed the New Redemptive Ensemble and was hired by Savoy Records in an administrative capacity. In 1983 he founded the Georgia Mass Choir, an organization that is at the vanguard of gospel music. Garnering numerous honors and acclaim, the Georgia Mass Choir's collaboration with Whitney Houston enjoyed wide commercial success with the release of the 1994 film and soundtrack for *The Preacher's Wife*. Biggham has served as pastor of the Mt. Vernon Baptist Church in Newark, New Jersey, since 1986.

1997: Gospel in the 1990s: The Reason Why We Sing, panelist, Distinguished Achievement Award recipient

Bown, Patti

(b. 1931) Born in Seattle, Washington, Patti Bown is a pianist, composer, singer, actor, and writer who has performed in clubs, festivals, and concert halls around the world. She was an original member of the Quincy Jones Orchestra and served as musical director for the vocalists Dinah Washington and Sarah Vaughan.

Bown has performed with many legendary performers, and her recording career covers many diversified styles of music, including jazz, r&b, soul, as well as gospel, country, pop, funk, and hip-hop.

1989: Black Music and Social Change, panelist

Boyer, Horace Clarence

(b. 1935) A professor emeritus of music theory and African American music at the University of Massachusetts, Amherst, where he taught for twenty-six years, Horace Clarence Boyer has had a long and distinguished musical career. He served as guest curator of musical history at the Smithsonian Institution in 1985–86, and in 1986–87 was the Distinguished Scholar-at-Large at Fisk University, where he conducted the famed Fisk Jubilee Singers.

Boyer served as advisor on gospel music to the *New Grove Dictionary of American Music*, edited the 1993 edition of the African American hymnal *Lift Every Voice and Sing II*, and is the author of the very popular *How Sweet the Sound: The Golden*

Age of Gospel.

As a scholar, Boyer has appeared in numerous television documentaries on gospel music and has lectured across the United States. As a singer, he has performed throughout his life as a soloist and with his brother James as a member of The Boyer Brothers. He has recorded on Savoy and Nashboro labels, and has appeared in over five hundred concerts, festivals, and television performances, and with such gospel luminaries as Mahalia Jackson, Clara Ward, Alex Bradford, James Cleveland, and Dorothy Love Coates.

1991–1999: Black Musicians Conference and Festival, artistic director.
1996–1998: panel moderator

Brown, Clarence "Gatemouth"

(b. 1924) From an early age Clarence Brown knew what it was like to adapt. His early years were spent on the Louisiana/Texas border — an area where categorization of music did not exist. Brown's father was an active musician on many instruments, and this versatility was passed on to the younger Brown, who developed into a virtuoso player on guitar, fiddle, and harmonica, all of which he incorporates into his live performances. Brown's versatility covers various genres as he performs all forms of American music, including country and western, blues, swing, cajun, and big band jazz — all with equal depth of interpretation and original flair.

In 1949 Brown became the first artist to sign with Peacock Records, one of the United States' first Black-owned-and-operated labels. Some of Brown's early major hits include "Okie Dokie Stomp," "Mary Is Fine," and "Gate's Salty Blues." In 1994 he signed a contract with Verve Records, for which he has actively recorded, including two Grammy-nominated albums. He has been the recipient of numerous W. C. Handy Blues awards and nominations, and is a multiple Grammy Award winner.

1999: The Blues Lives On, panelist, performer, Distinguished Achievement Award recipient

Bryant, Clora

(b. 1929) A native Texan who relocated to the West Coast, the trumpeter Clora Bryant is but one of many very talented female instrumentalists working in jazz today. As surprising at it may seem, Clora Bryant has released just one recording as a leader — *Gal with a Horn: Clora Bryant*, a 1957 release on Mode which was reissued on the VSOP label. Mostly a bop trumpeter, Bryant has also appeared on recordings featuring Jeannie and Jimmy Cheatham and Linda Hopkins, and she headlined a concert tour in the Soviet Union during the Gorbachev years.

Bryant began her career in the early forties with the all-Black, all-women Prairie View College Co-Eds at Prairie View College in Texas. A self-professed Dizzy Gillespie disciple, she composed a suite titled *To Dizzy with Love*, and has won two NEA awards for composition and performance.

1993: Great Women of Jazz, Distinguished Achievement Award recipient

Carrington, Terri Lyne

(b. 1962) Terri Lyne Carrington grew up in Medford, Massachusetts, and was called the "little drummer girl" by famous musicians who heard her play as a child prodigy. She studied at Berklee College of Music and began her career as a sought-after side player during the 1980s and '90s. She has released two recordings as a leader — the 1989 Verve recording entitled *Real Life Story* and *Jazz Is a Spirit* (2002) on ACT Music.

Carrington was the house drummer for the late-night Arsenio Hall Show and is considered one of the first significant female drummers in jazz. She has appeared as a percussionist on many recordings featuring the Doky Brothers, and has performed with such drummers as Max Roach and Keith Copeland. While she is most well known as a jazz funk drummer, her musical styles range from hard bop to easy listening instrumental pop, in addition to "macro-basic array of structured extemporization," a post-funk style known as M-Base.

1993: Great Women of Jazz, panelist

Carter, Benny

(b. 1907) A towering figure in jazz, Benny Carter is one of the music's first important alto saxophonists and big band arrangers. He worked with Fletcher Henderson and Chick Webb before forming his own band in 1932. He is a virtuoso multi-instrumentalist who helped to set the standard for the modern approach to the alto saxophone. He also plays trumpet, clarinet, piano, tenor saxophone, and trombone.

Although he spent much time in the 1950s and '60s composing, arranging, and leading his own big bands and sextet, including writing and arranging music for Hollywood, Benny Carter made a full "comeback" as a performer in the 1970s. He has maintained an active playing, writing, and recording career to this day.

1989: Black Music and Social Change, Distinguished Achievement Award recipient

Carter, Betty

(1930 – 1998) Betty Carter was one of the greatest jazz performers in music history. Her unique interpretation of standard and original repertoire was unmatched in its freshness and clarity of musical vision. She was born in Flint, Michigan, and began her career as a singer in Detroit during the mid-1940s. While she was on tour with Lionel Hampton's band in the late forties, she picked up the nickname Betty "Bebop" Carter. Later she moved to New York to start a family.

After two decades of near obscurity, Carter began her ascent to fame when she established a trio and her own record label (Bet-Car) in the late 1960s and early '70s. Betty Carter was a visionary artist and educator who toured the world and recorded over twenty albums between 1955 and 1996. Over time she became one of the best known and critically acclaimed jazz artists of the 20th century.

1993: Great Women of Jazz, performer and master class instructor

Cheatham, Doc

(1905 – 1997) Growing up in Nashville, Adolphus Anthony "Doc" Cheatham gained early experience backing such greats as Ma Rainey and Bessie Smith as a member of the house band at the Bijou Theater. Cheatham moved to Chicago in 1926 as a saxophonist and trumpeter in numerous bands, and was soon asked by Louis Armstrong to sub for him in King Oliver's group whenever he was out of town. It was a gig that spurred Cheatham to abandon the saxophone and develop his "voice" on trumpet and cornet.

Although he recorded and toured consistently with different groups, both in America and in Europe, Cheatham gravitated to New York and joined Cab Calloway for an eight-year stretch as lead trumpet in his band. In the early 1950s, Cheatham remained at the pinnacle of the music world when he joined forces with the Latin bands of Machito, Perez Prado, and Marcelino Guerro while still being recognized as a leader of small groups and as one of the finest lead trumpeters in the business.

Doc Cheatham remained active in touring and bringing American music to the world as a member of various bands, jazz societies, and repertory companies until June 1997 when he died after suffering a stroke.

1994: World Music and Jazz, Distinguished Achievement Award recipient

Donegan, Dorothy

(1924 – 1998) A virtuoso pianist who bridged various styles of jazz as well as classical music, Dorothy Donegan was a consummate artist and performer who did not receive the full recognition she deserved until her later years. Donegan's unique ability to create improvisational medleys of varied repertoire on the spot was her trademark in concert.

Born in Chicago, Donegan trained in the classics as a child and later studied at the Chicago Conservatory and Chicago Music College. She made her recording debut as a classical pianist in 1942, and after a serendipitous meeting with Art Tatum, became one of the world's greatest jazz pianists. She also made a notable appearance in the 1945 film *Sensations*. Donegan released twenty recordings on a variety of labels, but she was not widely known as a jazz artist until the 1980s.

1993: Great Women of Jazz, Distinguished Achievement Award recipient

Ennis, Ethel

(b. 1932) A lifetime resident of Baltimore, Ethel Ennis was exposed to music at an early age. Her family's religious values nurtured her especially close connections with her mother and grandmother. It was in church that she found her first job playing piano for Sunday school. By the late 1940s, Ennis began regular engagements with a range of local musicians through which she honed her piano and vocal skills. In 1950 she collaborated on composing a rock and roll number called "Little Boy," which was recorded by Little Richard.

As a professional musician, Ethel Ennis always questioned the value of life on the road, and although she has been performing and recording music since 1955, she worked to fulfill her goals while remaining on the periphery of the music industry. The late 1950s through the early 1970s found her closest to the public eye with the bands of Duke Ellington and Count Basie, a European tour with Benny Goodman, and as a staple at Newport and other jazz festivals. In addition, Ennis set a precedent by performing the National Anthem as a solo for Richard Nixon's reinauguration and performing at the White House for two presidents.

1996: The Revolution Returns: The Next Generation in Jazz, Distinguished Achievement Award recipient

Farmer, Art

(b. 1928 – 1999) Born into a musical family in Iowa, Art Farmer and his twin brother, the bassist Addison Farmer, began musical instruction at an early age. The family soon moved to Phoenix, where Farmer played cornet in a dance band. It was not long before he began participating in jam sessions and fell in love with the sophisticated styles of Duke Ellington and others. Before completing high school, Art and Addison visited Los Angeles, where the city's thriving music scene immediately won them over. Art Farmer got a job with bandleader Johnny Otis and traveled with him to New York, where Jay McShann hired him.

After establishing residence in New York City in 1953, Farmer's versatility won him high regard. He started to record as a leader and was very active as a sideman. At this time he also began collaborating on other projects, including the Jazztet, founded in 1959 with Benny Golson. Farmer made many visits to Europe, and in 1968 he settled permanently in Austria, accepting an invitation to join a Viennese radio orchestra. He remained fully active in the most respected musical organizations of New York and Europe until the time of his death in 1999.

1998: A Great Day in Harlem: A Tribute to Dr. Frederick C. Tillis, performer

Freelon, Nnenna

(b. 1954) The Grammy-nominated vocalist Nnenna Freelon recorded her debut album (*Nnenna Freelon*) for Columbia in 1992. After releasing two more recordings, Freelon left Columbia Records in 1996, signed with Concord Jazz, and released four more critically acclaimed recordings: *Shaking Free* (1996), *Maiden Voyage* (1998), the double-Grammy-nominated *Soulcall* (2000), and *Tales of Wonder: Celebrating Stevie Wonder* (2002).

Freelon's affiliation with the University of Massachusetts began in 1989 when she attended the Fine Arts Center Jazz in July Summer Music Programs and met the saxophonist/composer Yusef Lateef, whom she credits with teaching her to "sing from the heart." Before starting her international performing and recording career, Freelon raised three children, performed regionally, and worked in the health profession in Durham, North Carolina. She was born and raised in Cambridge, Massachusetts, and is a graduate of Simmons College with a bachelors degree in health care administration.

1993: Great Women of Jazz, performer and master class instructor

Garland, Phyl

(b. 1935) A professor in the Graduate School of Journalism at Columbia University since 1973, and a prolific author on Black music and African American cultural issues, Phyl Garland began her writing and teaching career in her hometown of Pittsburgh. She is the author of the highly successful book *The Sound of Soul*, and has written extensively for *Ebony* magazine and other publications. Her liner notes appear on recordings by Jackie McLean, Blue Mitchell, and Booker T.

1992: New Trends in Vocal Jazz, panelist and Distinguished Achievement Award recipient

Goines, Leonard

(b. 1934) Leonard Goines is a renowned scholar, performer, and professor of music at the Borough of Manhattan Community College, CUNY, and the Juilliard School of Music. A trumpet player, Goines has appeared on recordings featuring Yusef Lateef and Montego Joe, and has performed with Duke Pearson, Donald Byrd, Sy Oliver, and Ella Fitzgerald among others. He is the author of hundreds of articles, book reviews, program notes, and, album liner notes, including extensive liner notes for Alex Bradford and the Abyssinian Baptist Gospel Choir's recording *Shakin' the Rafters*.

Goines received his bachelor's degree in music from the Manhattan School of Music and his graduate degrees in music from Columbia University. He has received numerous awards and honors, including fellowships at Harvard University at the W.E.B. Du Bois Institute for Afro-American Research and from the National Endowment for the Humanities.

1995: Blues-Based Jazz: The Legacy of William "Count" Basie, panelist

Gourse, Leslie

(b. 1939) With numerous book, magazine, newspaper article, and album liner notes credits, Leslie Gourse has a well-established and glowing reputation as a jazz writer. Gourse began her career as a journalist in the late 1960s when she wrote for the *Morning Report* at CBS Network Radio News. Work at the *New York Times* eventually led to writing assignments about music and jazz musicians.

Gourse has written for many music magazines including *Down Beat, Jazz Times, and Modern Drummer*, plus liner notes on several major labels, covering such diverse artists as Mahalia Jackson, Joanne Brackeen, and Marian McPartland. Her long list of book titles includes biographies of artists such as Dizzy Gillespie, Joe Williams, Wynton Marsalis, Sarah Vaughan, and Nat King Cole.

Gourse's biography of Nat Cole, entitled *Unforgettable: The Life and Mystique of Nat King Cole*, was published in 1991 just prior to her Amherst appearance. In 1991, Gourse also received an ASCAP award for her series of articles about women jazz artists which appeared in *Jazz Times* magazine. She continues to write about musicians and currently lives in New York City.

1992: New Trends in Vocal Jazz, panelist

Green, Randolph

(b. 1921) Born in Tuskegee, Alabama, Randy Green began singing gospel music while he was serving in the armed forces. He relocated to the Boston area after military service and has been a resident of Roxbury, Massachusetts, ever since.

Green is the founder and director of the Silver Leaf Gospel Singers, an a cappella jubilee style all-male gospel octet. The Silver Leaf Singers have been local favorites in the New England area since 1945. He is a member of the Concord Baptist Church in Boston's South End, and he has been actively performing gospel music and serving his church for over fifty years.

1997: Gospel in the 1990s: The Reason Why We Sing, Distinguished Achievement Award recipient

Hampton, Slide

(b. 1932) As a young man in Indianapolis, Slide Hampton was a member of a family band led by his father, whose encouragement enabled his son to teach himself the trombone. At age 20,

Hampton began a musical career and took his first steps toward developing into a master of the trombone and a gifted bandleader, arranger, and composer. He has been a crucial part of the ensembles of Dizzy Gillespie, Thad Jones/Mel Lewis, and Maynard Ferguson, and has collaborated with the likes of Art Blakey, George Coleman, and Freddie Hubbard.

In 1968, at the completion of a European tour with the Woody Herman Band, Hampton stayed in Europe to participate in the thriving music scene there, joining other expatriates such as Art Farmer, Dexter Gordon, and Kenny Clarke. Hampton returned to the U.S. at the end of the 1970s to lead ensembles, compose, and perform full time.

1994: World Music and Jazz, performer and master class instructor

Handy, D. Antoinette

(1930 – 2002) Born in New Orleans and raised in both New Orleans and Texas, D. Antoinette Handy spent her later years in Jackson, Mississippi. She was director of music programs at the National Endowment for the Arts from 1990 to 1993. She attended Spelman College, earned her bachelor of music degree from the New England Conservatory of Music, and received her master of music degree from Northwestern University School of Music.

A noted historian, classical flutist, educator, administrator, and writer, she is the author of three books on African American music and musicians in the U.S.: *Black Women in American Bands and Orchestras* (1981), *The International Sweethearts of Rhythm* (1983), and *Black Conductors* (1994), all published by Scarecrow Press.

1993: Great Women of Jazz, panelist

Harrison, Daphne Duvall

(b. 1932) Chair of the Department of African American Studies at the University of Maryland, Baltimore County, at the time of her appearance on the "Celebrating the Blues" panel, Daphne Duvall

Harrison is also the author of *Black Pearls: Blues Queens of the 1920s* (Rutgers University Press, 1988). *Black Pearls* is a comprehensive study of Black female blues singers in general, and four singers in particular: Sippie Wallace, Edith Wilson, Victoria Spivey, and Alberta Hunter.

1991: Celebrating the Blues, panelist

Hemphill, Jessie Mae

(b. 1934) Born in Senatobia, Mississippi, Jessie Mae Hemphill, a singer and guitarist, is a self-taught musician who incorporates strong Delta traditions into her music. She began her career in the 1960s and '70s, when she performed with various bands around Mississippi, and in the early 1980s pursued a solo career singing and playing guitar and percussion.

Hemphill released her 1981 debut album, *She-Wolf*, on Vogue records in Europe, but it wasn't until 1987 that she released her first recording in the United States (*Feelin' Good*). She won the W. C. Handy Award for best traditional female blues artist for two consecutive years in 1987 and 1988, and continued to perform into the 1990s.

1991: Celebrating the Blues, performer, Distinguished Achievement Award recipient

Hendricks, Jon

(b. 1921) Jon Hendricks was introduced to music at a early age as a singer in the choir of his father's church. After moving to Toledo, Ohio, Hendricks gained experience by singing for a local radio station and performing in high school musical theater productions. During this time he developed a close friendship with pianist Art Tatum. After serving in the Army, he moved to New York with the aspiration of finding work as a lyricist. He developed a jazz vocal concept that later became known as "vocalese." This remarkable innovation evolved from performances at jam sessions where Hendricks sang his own lyrics to the exact pitches and rhythms of the saxophone solos he had learned from recordings.

In 1958 he recorded *Sing a Song of Basie* with Lambert, Hendricks, and Ross, the group that defined the vocal ensemble in American instrumental music. Beginning in the 1970s the scope of Hendricks's writing broadened to include such projects as the award-winning television documentary *Somewhere to Lay My Weary Head* and the internationally acclaimed musical theater productions *The Evolution of the Blues* and *Reminiscing in Tempo*.

1992: New Trends in Vocal Jazz, panelist and Distinguished Achievement Award recipient; 1994: World Music and Jazz, performer

Hinton, Milton J.

(1910 – 2000) Milt John "the Judge" Hinton was an integral contributor to the development of American jazz as one of its most highly regarded and sought-after bassists. He was also an educator, photo historian, and role model for generations of jazz musicians and bass players.

Beginning in the late 1920s, Hinton worked as a freelance musician in Chicago, appearing with numerous early luminaries including Art Tatum. In 1936 Hinton joined Cab Calloway's band, and for the next fifteen years collaborated with all of the legendary Calloway sidemen. Around this time Hinton relocated to New York and was in high demand as a bassist, performing and recording with virtually every major artist in jazz. His work has been featured on scores of classic recordings spanning decades and led by a cross section of musical legends.

Milt Hinton has been widely honored with memberships, appointments, honorary doctorates, and awards. In addition to his sublime artistry as a musician, he has contributed to jazz history through his efforts as photographer, having published two books of his work: *Bass Line: The Stories and Photographs of Milt Hinton* and *Over Time: The Jazz Photography of Milt Hinton*. The award-winning documentary *A Great Day in Harlem* features some of his photographs as well as a Hinton home movie

of the famous 1958 photo shoot.

1998: A Great Day in Harlem: A Tribute to Dr. Frederick C. Tillis, panelist and Distinguished Achievement Award recipient

Ibrahim, Abdullah

(b. 1934) The pianist Abdullah Ibrahim was born Adolph Johannes "Dollar" Brand in Capetown, South Africa, and began his music studies under the tutelage of his mother, a church pianist and choir director. He is credited with South Africa's first "modern jazz" recording, and his group, The Jazz Epistles, which featured trumpeter Hugh Masekela, enjoyed much success.

In the 1960s, South Africa's oppressive apartheid government forced Brand and his family into exile. In 1962 he moved with his wife to Switzerland, where he met Duke Ellington, who was in the middle of a European tour. With Ellington's sponsorship he was introduced to a world audience through a recording contract and numerous festival and concert appearances. All of these showcased his wide range of talents, including original compositions and contributions to the European classical repertoire which are highly influenced by African folk forms and lyricism. In 1965 Brand joined the vanguard of the music world in New York, leading his own groups and collaborating with Elvin Jones, among others. In 1968 Dollar Brand converted to Islam and adopted his Muslim name. He remained active in touring the world, and made a triumphant return to South Africa in 1990.

1994: World Music and Jazz, performer and Distinguished Achievement Award recipient

Jeter, Claude

(b. 1914) Born in Montgomery, Alabama, Claude Jeter organized The Four Harmony Kings, a gospel quartet that included his brother and two miners he met while working in the coal mines of West Virginia. Success brought the group to Knoxville, Tennessee, where they changed their name to The Swan Silvertones and released their first professional recordings.

The group eventually settled in Pittsburgh, where in 1966 Jeter left the group to enter the ministry and establish a solo performing career. The Rev. Claude Jeter's soaring and lyrical tenor voice influenced many gospel singers, and his use of falsetto was adopted by many performers who followed him, including Al Green and Eddie Kendricks of The Temptations.

1990: The Time Has Come: Gospel Music, performer and Distinguished Achievement Award recipient

Johnson, Luther "Guitar Junior"

(b. 1939) As a young man, Luther Johnson made his way north to Chicago from Itta Bena — the heart of the Mississippi Delta and birthplace of many other musical luminaries including B. B. King. He soon found himself in the midst of the Chicago scene during the development of the West Side guitar style, which is the foundation of modern blues and rock.

Johnson served an apprenticeship with Magic Sam, one of the kings of the West Side style, but it was his later association with Muddy Waters that gained him international recognition as a powerful vocalist and guitarist. Muddy would often turn the stage over to Johnson to lead the band in his own original tunes. After leaving Muddy Waters's band in 1980, Johnson signed a recording contract with Alligator Records and began fronting his group, Magic Rockers, full time, making numerous appearances throughout the world. Luther earned his first Grammy Award in 1984 for his rendition of "Walkin' the Dog" which appeared on Alligator Records' *Blues Explosion*, an anthology recorded live at the Montreux Jazz Festival. Luther Johnson has also been widely acclaimed, receiving a number of W. C. Handy Blues awards and nominations.

1999: The Blues Lives On, panelist, performer, and Distinguished Achievement Award recipient

Kahn, Paul

(b. 1949) As a youngster, Kahn was exposed to the art, theater, and music scenes of New York City through his parents, both of whom were avid supporters of the arts. His interest in music developed after he began playing guitar in high school, and during his college years he performed with a variety of bands influenced by blues, folk, country, and rock music. Kahn soon decided to pursue music full time as a bassist and subsequently recorded with such artists as Bela Fleck, Pat Enright, Stacy Phillips, and Jack Tottle from the bluegrass group Tasty Licks.

In 1979 Kahn established Concerted Efforts, a talent agency devoted to managing roots music artists. He later formed his music publishing company, Foggy Day Music, for which he has written (under a pen name) songs recorded by artists such as C. J. Chenier and Eddy Clearwater.

1999: The Blues Lives On, panelist

Lowe, Bill

(b. 1946) Besides contributing to jazz through his collaborations with Frank Foster, Thad Jones and Mel Lewis, Dizzy Gillespie, and Archie Shepp, Bill Lowe is also a prominent music educator and researcher. He has led numerous ensembles, plays trombone and tuba, and is a composer. He has taught at Northeastern, Yale, Wesleyan, and the City University of New York. Lowe brought American music to people in Japan as a member of Boston Blazing Orchestra, and was a member of the 1995 United States delegation to the Inaugural Conference in Cuba, were he lectured, presented a paper, and performed as a member of Joyful Noise.

Lowe released one recording as a leader, the 1993 Konnex release of *Sunday Train*, and he has appeared on recordings featuring the Aardvark Orchestra, Muhal Richards Abrams, Frank Foster, and others.

1995: Blues-Based Jazz: The Legacy of William "Count" Basie, panelist

Manuel, Peter

(b. 1952) Peter Manuel is a professor at the City University of New York and John Jay College in New York City where he teaches and writes about Indian music, Latin American music, and world popular music. Manuel received his bachelor's and Ph.D. degrees from the University of California, Los Angeles, where he studied music and ethnomusicology.

Manuel has received numerous grants and fellowships for his research and has published extensively, including *Cassette Culture: Popular Music and Technology in North India* (University of Chicago Press, 1993), *Caribbean Counterpoints: Caribbean Music from Rumba to Reggae* (Temple University Press, 1995), and most recently, *East Indian Music in the West Indies: Tan-singing, Chutney, and the Making of Indo-Caribbean Culture* (Temple University Press, 2000).

Manuel's articles have appeared regularly in the journal of *Ethnomusicology* among many other publications, and he has lectured extensively on various topics of world music. He is also an amateur sitarist, jazz pianist, and flamenco guitarist.

1994: World Music and Jazz, panelist

Maultsby, Portia

(b. 1947) Portia Maultsby is director of the Archives of African American Music and Culture and a professor in the Department of Folklore and Ethnomusicology at Indiana University. One of the leading ethnomusicologists in the country, she has conducted research on Black religious and popular music, their relationship to each other, and their connections to African traditions.

Maultsby has published numerous articles on these topics in American and European journals. She also has served as music consultant, advisor, and coproducer for three award-winning films: PBS's Black history documentary *Eyes on the Prize II*; *That Rhythm... Those Blues*; and the National Afro-American Museum's music documentary, *Music as Metaphor*.

1990: The Time Has Come: Gospel Music, panelist

McBride, Christian

(b. 1972) Christian McBride hails from the fertile music center of Philadelphia. At age 9 he started playing electric bass, and was encouraged to study music by his father, a professional bassist

for the Delfonics and Mongo Santamaria. At age 11, McBride took up the acoustic bass and began studying European classical music. He gained the attention of local Philadelphia musicians early on, and at age 14 began his association with Wynton Marsalis, who became a close friend and mentor.

McBride attended Philadelphia's High School for the Creative and Performing Arts, and upon graduation in 1989 was awarded a scholarship to the Juilliard School of Music. During his first semester living in Manhattan, he began performing nightly and touring with the likes of Bobby Watson. He attended Juilliard for only one year before electing to tour with the bands of Roy Hargrove and Freddie Hubbard. McBride has recorded as a leader with Verve Records since 1994 and has been a featured rhythm section player on scores of recordings and special projects. He has also been a member of the trio Superbass with Ray Brown and John Clayton.

1996: The Revolution Returns: The Next Generation in Jazz, performer and master class instructor

McFerrin, Bobby

(b. 1950) Bobby McFerrin is an extraordinarily talented vocal artist who has enjoyed both critical and commercial success in pop, jazz, and classical genres. With his flexible voice and incredible range, his musicianship is legendary. McFerrin made his vocal debut in 1977 with the group Astral Projection. After appearing at the 1980 Playboy Jazz Festival (courtesy of his mentor, Bill Cosby) and the 1981 Kool Jazz Festival, he landed a recording contract with Elektra. But it wasn't until the release of *The Voice* (1984) that he achieved a prominent place in jazz history with the first-ever solo vocal album.

McFerrin garnered mainstream exposure with memorable performances of the theme song to the hit television series *The Cosby Show*, and also with his 1998 pop hit "Don't Worry, Be Happy." Shortly thereafter McFerrin formed the ten-member a cappella group *Voicestra*, which appeared at the Fine Arts Center in February 1992.

After his Amherst appearance, McFerrin released the chart-topping classical recording entitled *Hush* with the cellist Yo-Yo Ma. He has released two jazz recordings in collaboration with Chick Corea and has also recorded and performed classical repertoire with the Saint Paul Chamber Orchestra and jazz tunes with the Yellowjackets. In recent years McFerrin has continued a career that explores the boundaries of classical and jazz in addition to the solo vocal stylings that made him famous.

1992: New Trends in Vocal Jazz, performer

McLean, Jackie

(b. 1932) Since the 1950s when his career was just getting started, alto saxophonist Jackie McLean has been one of bebop and post-bop's preeminent musicians. He grew up in Harlem during one of the most prolific eras of jazz, and has performed and shared the stage with many of the music's greats, including Miles Davis, Charles Mingus, and Art Blakey.

Although his distinctive sound is rooted in bop, McLean's music is also influenced by elements of free jazz and the avant-garde. As a leader, McLean began recording and touring with his quintet in the late 1950s. In the late 1960s he began his teaching career as a faculty member of the Hartt School of Music. McLean and his wife, Dolly, later went on to establish the Artists Collective, a renowned community arts school and performance center based in Hartford, Connecticut.

1989: Black Music and Social Change, performer; 1996: The Revolution Returns: The Next Generation in Jazz, Artists Collective performers

Mighty Clouds of Joy

A leading voice in gospel music for over forty years, the group is the brainchild of its lead singer, Willie Joe Ligon. The all-male ensemble formed in Los Angeles in 1959 when its members were still in high school. With dozens of recordings to its credit, Mighty Clouds of Joy uses amplified instruments to accompany a gospel style that blends elements of popular music and rhythm & blues with traditional gospel repertoire.

Mighty Clouds of Joy was the first gospel crossover group to appear on the hit television series *Soul Train*, where they performed their disco hit "Mighty High." The group has also toured with pop acts such as Paul Simon, the Rolling Stones, and Marvin Gaye.

1990: The Time Has Come: Gospel Music, performers

Murray, Albert

(b. 1916) Born in Kokomis, Alabama, Albert Murray is a brilliant author, critic, novelist, biographer, and blues expert who has published extensively beginning with *The Omni Americans* in 1970. Although he began his writing career while teaching at Tuskegee Institute, Columbia University, and the University of Missouri, he began writing full time while he was in his mid-40s. Among his many books are *Stompin' the Blues* and *Jazz Lips*.

1991: Celebrating the Blues, panelist

Myers, Amina Claudine

(b. 1942) As a member of the Association for the Advancement of Creative Musicians since 1966, Amina Myers's artistry has found her in the fields of music, theater, and education. Growing up in Blackwell, Arkansas, and Dallas, Texas, she began her piano training at age 7 and soon began participating in gospel groups as singer, pianist, choir director, and as cofounder of two groups. She attended Little Rock's Philander Smith College as a student of piano and music education, and upon graduation moved to Chicago where she taught music for four years in the city's public schools.

In 1970 Myers joined Sonny Stitt's group as pianist, and later worked with the Gene Ammons Quartet. Since moving to New York in 1976, she has premiered a number of works in theater, musical theater, and improvisational and mixed media, has fronted various small ensembles, and has assembled a substantial discography. She has worked with artists such as Lester Bowie, Henry Threadgill, Muhal Richard Abrams, and Leroy Jenkins.

1995: Blues-Based Jazz: The Legacy of William "Count" Basie, panelist

Odetta

(b. 1930) A dynamic force on the American folk music scene for more than fifty years, Odetta Gordon was born in Birmingham, Alabama, and has appeared at most of the world's major festivals and in concert around the globe since her performing debut in San Francisco.

Odetta has recorded on Vanguard, RCA Victor, Verve, and Polydor labels among others, and has received honorary degrees from many institutions of higher learning. She is also an actor, having appeared in Toni Morrison's musical, *New Orleans*, as well as in *The Crucible* and *The Effects of Gamma Rays on Man-in-the-Moon Marigolds*.

Odetta's most celebrated period as a recording artist was in the 1960s, but in 1999 she released *Blues Everywhere I Go*, her first studio album in almost two decades. In 1999 she received the National Medal of the Arts from President Bill Clinton.

1989: Black Music and Social Change, performer and Distinguished Achievement Award recipient

Placksin, Sally

(b. 1948) Sally Placksin, a noted jazz historian and radio personality, is the author of several books and articles on women in jazz, including *Women in Jazz, 1900 to the Present: Their Words, Lives and Music* (Putnam Publishing Group, 1982). She currently hosts "What's the Word" on Newark Public Radio, WBGO 88.3 FM.

1993: Great Women of Jazz, panelist

Reid, Vernon A.

(b. 1958) Born in England of West Indian heritage, Reid moved to Brooklyn, New York, and delved into the jazz and rock music scenes at an early age. He studied with jazz guitarist Ted Dunbar as a teenager, and later served an apprenticeship with Ronald Shannon Jackson's Decoding Society.

Reid has performed with a rainbow of diverse artists and groups such as John Zorn, Geri Allen, Tracy Chapman, Public

Enemy, and Mick Jagger, but he is most well known as lead guitarist for the rock band Living Color, which disbanded around 1995. He is also a founding member of the Black Rock Coalition, an organization dedicated to combating racial stereotypes in the music industry.

1989: Black Music and Social Change, panelist

Roach, Hildred

(b. 1937) A professor and concert pianist, Hildred Roach was born in Charlotte, North Carolina, and began her piano studies at an early age. She received her master's degree in music from Yale University and has also studied at the Juilliard School of Music and the University of Ghana. Roach has been on the faculty of several universities, including Tuskegee Institute and Howard University, and she currently teaches at the University of the District of Columbia. She is the author of the celebrated *Black American Music: Past and Present*, and has toured widely as a pianist and lecturer.

1994: World Music and Jazz, panelist

Smallwood, Richard

(b. 1948) Richard Smallwood formed the Richard Smallwood Singers in 1977 in Washington, D.C. He began his piano studies as a child and graduated with honors from Howard University. The Richard Smallwood Singers' self-titled first recording spent eighty-seven weeks on the gospel chart of *Billboard* magazine, and their second recording, the Grammy-nominated *Psalms*, which was released in 1984, was number 1 for fourteen weeks.

The Richard Smallwood Singers formed the core of the 1985 tour of the musical *Sing, Mahalia, Sing*, of which Richard Smallwood served as both composer and musical director. When the Singers signed with Rejoice Records in 1986, their debut album, called *Textures*, introduced the song "Jesus Is the Center of My Joy," which is now a staple of many gospel church choirs. When the Richard Smallwood Singers appeared in the Fine Arts Center Concert Hall along with Mighty Clouds of Joy, they had just released their recording entitled *Vision*. They subsequently have released many other award-winning recordings and enjoy an active touring schedule.

1990: The Time Has Come: Gospel Music, performer and master class instructor

Staton, Dakota

(b. 1931) Dakota Staton began singing at age 4, and at age 16 she was hired to sing by Joe Wespray, leader of Pittsburgh's top big band. She later moved to Detroit and began touring the night club circuits of Detroit, Cleveland, Cincinnati, Milwaukee, Montreal, and Toronto before settling permanently in New York. In 1954, while singing at Harlem's Baby Grand, she was approached by a producer at Capital Records and was signed to a recording contract.

In 1955, Staton won a *Down Beat* magazine award as most promising newcomer. Her legendary 1958 recording, *The Late, Late Show*, is among the best of her twenty-plus recordings. Through her international tours she has brought American music to China, Japan, Southeast Asia, Europe, South America, and Australia.

1995: Blues-Based Jazz: The Legacy of William "Count" Basie, Distinguished Achievement Award recipient

Taylor, Billy

(b. 1921) Billy Taylor is internationally recognized as a performer, educator, author, recording artist, and legend of jazz, an art form that he calls "America's classical music." Since the 1950s he has been devoted to making African American music accessible to all. He is a pioneer of jazz education, having established such programs as New York's Jazzmobile and television's first jazz education program called *The Subject Is Jazz*. More recently, *Billy Taylor's Jazz at Lincoln Center*, CBS's *Sunday Morning*, the Metropolitan Museum of Art's *Jazz Models and Mentors*, and his National Public Radio program have given jazz national prominence and exposure.

Billy Taylor moved to New York in the early 1940s and began his career as one of the staples of the city's music scene. He was house pianist at Birdland from 1949 to 1951, and along with leading a trio for decades he has worked with many luminaries in the world of American music. He has produced a number of commissioned works for organizations including the Kennedy Center, the University of Illinois, and the Atlanta Symphony.

Billy Taylor received his doctoral degree from the University of Massachusetts, Amherst, and is a founding faculty member of the University's Jazz in July Summer Music Programs.

1996: The Revolution Returns: The Next Generation in Jazz, panelist and Distinguished Achievement Award recipient

Thokoza

Formed in 1965 in Durban, South Africa, by the playwright Welcome Msome, Thokoza (Zulu for "happiness") performs a chorale singing style known as "ingoma ebusuku." Based on Zulu song and dance traditions, Thokoza's vocal interpretations incorporate Western hymn, choral singing, and elements of Black gospel.

Since moving to New York in 1979, Msome and the singer Thuli Dumakude have been involved in many theatrical and music and dance productions that celebrate the culture and arts of South Africa's Zulu people.

(1989: Black Music and Social Change, performers

Tillis, Frederick C.

(b. 1930) Frederick Tillis is a renowned artist, educator, administrator, and poet, and is a lifetime member of the International Association of Jazz Educators, an organization that honored him with an award for outstanding service. He is a Danforth Associate and is currently director emeritus of the University of Massachusetts Fine Arts Center, where he served for twenty-three years as director. At the University, Tillis has served as associate chancellor, professor of music composition, and director of the

African American Music and Jazz program. He earned his Ph.D. in music composition from the University of Iowa, and has written more than 120 pieces in various media, including orchestral, vocal, jazz instrumental, choral, and chamber music. His compositions explore a variety of musical contexts from throughout the world including African, African American, and classical European traditions.

The works of Frederick Tillis have been performed internationally and in the United States. Such pieces include *A Festival Journey* (1992); *Ring Shout Concerto* (1974) for percussion, written for and performed by Max Roach and symphony orchestra; and *Concerto for Piano (Jazz Trio) and Symphony Orchestra* (1983), written for and performed by Billy Taylor. He has produced seven books of poetry and a text, *Jazz Theory and Improvisation*. In addition, Tillis is an accomplished instrumentalist, offering a distinct and personal interpretation of the soprano and tenor saxophones.

1989 – 1995: panel discussion moderator; 1998: A Great Day in Harlem: A Tribute to Dr. Frederick C. Tillis, Distinguished Achievement Award recipient

Titon, Jeff Todd

(b. 1943) A professor of music and director of the ethnomusicology program at Brown University, Jeff Titon is also an accomplished author, editor, fiddle player, guitarist, photographer, and filmmaker. He is the author of *Early Downhome Blues: A Musical and Cultural Analysis*, which won the ASCAP Deems Taylor Award. From 1990 to 1995 he was editor of *Ethnomusicology*.

Titon received his B.A. from Amherst College and both his M.A. and Ph.D. from the University of Minnesota, where he studied ethnomusicology and wrote his dissertation on blues music.

1991: Celebrating the Blues, panelist

Tracy, Steven C.

(b. 1954) Steven C. Tracy is an associate professor of Afro-American Studies at the University of Massachusetts, Amherst, and a highly regarded scholar of blues music and American literature.

Tracy fronts his band, Steve Tracy and the Crawling Kingsnakes, on vocals and harmonica; the group has recorded and performed throughout Europe and the United States. Tracy has also performed in the bands of Big Joe Duskin, Albert Washington, and Pigmeat Jarrett, as well as appearing with the Cincinnati Symphony Orchestra in performances of *Three Pieces for Blues Band and Symphony Orchestra*.

Steve Tracy is a respected expert on the work of Langston Hughes, and has written numerous articles, reviews, and liner notes concerning Hughes's works. He is the author of *Langston Hughes and the Blues* (University of Illinois Press, 1988), and served as editor for *The Collected Works of Langston Hughes* and *A Historical Guide to Langston Hughes* (Oxford University Press, 2002). Tracy's publishing credits on the subject of blues music include *A Brush with the Blues* with visual artist Jack Coughlin, and *Going to Cincinnati: A History of Blues in the Queen City*, for which he won the ARSC Award for best research published in jazz, blues, and gospel.

1999: The Blues Lives On, panel discussion moderator

Turre, Steve

(b. 1948) Steve Turre has contributed much to contemporary music. He has performed and recorded with many great artists, and he exhibits a masterful technique on trombone and on the conch shells. He pushes the limits of both instruments much in the vein of his former employer and mentor, Rahsaan Roland Kirk.

Turre has been a regular member of the *Saturday Night Live* Band since 1985 and has been featured with the Thad Jones/Mel Lewis Big Band, Art Blakey and the Jazz Messengers, Van Morrison, Santana, and Ray Charles, as well as Dexter Gordon, McCoy Tyner, Slide Hampton, and Bobby Hutcherson. He is also one of the most respected trombonists of Latin music, having worked with a score of great artists, including Hilton Ruiz and Tito Puente.

1998: A Great Day in Harlem: A Tribute to Dr. Frederick C. Tillis, performer

Ward, Willa

(b. 1922) With a career that began in the 1930s, Willa Ward Royster has the distinction of being a founding and last surviving member of The Ward Singers from Philadelphia — the first famous female gospel group in the history of Black gospel.

Along with Marion Williams and Henrietta Waddy, the Ward family brought gospel music to the masses. With Willa on vocals and piano, her sister Clara as the group's creative leader, and their mother, Gertrude, handling both vocal and business matters, The Ward Singers were one of the first groups to take gospel music out of the church and bring it to clubs and the concert stage. They enjoyed extraordinary commercial success in their heyday, and while their theatrical flamboyance and show business aplomb had both its detractors and supporters, their musicianship was innovative and legendary.

Although Ward is now semiretired and performs just occasionally, she is coauthor with Toni Rose of *How I Got Over*, a memoir of the Ward family's rise to fame (Temple University Press, 1997).

1997: Gospel in the 1990s: The Reason Why We Sing, Distinguished Achievement Award recipient

Watrous, Peter

(b. 1958) Peter Watrous is a prolific writer and critic who has written extensively about jazz and other styles of Black music in the *New York Times* among other publications. Other writers often cite his articles and reviews, which appear frequently in a variety of performer biographies.

Watrous received his B.A. in English from the University of Massachusetts in 1982, and although he did not receive his academic degree in music, he performed in various jazz ensembles under the direction of Frederick C. Tillis. His liner notes appear on recordings of Kenny Barron, Sun Ra, Cecil Taylor, and Marty Ehrlich, among others.

1996: The Revolution Returns: The Next Generation in Jazz, panelist

Williams, Claude

(b. 1908) Claude "Fiddler" Williams was born in Muskogee, Oklahoma, and by the age of 10 was proficient on guitar, mandolin, banjo, and cello. He was inspired to play violin after hearing Joe Venuti's sound rise above an entire band at an outdoor concert. In 1928 he moved to Kansas City, and as a member of Twelve Clouds of Joy, made his first recordings on guitar and violin. He then lived for a time in Chicago, where in 1936 Count Basie recruited him as guitarist for the first Count Basie Orchestra, luring him away from the guitar chair of Nat King Cole's band. Williams won a *Down Beat* poll for his work with Basie, but soon gave up his spot to Freddie Green, the legendary pulse of the Basie rhythm section for the next forty years.

Williams has fronted many national and international tours including the National Council for the Traditional Art's "Masters of the Folk Violin" and the Tony Award-winning show *Black and Blue*. In 1989 he was honored as the first inductee to the Oklahoma Jazz Hall of Fame, and in 1994 he was awarded the first and only Charlie Christian Award from Black Liberated Arts, Inc.

1995: Blues-Based Jazz: The Legacy of William "Count" Basie, performer and Distinguished Achievement Award recipient

Williams, Marion

(1927 – 1994) Born in Miami, Florida, Marion Williams began singing as a child in her local church, and twenty years later became a member of the famous Ward Singers. Her electrifying delivery of "Surely God Is Able" contributed much to the success of The Ward Singers' first hit recording, which was also the first million-selling Black gospel record.

Williams remained with the Ward Singers until 1958, when she organized Stars of Faith, which appeared in the hit off-Broadway musical *Black Nativity*. When she left that group in 1965, she began a successful solo career, touring worldwide and releasing recordings up until the early 1990s. Literally months before her death, she became the first gospel performer to win a

MacArthur "Genius" Grant and the first gospel singer to receive a Kennedy Center Lifetime Achievement Honor.

1990: The Time Has Come: Gospel Music, performer and Distinguished Achievement Award recipient

Winans, Marvin L.

(b. 1958) A dedicated preacher, gospel icon, and since 1989 pastor of Perfecting Church in Detroit, Marvin Winans's life work has been devoted to God and music. He was a founding member of the quartet bearing his family name — the first veritable dynasty in contemporary gospel music. With their pioneering and sometimes controversial use of melody, harmony, and instrumentation, the Winans's musical influence is now legendary in Black gospel music.

Winans is a talented vocalist, pianist, composer, and producer for Winans family projects, as well as for other gospel performers. Winans led The Perfected Praise Choir in its 1992 debut recording, *Introducing Perfected Praise*, and followed up that album with *Friends* in 2001. As a vocalist, Winans has made guest appearances on recordings of such diverse artists as Vanessa Bell Armstrong, Michael Jackson, and Ladysmith Black Mambazo.

1997: Gospel in the 1990s: The Reason Why We Sing, panelist and Distinguished Achievement Award recipient